With a Narrow Blade

With a Narrow Blade

Faith Martin

ROBERT HALE · LONDON

© Faith Martin 2007
First published in Great Britain 2007

ISBN 978-0-7090-8443-3

Robert Hale Limited
Clerkenwell House
Clerkenwell Green
London EC1R 0HT

www.halebooks.com

2 4 6 8 10 9 7 5 3 1

Typeset in 11/13½pt Sabon
Printed and bound in Great Britain by
Biddles Limited, King's Lynn

chapter one

At twelve minutes past eight that Tuesday morning, two people closed the front door behind them, and set out to face another day. Both had appointments with murder, though in very different capacities. One was Detective Constable Keith Barrington, who'd just left his temporary digs in Summertown, a suburb of Oxford, and the other was Caroline Weekes, a wife, wannabe mother, and PA to the owner of a local coal merchant. She lived in a small, privately owned semi in King's End in the small market town of Bicester. Neither knew the other, but both, for vastly different reasons, faced the day with a certain amount of trepidation.

DC Barrington nodded pleasantly to the owner of a small newspaper shop as he passed him on the way to where he'd parked his ten-year-old banger just off a nearby slip road, and received a brief smile in reply. The early December morning was still dark and he was glad of the orange glare of a street light as he reached for his car keys and fumbled for the lock. The sky was full of ominous dark clouds, and a chilly wind brought with it the first spatter of raindrops. He ducked quickly into the shelter of his car and reached for the seat belt.

When he pulled out onto the main road, the rush hour traffic was already building up, but since he was travelling out of the suburbs rather than into the city proper, he was going against the tide, and the roads on his side were almost clear. Something, he thought with a pang of nostalgia, that would never happen back in London. There, the rush hour clogged every artery at every point of the compass regardless, bringing gridlock and road rage for nearly three solid hours, and as he drove towards Thames Valley's Police Headquarters in Kidlington, he tried to fool himself that he was enjoying the sensation of being a fish swimming against the tide, that it was a perk, or at least a pleasant change in circumstances that anyone with even half a brain would be pleased to accept. He didn't quite succeed. Even though he never quite left the signs of suburbia behind him on the short commute, there were still too many bare-twigged trees, too much greenery hovering at the edges, reminding him that he was out in the sticks. Rural Oxfordshire lurked, never far away, never out of mind. For a boy who'd been born and raised in the mighty blight of a capital city, the sight of a grazing horse in a small paddock just before he got to the Kidlington roundabout hit him with a jolt of culture shock that made him miss his gear change.

As he filed into the traffic heading down Kidlington's main road, he tried to remember the last time it had been his 'first day' at a new nick, but it was too many moons ago now to be clear in his memory. He'd entered the police force straight after he'd finished his A levels, joining his local nick and staying there until his abrupt and ignominious departure last month, after more than seven years of exemplary service. An image flashed into his mind of his snarling, jeering DS, but he quickly thrust it away. Far better to remember the sincere sympathy of his friends, and the atmosphere of resentment that had pervaded the once-friendly nick on his behalf when it became clear that he wasn't going to be allowed to stay on.

Of course, not everyone had been on his side – most of the brass seemed to think he was bloody lucky to keep his position of DC at all, and not be demoted back down into uniform. Or even prosecuted. But there would have been one hell of a stink if they'd tried that on, Keith thought with some satisfaction, and then caught sight of his defiant grin in the driving mirror. Quickly, he wiped it off. He hadn't met his new DI yet, but he was damned sure a cocky grin wouldn't go down too well.

As his dad had kept on saying only last weekend, as he'd helped his son move his stuff from the East End of London to the rarefied suburb of the university city, he needed to keep his head down and play it clever. Maybe even eat humble pie for a while, if need be. But most of all to think of it as a new start and a new chance to shine.

Ever since joining the force, Keith had been determined to get out of uniform and start doing some real detective work. Locking up the bastards who preyed on ordinary decent folk, like his own mum and dad. To actually make a difference to some poor sod's quality of life, by collaring hooligans and vandals, who specialized in tyrannizing the elderly or young. The fact he could still feel that way, even after how he'd been treated back at Blacklock Green, was, he supposed, at least something. He hadn't let that bastard of a sergeant wear him down completely.

He carefully kept an eye on the buildings leading off on his right, remembering from his brief orientation interview last week that the HQ was situated nearly halfway down the main road, not far from a big comprehensive school. Spotting the large signpost at last just outside a narrow access road, Keith indicated and pulled in, but struggled to find a parking space.

His shift didn't officially start until 8.30, and he had a good ten minutes to spare, but it didn't do to be late on his first day.

As he climbed out of the car, he wondered yet again what his new boss was going to be like. Detective Inspector Hillary Greene. He'd done the usual asking around, of course, but information had been sketchy. Not many of his still-loyal mates back at Blacklock Green knew much about Thames Valley. So what he'd managed to glean had been mostly trawled from the Internet, scuttlebutt and guess-work. His friends had ribbed him a bit about working for a woman, but Keith thought it might not be such a bad thing. He certainly didn't think he had any hang-ups about taking orders from a woman, unlike some. Who knows, it might even work out.

As he walked towards the entrance and pushed through the door, he thought, fatalistically, that she could hardly be worse than the last bastard he'd worked for.

About ten miles away, Caroline Weekes walked down her short, concrete pathway, and pushed open her garden gate. She was a tall woman, with short dark hair and large choco-late-coloured eyes, and wore a long beige Burberry, belted tightly against the wind and threatening rain. The neigh-bour's cat, a large fat ginger tom, spotted her coming and jumped up onto the top of the neat brick garden wall that surrounded her property and arched his back, already antic-ipating the warm caress of her hand. The sight of the friendly moggy lifted her vague sense of depression and brought a smile to her face.

'Hey there, Spartacus. Not been after the sparrows, I hope?' She stroked the hard, furry head that butted into her palm with typical cat-like ecstasy, and listened to the loud rumbling purr. Every morning she left for work, and more often than not, had to pay the cat the usual toll. She smiled at her neighbour who was climbing into his car, then gave the cat a final chuck under the chin and moved off down the road. She usually caught the bus at the end of the street, since she only worked in the market square and it never seemed worth the bother to take the second car. Once at the bottom of the road, however, she crossed over at the corner and after a short while, veered off the pavement to enter a little cul-de-sac of council houses.

Caroline was thirty-nine, but managed, with a strict exercise regime and careful dieting, to look much younger. A flair for clothes and an expert hand with make-up also helped, and her short bob of brown hair was always maintained in a careful cut. Those who knew her had never been able to understand why her first husband had left her for, of all people, his rather overweight secretary. Caroline had felt proud of herself for taking it more or less in her stride and had promptly divorced him, then re-trained as a secretary herself. She had taken a job as a humble secretary and admin assistant in Johnson Coal, but was now, three short years later, PA to the man himself. She had also remarried just recently, to a man ten years her junior, who was an up-and-coming 'something' in advertising, working out of an office in High Wycombe.

Anyone watching the attractive brunette walking down the street on that cold and wet December morning might have supposed that she was a woman who'd taken life by the throat and shaken it into a position that suited her.

They would have been wrong.

As she walked to number 18, in the rather grandly named Holburn Crescent, Caroline Weekes was a woman with plenty on her mind. She felt slightly sick for a start, but knew that it was probably only the new pills her specialist had put her on last week. She felt cold, maybe because she'd started her period that morning – a circumstance that had in itself filled her with a deep sense of gloom. Soon she'd have to start on the treatments, and a vague sense of terror momentarily paralysed her. What if they didn't work? She bit her lip and told herself to get a grip. Take things one step at a time.

She sighed, glancing up at the house in front of her. For over five years now, she'd been dropping into number 18, usually with some shopping, sometimes with a box of biscuits or other treats. Hers and Flo Jenkins' was an odd sort of friendship, and most people took it for granted that the youthful, successful Caroline was merely playing the good Samaritan to a 76-year-old who needed a helping hand. It wasn't as one-sided as that, though, and many was the time that Caroline had sat at Flo's kitchen table, pouring out her various woes, and slowly feeling better.

'Hello, love, nice weather for ducks innit?' The cheerful voice of the woman across the street, picking up a milk bottle, made her jump.

'Certainly is,' she said with a wry smile, as the first of the raindrops began to splatter down. Not wanting to get her shoulders damp and cold, she half ran up the path to the shelter of Flo's meagre porch and rang the bell.

And waited.

Back in Kidlington, Keith Barrington looked across the expanse of the lobby and instantly caught the eye of the curious desk sergeant. There was no getting around him, of course, and taking a deep breath, deciding it was best to just get it over with, he walked on over.

'Searge,' he said pleasantly. 'DC Barrington. I'm looking for DI Greene's billet?'

The desk sergeant's face tightened, and Keith felt his heart sink. So it was beginning already. It had been too much to hope, of course, that the plods out here in the sticks hadn't heard the rumours that must have been seeping out of Blacklock Green. He only hoped they were halfway accurate, but the fact that he'd be painted as black as possible was far more likely to be the case.

'Oh, so you're the lad then,' the desk sergeant said heavily, confirming Keith's worst fears. He was the usual type for the breed, middle-aged, with a comfortable middle-aged spread and that certain smugness that comes with someone who's been on the job for over twenty years and has earned their stint out of the firing line.

Keith met the curious, watery blue eyes with a slightly stiffened back and met the gaze head on. 'DC Keith

Barrington,' he repeated expressionlessly. He tensed even further as he felt someone behind him, and turned quickly to see another of the breed closing in. Of course, the day shift was just coming in to replace the owl watch.

'Morning Cliff,' the present incumbent said, lifting the hatch and moving around to make room. 'Quiet night, nothing to worry about. This here's Hillary's new recruit,' he added by way of introduction.

The other man nodded at him as he glanced down at the log book. 'She'll be glad to get the extra help I reckon,' the newcomer said amiably enough. 'Her last DC left in the summer. Got married and moved to Headington. Not sure which fate is worst,' he added, and his crony gave a loud laugh. 'She was supposed to get someone right away, but you know how it is. Now her DS is leaving too – another one getting married. Must be a bloody epidemic up there.'

Keith smiled, just to show willing. They were obviously going to have their say, so he might as well get his licks in as well, just to test the waters. 'I was told at orientation that there are two DS's in her team. Bit unusual that, isn't it?'

The two desk sergeant's shot each other a knowing grin. 'Ah, but DS Ross doesn't count,' one of them said succinctly.

'Oh,' Keith said warily. Just what the hell was that supposed to mean? Was he a burn-out, or a booze hound or what?

'You know what I was thinking the other day?' the night-shift sergeant mused, with all the subtlety of a mating moose. 'That time Hill arrested that drug-dealing toerag off that canal barge.'

His oppo grinned widely. 'Oh yeah, I remember that too. Running away up the tow path he was, dodging all the uniforms like a scrum half at Twickenham. Bowling over beefy constables like they were nine pin bowling skittles.'

'Then he comes to the bridge, and there's only DI Greene stood there.' The other one took up the tale with all the panache of a straight man playing off a long-established comedy partner. 'Of course, he sees this woman in civvies stood there, and he thinks he's got it made, right? Get past her and he can leg it into any of the side streets and disappear like a rat up a drainpipe.'

Keith Barrington could see the punchline coming a mile off, and patiently waited for it, neither smiling nor frowning.

'So Hill just stands there, right, waiting for him to come to her, then lets off with a high kick right between the legs.'

'He was nearly wearing his balls for earrings,' the other man said, both of them laughing hard, but both of them watching him closely. Just to make sure he'd got the message.

Keith nodded shortly. 'Sounds like she knows what she's about,' he said blandly.

The two older men nodded, catching each other's eye, before the night-duty man shrugged. 'Well, must be off. Supposed to be a match on Sky One this afternoon I wanna catch. See you, Ted.'

They both watched as he made his way to the door, then the newly arrived desk sergeant cleared his throat. 'You'll find your new boss is highly respected around here, laddie,' he said flatly, all pretence at subtlety going out the window. 'She's well liked, and one of the best thief-takers and SIO's in the business. Chief Superintendent Donleavy rates her.' He paused, just to make sure it was all sinking in.

Keith Barrington nodded wearily. So the gloves were off already. Well, sod 'em. Sod 'em all. 'Sounds like she can teach me a lot,' he said flatly. 'I'm looking forward to working for her.'

The older man held his gaze for a moment, then smiled briefly. Perhaps something about the youngster reminded him of a stag at bay, because he suddenly felt rather sorry for him. 'Look lad,' he said quietly. 'Hillary Greene's one of the best there is. She's clever, she's fair, she knows the ropes, and if you treat her right, she'll do the same to you. Do yourself a great big favour and just watch, listen and learn. Keep your head down, get some good years in, and things could look up. Know what I'm saying?'

Keith smiled grimly. 'Sure,' he said.

Well. They would see.

'Flo, love, you not up yet?' Caroline Weekes called through the letter box she'd just opened, and squinted into the empty hall. She waited, called again, then, conscious of the neighbour across the street still watching curiously, stood back a little and looked up.

The terraced houses were simple two up, two-downs, and all the windows at number 18 had curtains drawn firmly across. Even the ones downstairs.

'She not up yet then? That's funny, Flo's usually up by now,' the woman with the milk bottles called.

'I know,' Caroline called back. She could almost remember the woman's name, but not quite. 'I wanted to ask her if she needs me to bring anything back from Tesco's for her.'

The neighbour, another old-age pensioner who had always envied Flo a friend like Caroline – someone young, willing, with a car – frowned, obviously beginning to get a little worried herself now. Flo Jenkins had lived across the road from her ever since the council had moved her into her house just over ten years ago, and she had always been a friendly soul. 'She's not been very well recently,' the old woman said nervously, and Caroline bit her lip.

'No, I know,' she said. 'I think I'll use the spare key she gave me. Just to make sure. She's probably just overslept.' And so saying, Caroline Weekes reached into her bag and withdrew a large set of keys. On it were her own house keys, her car keys, and Flo Jenkins' front door key. She inserted a silver Yale key and pushed open the door, calling loudly, 'Flo? Flo, it's me, Caroline.' She shut the door behind her, noticing that the old woman across the way hadn't gone in, even though it had now begun to rain in earnest.

DI Hillary Greene parked Puff the Tragic Wagon, her ancient Volkswagen, as close to the entrance as she could get and swore softly at the rain as she ran across the car park. As ever, she'd left her umbrella somewhere, and made a vague mental promise to buy a new one soon. She shook herself off just inside the door, where a growing wet patch signalled that she wasn't the only one to have done so recently.

'Mornin',' the desk sergeant said cheerfully as he spotted her. 'Your new DC's just reported in,' he added, opening his mouth as if to say something, then closed it again. It probably wouldn't do to tell her that he and Ted had already warned him what was what. Hillary Greene was well able to take care of herself, and probably wouldn't appreciate it.

'Oh, right. About time I got some help,' she said, but with a distinct lack of enthusiasm. The desk sergeant watched her go, then shrugged. If anyone could handle the likes of Keith Barrington, it was her. The brass around here seemed to have got into the habit of sending her the lame ducks, the unknown quantities and 'sensitive' appointees. But with Barrington, they might just have taken it too far.

Hillary climbed the stairs, having forsaken the lift years ago, when the size of her hips and thighs threatened to match her age. Which was in the forties. Now, as she climbed the stairs, she was thinking about her new DC with just a tinge of unease.

She used her key card to get into the main office, and was instantly hit by a barrage of noise. The big open-plan office held clusters of desks that housed uniform and plain clothes alike, most of whom were busy on the phone, typing up reports, scanning computers or chatting over the first morning cup of tea. One of them, a DS who'd migrated over from Juvenile Crime Squad, waved her over as she came in. Sandra Pierce was about Hillary's age, and they had known each other since the year dot. She was at Sam Waterstones's desk, and Sam, another old friend, grinned at her as she approached.

'We were just talking about our mystery millionaire,' Sam said, and added, in obvious mimicry of someone else, 'It could be you!' He pointed dramatically at Hillary, who looked back at him blankly.

'Huh?'

'Crikey, don't say you haven't been following the drama,' Sandra said. 'Don't you read the local papers?'

Hillary grunted wryly. 'I don't read any papers if I can help it. I'm depressed enough as it is.'

'Ah, but this is a good-luck story for a change,' Sam said, then grinned. 'Well, not so much good luck really. Somebody around here's won the lottery.'

Hillary blinked. 'Around here? You mean in this nick?' she squeaked. 'Who? And how much can I touch him up for?'

'No, not here, you nit. Well, maybe here,' he added thoughtfully. 'Someone in the "Oxfordshire area" had the winning ticket a while back, but never claimed it.'

'Nearly 180 days ago, to be exact,' Sandra corrected. 'Apparently, Camelot give you exactly 187 days to claim it, the stingy sods. The *Oxford Mail* came out with a piece about it yesterday. You really not seen it? You know, "Do you have the three million pound ticket in your coat pocket?" sort of thing.'

'Yeah. Here, Hill, you checked your old tickets lately?' Sam asked. 'The missus has had the drawers out at our house, I can tell you. Driving me barmy. Even looking in flower vases and everything. I mean, who'd put it there, even if we had it? The numbers you want are,' he picked up yesterday's edition of the paper, which had run the numbers, '2, 9, 12, 14, 30 and 49.'

'Yeah, do those numbers ring a bell, Hill?' Sandra said.

'Nope,' Hillary grunted, glancing across to her nest of desks near the side wall. She could see Janine Tyler's blonde head bent over some paperwork, and, sitting beside her in Tommy Lynch's old place, an unfamiliar, red head. Her new DC.

The one who liked to beat up his superior officers.

'Just think, if whoever it is knows it's their numbers but can't find the ticket ...' Sandra was saying. 'I'd feel as sick as a dog.'

'Don't bear thinking about,' Sam agreed. 'Hey, Hill, you sure you ain't got an old ticket lurking about? If it's yours, you can treat us all to a holiday in Bali.'

'Yeah, Hill, what about it? Wouldn't you be surprised if you went back to that boat of yours and found the winning ticket tucked up in a letter rack or something?' Sandra teased.

'Surprised? I'd be bloody astounded,' Hillary said, beginning to walk off, then saying over her shoulder with perfect timing, 'I don't play.'

The wave of laughter that shot across the office lifted Keith Barrington's head. The woman he saw walking towards him was dressed in a plain dark-grey skirt and blazer, with a white blouse and flat black shoes. She carried a large, black leather handbag, and her chestnut-tinted brown hair was cut in a long, bell-shaped bob. She had a surprisingly lush, hourglass figure. The fact that she was headed straight for their group of desks, and hadn't taken her eyes off him, told him that he was about to meet his new boss. The one who'd recently been awarded a medal for bravery after being shot during the take-down of Oxford's most notorious drug dealer. The one who could make his life hell, or give him a second chance.

He rose carefully to his feet and waited for her to make the first move.

*

The house was totally quiet, and Caroline Weekes paused in the hall at the bottom of the stairs. She didn't go up them, but instead walked a short way down the little hall and pushed open the first door on the right, which, she knew, would take her into the lounge.

The curtains were drawn and the electric lights were on. The telly was turned down low, showing a couple sitting on a sofa as breakfast telly in all its glory was beamed into the living room. Facing the telly was an old but comfortable armchair. On it, sat a grey-haired woman. Her feet were encased in comfortable carpet slippers, her nylon tights a little wrinkled and baggy around the calf. She was wearing a dress of some heavy, rather itchy-looking material that was probably very warm, and a hand-knitted cardigan in the same colour as the flowers on her dress. She seemed to be watching the television. But Caroline Weekes knew that she wasn't. Her eyes didn't move, her chest didn't rise and fall. She sat in her chair so incredibly still.

A gas fire burned in the grate, and the room felt hot and stuffy. She was finding it hard to breath. Caroline stepped a little further into the room and stared down at her old friend. She seemed to be wearing what looked like some strange, large, ornamental metal pin, right in the middle of her chest.

Caroline Weekes turned and walked out of the room into the hall, and out to the front door. This she opened, then walked a little way down the path, then stopped for a moment, then walked a little way more until she reached the gate. There her knees seemed to give way, for she found herself clutching at the gate to stop herself from falling over.

A car went by in the road, the sound of the tyres hissing on the wet tarmac loud in her ears. Across the road she thought the old woman, still standing in her doorway, called out something, but she couldn't seem able to make out what it was.

After a few moments, she reached into her bag, only then

aware that she was getting soaking wet, as the rain ran off the red leather of her bag and dripped onto the concrete beneath her feet.

With shaking hands she got out her mobile phone, turned it on, took a deep breath, and dialled 999.

chapter two

Hillary Greene put her bag down on the table and held out her hand. 'You must be DC Barrington?'

'Yes ma'am.'

'Guv.'

'Yes, guv.'

From his file, Hillary knew he was twenty-five years old, but he looked younger. It was possibly his colouring that made him appear so, for his sandy hair bordered on the ginger, and he had very pale skin with the usual smattering of freckles that went with it, reminding her of a schoolboy Just William type. He also had round, pale green eyes that looked disproportionately large in a triangular-shaped face. But looks, in this case, were almost certainly deceiving. There was nothing innocent about this young man.

'I see you've met Sergeant Tyler,' Hillary said, glancing down at Janine, who didn't appear to hear her. She was reading a file, probably on her battered wife case, but Hillary got the feeling that the younger woman wasn't really paying attention to that either. She'd noticed this air of distraction about her before, and had assumed it was down to pre-wedding jitters. Now she was not quite so sure.

'Janine is getting married on Friday.' She turned back to Keith Barrington, a definite warning in her voice now. 'To Detective Superintendent Mallow. He's known around here as Mellow Mallow, or Mel for short. Our Super,' she added, just in case he hadn't twigged yet. 'It means she's leaving us to go to Witney nick, so we'll be short-handed. I hope you like hard work.'

Keith smiled. 'I like it better than being bored, guv,' he admitted.

Hillary nodded, not missing the quick, assessing look he shot down at Janine, who, at last, had realized she was being talked about, and was staring right back at him. Good, he'd got the message. The last thing the new boy wanted to do was run foul of his superior's soon-to-be missus.

'Ross phoned to say he'd be late, boss,' Janine said, and Hillary raised an eyebrow. Frank Ross never usually bothered to explain himself.

'He say why?' she asked curiously.

'Of course not,' Janine said, as if surprised she should even ask.

Hillary grunted, then seeing the new boy follow this byplay, nodded to a chair. 'Sit down, let's have a chat. I like to keep things up front and clear. That way we can avoid sticking our foot in it.' She took her own seat, pushed her towering In tray to one side, and regarded the London boy closely.

'I don't know whether you've heard about my late husband, Ronnie Greene, or not,' she began, seeing by the fleeting look of surprise to cross his face that he either hadn't, or hadn't expected her to mention him. She smiled wearily. 'I don't want you putting anyone's back up because you're not up to speed, that's all. I was on the point of divorcing my husband, when he was killed in a car crash and allegations of serious corruption against him came up. These were investigated and substantiated.' She stated the facts boldly, and without any emphasis.

Keith blinked, but said nothing.

'I also was investigated, as was DS Ross, who was my husband's bosom pal,' she added dryly. 'I was exonerated, and no mud was able to stick to Frank Ross.'

Janine, listening with half an ear, smiled thinly. Nicely worded, boss, she thought grimly. It made it clear that she was innocent, whilst Frank Ross was as guilty as hell, without her actually saying so.

'You'll soon discover that Sergeant Ross is not popular around here,' Hillary went on flatly. 'But from time to time you'll have to take orders from him,' she added. 'Your predecessor, Tommy Lynch, had to, and his before that, so you're not coming in for any unusual treatment.' She stressed the last few words just enough for a delicate wash of red to colour the youngster's cheeks. 'Tommy's now a DS out of Headington. He kept his cool, worked hard, learned and studied. If you do the same, I don't see any reason why your story should be any different.'

She paused and looked across at him steadily. She doubted she could make things any plainer than that, but added, nevertheless, 'If you think you're going to have any problems taking orders from someone you may not personally respect, it would be better if you just up and left now. I won't stand for any insubordination here.'

Janine raised an eyebrow, but wasn't particularly surprised that Hillary had thrown down the gauntlet so early or so clearly. Mel had told her all about the new boy, and how he'd decked his old sergeant back in the Smoke. Rumour had it that the sergeant had it coming, which was why Barrington wasn't prosecuted, but still. Hillary couldn't have been any too pleased to learn that Blacklock Green's troublemaker was being seconded onto her team.

Keith Barrington met Hillary Greene's dark brown eyes without flinching. 'I don't think it'll be a problem, guv,' he said. But he had to wonder. Had the brass back in Blacklock Green arranged for all this? Did they know DI Greene's resident sergeant was a wrong 'un, and deliberately made sure he got posted here, just to see if he'd lose control and clock this Ross character too? Were they *that* determined to get him booted off the force? Because his career would never survive another incident like that last one.

If so, they were in for a nasty disappointment, Keith thought grimly. He was damned if he was going to let them get him down.

Especially since his new boss seemed to be all right. He found himself inclined to like her, but first impressions weren't always reliable, he knew. And there was still that problem with her bravery award. It worried him. It worried him a lot. If she was the gung-ho sort who liked to take chances and grab the glory, and sod the consequences to those around her, then it might not be Frank Ross he felt like clocking.

Hillary's eyes narrowed slightly. It was almost as if she could read his mind, and he shifted uncomfortably in his seat. He didn't know it, but he was only one of a long line of people who half-believed Hillary Greene could do just that. Many was the villain, and underling, who'd faced her questions and felt as if he was being read like a book.

Hillary abruptly nodded and reached for a folder from her In tray. 'OK then. Janine, bring ... you want to be called constable, Barrington or Keith?' She turned back to the new boy, who hesitated a moment, then replied.

'Keith's fine, guv.'

Hillary nodded. 'OK. Janine, bring Keith up to speed with our ongoing cases. Your paperwork all up to date?'

'Boss,' Janine said flatly, giving her a hard-eyed look. She'd never referred to Hillary as 'guv' and, in truth, resented just a little having to work with another woman. But she'd never given DI Greene cause to complain about her standards of work. And just because she was getting married in a few days' time didn't mean she'd been slackening off either. A few months ago, she'd failed her first sitting of the Inspectorship Boards, exams that she thought she'd aced, and she was still smarting from that. But she knew she could do her job standing on her head, even with all the hassles from her anonymous bloody friend. The bastard might have succeeded in distracting her now and then, but she could handle it.

Hillary, used as she was to Janine's prickly character, wondered again what was eating at her, because something definitely was. Far more than usual. There was little chance of the blonde woman confiding in her, she knew, so she'd have to keep an eye out and see what she could discover. Right now, however, work beckoned. She opened the folder containing a hit-and-run case that was almost certainly going into the 'open' file before long. A young lad on a bike, on his way to Technical college, had been knocked off it into the roadside ditch, and lain undiscovered for several hours. Luckily he was making a good recovery, but with no witnesses and very little by way of forensics except for a paint scraping that could match over a hundred thousand vehicles, she couldn't see it going anywhere. Reluctantly, she signed off on it, then glanced across at Janine. There were dark patches under her eyes, and she'd noticed for several weeks now that she seemed jumpy, and far more aggressive than usual. She dreaded to think who the brass would assign to replace her. What she sorely needed was an experienced sergeant, preferably without any baggage. Ross was useless, and the new boy was very much an unknown quantity. She found herself missing Tommy Lynch more than ever.

She was just reading her notebook on an arson case she was due to testify on in court next week, when she saw Chief Inspector Paul Danvers come out of his cubby hole and walk quickly across towards them. He was a tall man, lean, blond and classically handsome, and today was wearing a dark blue suit so severe it must have cost a bomb.

He was also the man who'd once investigated her for corruption. And was now her immediate superior.

He was already smiling at her as he approached, though a paradoxical frown seemed to tug at his eyebrows. Danvers stopped at her desk and held out a piece of paper. His eyes skimmed over her with their usual welcoming warmth, which Hillary habitually ignored, hoping it would go away.

'This just came in,' Danvers said. 'Report of a suspicious death in Bicester. I'd like you to take it.'

Janine perked up instantly, and Keith felt his heart beat quicken. He'd not been here an hour, and already they had a possible murder on their hands. Some action already. Unless the new boss made him stay and play catch-up.

But Hillary Greene was already reaching for her bag, and her look took in the both of them as she said, 'Right. Drop everything else. Guv, if DS Ross comes in, can you point him our way?'

Danvers nodded, glanced at the new boy, seemed about to say something, then thought better of it. Instead he merely nodded, turned, and went back to his office. But he wasn't happy. He'd argued strongly against Barrington being foisted on Hillary Greene, but had been overruled. Just let the violent little sod lay one finger on her, he thought, and he'd be out on his ear so fast he wouldn't touch the floor on his way out.

As Hillary lead the way through the large open-plan office towards the exit, Janine said to Barrington out of the corner of her mouth, 'Unless you missed that, Danvers has the hots for Hillary. Everyone knows it, but she's got her head stuck in the sand at the moment, so don't get in the middle of it. Danvers might look like a walking advertisement for the Chippendales, but he doesn't take no for an answer. He'll wear her down, and he won't want any interference from the likes of us. So watch your back.'

Keith, who hadn't missed the way the CI had eyed up his new boss, sighed deeply. This was just great. He felt like he was stepping into a bloody soap opera. Tyler was marrying the Super, the CI had the hots for his immediate boss, and Frank Ross was probably going to be a twin of his bastard of a sergeant back at Blacklock.

So much for a new start.

'I don't suppose you know the area just yet,' Hillary said to Barrington as they dashed across the wet and squally car park towards her car. 'So I'll drive.' It was usual protocol for the senior officer to be driven. Once inside the car and buckled up, she started the engine, and added, 'But if I were you, I'd spend some of my spare time just riding around, getting a feel for the geography.'

'Guv.'

As she pulled out of the car park, headed to the roundabout, then motored quickly down the main road towards Bicester, she gave him a quick lesson. 'Bicester's one of several market towns that fall in our catchment area, about ten miles from here. It's grown a lot in recent years, and is popular with commuters, being close to both Birmingham and London with the motorways right on its doorstep.'

She glanced in the mirror, saw Janine's 'new' mini close behind and swore as the wind took the car and pulled it towards the centre of the road. She fought it back, and reluctantly lowered her speed a little. The windscreen wipers of the old car battled to keep the glass clear as the rain suddenly became torrential. She swore under her breath again, and lowered her speed even more, knowing that Janine, behind her, would probably not approve. Janine was the kind who liked to get where she was going fast.

Barrington, however, relaxed a little as she reduced speed, and inside, he felt a lessening of the tension that had been building up ever since his hostile reception at his new nick. At least his new boss wasn't going to wrap them around a telegraph pole.

'Know anything about the vic, guv?' he asked a few minutes later, but Hillary shook her head.

'Not much. Female, the only resident of the house where she was found. It might turn out to be a domestic accident or suicide.'

Barrington nodded, looking out of the streaming

windows nervously. More green fields. Bare twigged hedges. Cows. Actual cows, grazing. Now sheep. Apart from the road ahead, with its steady stream of oncoming pale head-lights, there wasn't a manmade thing in sight. He sighed heavily, caught his new boss looking at him, and clamped his lips hard together.

Hillary gave a mental shrug and concentrated on driving. In front of her a Peugeot started to aquaplane, and she touched her brakes gently.

This was going to be a long morning.

The house was a small two-up, two-down, in a row of terraced council houses in the King's End area of Bicester. She found it by asking a postman, who'd parked up and was staring gloomily out of his window at the sky.

The rain was easing just a little as they parked behind a patrol car. The uniform posted at the door watched her approach, nodded as she showed her ID, and entered her name into the log. Behind her, she heard Janine and then Barrington go through the same procedure. Inside, the tiny passageway was dark, and plastic sheeting already covered the carpet, put down by SOCO to preserve any signs of footprints on the carpet. She moved towards the first open door and glanced inside. Here, also, protective polythene had been laid, and the flash of a police photographer briefly lit the dim grey light filtering into the room.

A man dressed in white overalls was dusting a mantel-piece for prints. She was slightly surprised to see SOCO already in place. Contrary to popular public belief, almost any death was labelled 'suspicious' until a senior investi-gating officer had declared it otherwise. He or she usually relied on a mixture of experience, common sense, and the initial report of a police doctor, before deciding on how to proceed. The fact that SOCO was here meant that there could be very little doubt that this was a murder. The uniforms who'd first arrived at the scene must have reported it in as such.

Rather than go inside and interrupt them, she turned and made her way to the second door, which lead into a tiny kitchen. SOCO had already been here, for two constables stood around the kitchen table, drinking tea from their thermos flasks. One looked about eighteen and a bit green around the gills, the other was older, and far more sanguine. Both straightened up when they spotted her.

'DI Greene, SIO,' Hillary introduced herself. 'You first up?'

'Yes ma'am.' The taller, older of the two, reached unasked for his notebook and commenced to give a short but detailed account. Behind her, Janine got her own notebook out, ready to start transcribing. 'We received a 999 call at 8.27 this morning from a female person, who gave her name as Mrs Caroline Weekes. She reported finding the body of her friend, in her house, and said she'd been stabbed to death. We were dispatched, and found a woman waiting at the gate. She appeared pale and had been crying, but was able to confirm her identity and the telephone call and told us where to find the victim.' He cleared his throat, and turned the page. 'I told Constable Myers here to stay with Mrs Weekes, and proceeded inside. I could see only one set of footprints, still wet and approximately size five, leading down the hall to the lounge. I took these to belong to Mrs Weekes. Inside, I saw the body of an elderly woman, sitting in her chair. Life was extinct. She had what appeared to be the hilt of some sort of ornamental knife or dagger protruding out of her chest. I immediately reported back in, and asked for SOCO and detective division. When back-up came, I had a WPC escort Mrs Weekes back to her home. I have her address. The victim, according to Mrs Weekes, is Mrs Florence Jenkins, 76, widow and sole resident.' He closed the notebook and glanced at Hillary.

'You said life was extinct. You checked this with a finger to the side of the neck?'

'Yes ma'am.'

'You didn't touch the body or anything else?'

'No ma'am, I was careful. Hands firmly in pockets,' he repeated the policeman's mantra with a smile, and Hillary grinned back. She recognized him vaguely from around, and no doubt he knew her as well.

Barrington, who'd been listening and looking over Janine's shoulder, noted the uniform's easy manner around Hillary Greene, and felt yet more of the tension leave him.

'Right. Well, you can't stay here in the warm and dry all morning. Might as well start on house-to-house, and make yourself useful,' Hillary said. 'It's almost stopped raining.'

The younger one hastily emptied his plastic mug and screwed the lid back on his thermos.

'Since we don't have an approximate time of death yet, keep it vague,' Hillary advised. 'Did anyone see or hear anything unusual? Did she have any visitors in the last forty-eight hours. General gossip. Was she well liked, or was she the neighbour from hell? You know the drill,' she added. 'Keith, you can help them out. I want a list of those who seem to know her the best. I might need to do some follow-ups. As soon as DS Ross deigns to show up, I'll get him to help you out too.'

'Guv,' Barrington said.

'Janine, I want you to do a thorough search of the house, see if you can find any signs of a break-in or illegal entry. And I want a full inventory of the contents of the house. We'll have to get somebody, a relative or close friend, to go through it and see if anything's been stolen.' It didn't quite have the feel of a burglary gone wrong to her, but it had to be checked out, nonetheless.

'Boss,' Janine said heavily. More scut work.

'Then get on to doing a background check on her.'

Janine nodded, and Hillary watched them all troop out, then walked to the door to the lounge again.

So, it was an old lady. She couldn't see much from her position in the doorway, for a white-overalled figure was knelt down in front of the chair, concealing the body from her view as he dusted the chair arm for prints and traces, but there was always something particularly sad about the old meeting a violent end. They always seemed so ill-equipped to deal with it. Especially the women. She'd probably been someone's mother and grandmother. Had she been looking forward to spending Christmas with her family? Had she been busy knitting sweaters that embarrassed family members would only ever wear when they knew she was going to be around?

Hillary shook her head. This was pointless, and only making her feel depressed. She turned instead and left them to it, walking to the front door and then stepping out into a light drizzle. Even the wind seemed to be dying down. She glanced around the tiny rectangle of bare winter garden, and across a ragged privet hedge, and saw an old man in the house immediately abutting on the right, staring out at her from his window. She saw Keith Barrington start up the pathway, and on impulse called him back. 'It's OK, I'll take this one. Try the next.'

'Guv.'

The old man had the door open by the time Hillary got there, and instantly stood aside to let her in. 'Something's happened to Flo then?' he asked flatly, as she passed.

Hillary nodded, watched him close the door, and glanced around. The tiny corridor was an exact replica of next door, and when the old man indicated she was to go in through the first door, she wasn't surprised. Inside, a single comfortable armchair was pulled up close to a gas fire. Sleeping on the mat in front of it was a large black cat. Hillary took a hard-backed wooden chair and moved it forward, careful not to disturb the slumbering feline, and looked around. Pale apricot-coloured walls and a somewhat dirty beige carpet blended together and was soft on the eye. An original but not very good seascape was the only painting on the wall, and a large-faced clock ticked ponderously from over the fireplace. On the mantelpiece were two pictures – one of a couple on their wedding day, their style of dress straight out of the forties. The other was a group picture of men in uniform. Commandos, by the look of them. One of them, no doubt, was now the current home owner.

'She dead then?' The old man slowly lowered himself into his chair. He had sparse white hair and was wearing a heavy grey knitted cardigan, a clean white shirt, and a pair of dark grey trousers. He looked neat and smelt clean. Obviously a man fully in charge of both his faculties and his living conditions. Good. Such people usually made excellent witnesses.

Hillary got out her notebook. 'Can I have your full name, sir?'

'Sure. Walter Mitchell Keane.'

'You've lived here long?'

'Since the council built 'em back in 1948.'

'So you knew Mrs Jenkins well?'

'Course I do. Her and Clive moved in same time as we did. Clive was her old man, dead now twenty years. My own gal, Phyllis,' he nodded at the wedding picture, 'went a few years after. Why are you lot here, then?' he asked sharply. 'She didn't die in her sleep, did she? Not with you lot out in force.'

While his words might have been belligerent, Hillary didn't think they were meant to be. Walter Keane was just one of those men who spoke in a simple and forthright manner that was probably leftover from his army days. Someone who had little time for the pleasantries in life. 'I can't discuss an ongoing case, sir,' she said, but showed her ID. 'I'm Detective Inspector Hillary Greene from Thames Valley Police, and I'm the Senior Investigating Officer here. I'd appreciate it if you could answer some questions for me.'

She had an idea he'd respond automatically to authority, and wasn't disappointed. He was a tall, thin, stoop-shouldered man, the kind who'd be unexpectedly wiry and tough, and as expected, his back straightened a little at her crisp, no-nonsense tone.

'Do all I can to help,' he said gruffly.

'Did you hear anything odd from next door, within, say the last forty-eight hours?'

'No. I heard Flo's telly come on last night at the usual time, about six o'clock. She liked to listen to the news.'

'Did you hear it go off again later that night?' Hillary asked sharply, remembering that the television had still been on when she'd popped her head around the door for a look.

'No, but then I wouldn't. I always went to bed before she did, see. Told her she was the spring chicken, but us older bods needed their shut-eye. I'm eighty,' he added.

Hillary nodded. 'Did she usually watch breakfast TV?' she asked next, blessing the thinness of the walls.

'Never,' Walter Keane said firmly. 'Neither of us could stand them blathering, all those smiley faces first thing.' He shuddered.

Hillary nodded thoughtfully. So, if the telly was still on, it probably meant it had been on all night. In which case, Flo Jenkins had been dead for some time. 'Do you know when Mrs Jenkins usually went to bed?'

'Eleven or thereabouts.'

So, the killer probably came some time between six and eleven, Hillary mused. It would be interesting to see if Doc Partridge's findings, when he came, confirmed her working theory.

'And you never heard someone come to the door last night? She have a doorbell or a knocker, by the way?'

'Both. And now you mention it, I did hear the doorbell go next door last night. About 6.30, 6.40. Something like that.'

'Did you hear whoever it was talking to Mrs Jenkins? Did they argue?'

'No. Not loud, at any rate. You can't hear normal human voices so much. The telly, yeah, and the doorbell. And when she plays that bloody awful music of hers – Des O'Connor. I ask you! But no, I didn't hear no voices.'

Hillary underlined the last sentence in her book. Find out who called last night at 6.30. 'Did Mrs Jenkins have any enemies that you know of? Did she ever mention any ill feeling between her and her family perhaps? Or a neighbour?'

'Flo? Any enemies? Don't be daft,' Walter Keane snorted. 'Salt of the earth, Flo. Always willing to help out – not that she could do much, mind. Not been well lately. But she would lend you the shirt off her back if you needed it more'n her. She didn't gossip nasty about you neither, behind your back, unlike some around here.'

'And her family?'

'Her and Clive only had the one. Daughter, Elizabeth, though everyone called her Liza. Not that she was much good to her old mum. Hit the sauce, didn't she, when her husband left her. Drank herself to death, I reckon, though they did say it was cancer of the liver. She only had the one boy – Dylan. And he's worse than his mum, only with him it's the drugs, see. A proper little druggie. Layabout, idle good-for-nothing bum. He was always cadging off Flo, and all she had to live on was her own pension, and a little money Clive left her.'

'Dylan. Do you know his last name?'

'Hodge.'

'I don't suppose you know where he's living, do you?'

'Squatting somewhere I 'spect,' Walter Keane said flatly, then added, more plaintively, 'She's really gone then, Flo?' His voice trembled slightly, and Hillary slowly reached out and touched the old man's knobbly hands, where they rested on top of his knees.

'I'm sorry,' she said softly.

'Pity,' Walter said, his eyes suspiciously bright. 'She was looking forward to her birthday at the end of the week. "I'll be all the sevens, Walt," she said to me a while ago. "My lucky number, seven." And then she laughed.' Walter shook his head. 'Christmas too. She loved Christmas – like a big kid she was. Always put up a tree, and lights, and those colourful twirling things hanging from the ceiling. She couldn't get up a stepladder no more, so it was usually me she had round to help her put 'em up. She was really looking forward to it this year, especially.'

Hillary swallowed hard, was about to say something, then heard a car pull up outside. She got up, and a quick look through the window revealed a low, classic sports car. She smiled wryly. Doctor Steven Partridge had just arrived.

She turned back to look at Walter, and said softly, 'Do you want me to call anyone for you? To come and sit with you perhaps?'

At this, Walter Keane stiffened almost to attention in his chair, and shot her an upbraiding look. 'Of course not,' he said, with immense dignity.

Hillary nodded. 'Well, I have to go now, but I expect we'll talk again, Mr Keane. Thank you for your help.'

Walter got to his feet with surprising agility for one so old, and again, Hillary was left with the feeling that this old man was actually quite fit. Maybe he was even one of those octogenarians that ran half-marathons and what not.

'You just find out who did for her,' Walter said grimly. 'It's not right that she didn't get to have her birthday party, or Christmas. You just find out.'

Hillary met the watery blue eyes, and nodded grimly. 'I intend to, Mr Keane,' she said.

chapter three

She doesn't look very well, was Hillary's first impression on seeing the corpse of Florence Jenkins. Which wasn't as incongruous a thought as many people might have assumed. In her time, Hillary had seen many dead people – some whose image still haunted her today. But from all she'd heard about this latest victim, she'd died of a neat, single stab wound to the chest, and she'd been half-expecting the body to look as if it might get up and speak at any moment.

In truth, there *was* an air of peaceful patience about Florence Jenkins. She was dressed in one of those pinafore flower dresses that Hillary's grandmother had favoured, and had on over it a warm cardigan. Her wispy white hair was done up on the back of her head in a bun that had become skewed to one side of her head after a night of being pressed against the back of the chair. She wasn't wearing make-up, but even now, the aroma of 4711 still emanated from her. She looked, in fact, as if she'd just fallen asleep.

But she still didn't look well.

Her skin, wrinkled and pale, hung on her face in a way that told Hillary she'd recently lost a lot of weight, much too fast. Her eyes had dark sunken circles around them. The shape of her skull was clearly, and eerily, pronounced.

Hillary sighed, feeling uncomfortably warm in the small room, and watched Steven Partridge as he worked. He was both meticulous and careful and watching him was somehow strangely pleasant. He wasn't a big man, and his hair was carefully coloured. Hillary wasn't sure how old he was, but she'd put him nearer sixty than the forty he actually looked. His clothes, as ever, were impeccable and costly. He rose at last, and carefully dusted off his knees before turning to Hillary and shrugging.

'Well, pretty much everything is as you see,' he murmured. 'I'd put her in her mid-seventies. I can't find a single wound or mark of violence on her, save for that.' He pointed with distaste to the intricate metal dagger head protruding from her chest.

'Any idea what that is?' Hillary asked curiously, bending down for a closer look. 'It looks like a base metal of some kind.'

Doc Partridge grunted. 'Wouldn't be surprised if it isn't an ornament of some kind. It's got the look of a fancy paperknife, or some sort of fancy dagger someone brings back from Spain with them. Toledo steel, wouldn't be surprised. Whatever it is, I think it's very sharp. I can see very little sign of snagging in the flesh – still, can't say for sure till I get her on the table.'

Hillary nodded. She was lucky it was Steven Partridge who'd taken the call. Some police surgeons wouldn't speculate so much as a word at a crime scene. But she and Doc Partridge were friends of old, and he nearly always trusted her with his preliminary thoughts, knowing she was too wise to take them as gospel before they'd been confirmed. 'Did it require medical knowledge, do you think?' Hillary asked next. 'The blow seems very well placed.'

The medical man shrugged, pulling off his rubber gloves carefully and dropping them into his open bag. 'I'm not sure. Could have been just a lucky blow. Mind you, she's old. The knife needn't even have perforated the heart to kill her straight away. The blade could have missed her aorta altogether, come to think of it. Depends how long the blade is. Besides, the shock alone would probably have been enough to finish her off.'

Hillary sighed. 'You think she was knifed where she sat?'

'Almost certainly, I should say. The angle of the blade appears to be downwards.'

Hillary nodded. 'I can't see any sign of blood on the carpet either. So it's unlikely she was killed somewhere else and moved here.' She was talking more or less to herself by now. 'Any guess on time of death?' she asked sharply, focusing once more on the dapper medico.

Partridge smiled. 'Knew you'd ask me that. You got any guesses yourself, from preliminary interviews?' he asked, obviously edging.

Hillary smiled. 'Between seven and eleven last night?' She raised her voice at the end, making it a question.

The doctor smiled. 'I'll go along with that.'

'Why so cagey?' she asked curiously, and Partridge turned and pointed at the gas fire.

'That,' Steven Partridge said succinctly. 'The victim's been sitting close to a constant heat source, for who knows how long. Plays bloody havoc with rigor and the whole science of predicting time of death, I can tell you.'

It *was* very warm in the room, and no wonder, if the fire had been going all through the night. Especially if the door had been shut as well. Hillary sighed. 'Great.' She wondered if the killer knew that, and was that why he or she had left the fire on? Or had they simply not given it another thought, and simply left it burning? It was possible the killer had turned the fire on when they left, but Hillary didn't think it very likely. It was the middle of winter, after all, and the old felt the cold more than most. It was almost impossible to think that Flo Jenkins herself hadn't turned the fire on, and kept it on all day.

'Is it just me, or doesn't she look well?' Hillary finally had to ask, and wasn't all that surprised when Steven shot her a quick, interested look.

It was a sign of how much he respected her that he never even suspected she was being facetious. Some coppers he worked with could be brutal sods, often hiding discomfort behind coarse humour. But since it was Hillary Greene asking, he shot the corpse another, less functional glance, and slowly frowned. 'No, it's not just you. Sudden weight loss, bags under the eyes. Irregular sleeping habits. Hmmm … I think, when I get this old girl on the table, she might have lots to tell me. Mind you, it might be a while. I've got two days backlog as it is.'

Hillary sighed. 'I'll let you get on with it then,' she said wearily. 'Oh, and doc, can you make removal of the murder weapon a priority, please? I don't want it sitting in her for a couple of days when I can get cracking on it.'

Steven shut his bag with a snap. 'I'll get it photographed and removed, bagged and tagged on its way to you before you leave tonight.'

'You're a prince Doc.'

'So kind. Oh, and talking of princes, I think I can see Sergeant Ross arriving,' he said drily, grinning as Hillary groaned.

She became aware of Janine hovering behind her, just as Frank Ross came through the open doorway. He was a round, fat-faced man in his fifties, with very deceiving Winnie-the-Pooh placid features, and a shabby way of dressing.

'Decided to turn up then?' Hillary said shortly, then held up a hand, before he could start whining excuses. 'Forget it, I can't be bothered,' she said. 'You can join the new boy on house-to-house. And Frank, I expect you to work through the lunch hour. Don't let me find you in a pub somewhere.'

Frank merely shrugged. At one time he might have mumbled something obscene under his breath, or even shot her the finger if she thought she wasn't looking.

His hangover must be particularly vicious this morning, Hillary mused to herself, then glanced behind her. 'Got something for me?'

Janine nodded. 'Boss. Victim's handbag. I found it on the

sofa opposite where she was sitting. Usual stuff, but her purse only contained twenty-three pence in change. No pound coins or folding stuff at all. Now it might just be she was skint, but it was pension day yesterday. If she collected it, or had it collected for her, where is it?'

Hillary nodded. 'Any other signs of robbery?'

'Not definite, boss, but her jewellery box is almost empty. Only some obvious cheap stuff in the bottom drawer. But until we know if she even had any good stuff in the first place ...' She trailed off with a graphic shrug.

Hillary nodded. 'OK. I'm going to interview the finder of the body. See if she knows what Flo Jenkins had by way of goodies. Any sign of a break-in?'

'No boss.'

Hillary nodded. 'OK, keep at it.'

Janine nodded, and watched her from the window as her superior officer walked down the short concrete path. The pretty blonde woman bit her lip as she stood there, an unconscious habit she had when she was anxious. Should she tell Hillary what was going on? Janine was almost positive that she'd know how best to handle it. And once or twice she'd caught Hillary Greene looking at her oddly, almost as if she'd guessed anyway. It was almost spooky when she did that. Instinctively, Janine felt she could trust her. She'd worked with the woman for four years now, and if she trusted anyone, it was Hillary Greene. Only her pride, and a contrasting sense of humiliation, stopped her. Hell, she doubted anyone would ever have the guts to stalk Hillary Greene! Besides, it was something she could deal with herself, right? She was a bloody sergeant, for pete's sake, soon to be married to a super, and, when the next chance to take her Boards came along, a DI herself. She could handle some wanker who liked to leave silly messages. Hell yes.

With a shrug, Janine got on with listing the contents of Flo Jenkins' life.

The uniform guarding the front gate told Hillary where she could find Caroline Weekes, which turned out to be just a short distance to the end of the road, where she crossed over and went a few hundred yards up the next street. As she walked, however, she might have been crossing a border to another country.

Here, the cramped, identical houses built by the council, suddenly gave way to far more modern, detached and semi-detached private houses. The gardens were smaller, more well tended, the cars that were still parked on the road, more expensive and up-market.

Caroline Weekes' house was one of those trying to look like a miniature Tudor mansion. Bushes that had seen topiary clippers stood like sentinels beside a slate grey concrete path. When she rang the door bell, the WPC who answered straightened up a little at the sight of Hillary's warrant card, and ushered her through to the lounge. The room was long and full of light, one end opening onto the back garden through a large set of French doors, the other having a large panoramic window that gave a great view of the road. A mock fireplace that had no actual chimney, played host to a gas fire that looked like real logs and flames, and a large winter landscape painting dominated one wall. The flooring was modern wooden planking, with scattered black and white throw rugs scattered strategically around. From the depths of a white leather sofa, a pale-faced woman looked up at her.

'Mrs Weekes, this is Detective Inspector Hillary Greene.' It was the WPC who introduced them. 'She's the senior investigating office of Flo's case. Can I make you a cup of tea, ma'am?' she added to Hillary, who nodded back. She knew the uniform wouldn't come back with tea unless she actually indicated that she wanted it. It was just a way of leaving them alone, whilst she got on with the interview.

'Hello Mrs Weekes. I'm sorry to bother you so soon. I know it must have been quite a shock for you.' As she spoke, she walked forward and, uninvited, sat down in a large, black leather chair. It faced the sofa across the expanse of a wide, glass-topped coffee table, on which rested a luxuriant spider plant and one of those books full of stunning photography. The whole place reminded Hillary of one of those ideal homes exhibitions. Did anybody really live in such spotless elegance? Well, evidently Caroline Weekes did.

The witness was dressed imaginatively and well, but her eyes were large and hollow looking, and she noticed that the woman sat with her hands under her armpits as if trying to warm them. All signs of distress and shock.

But, as the statistics showed, the person who first found a body had to go straight to the top of any investigator's list. Any trace or forensic evidence found on such a person could so easily be explained away, which was why many killers opted to 'find' their victim before anyone else had the chance to. She hoped the WPC had explained to Mrs Weekes that they'd be needing the clothes she'd been wearing when she found Flo Jenkins.

'So, perhaps you can just talk me through what happened this morning,' Hillary began, keeping her voice friendly and light. 'You woke up at your usual time?'

'Yes. Seven. John has to get up that early to make the commute. He works in High Wycombe.'

'John's your husband?'

'Yes.' She gave his details and Hillary wrote them down, though she doubted they'd be needed. But it was often useful to slide into these things gradually.

'You had breakfast?' she prompted.

'Yes. Cornflakes. Tea. I left the house to go to work about ten past, quarter past eight. Something like that.'

'You didn't drive?'

'No, I usually catch the bus. I only work in town, so it's easier. Parking and all.'

'But you called in to see Mrs Jenkins. You usually do that?'

'Yes, couple of times a week. Just to see if she needs anything – shopping, her rubbish bin taken out, that kind of thing. I can pop into Somerfield, which is just over the road from work, then nip on the bus, take it to her, and still have a decent lunch hour. Sometimes she used to do me soup and toast at her place.' Her voice sounded wistful, as if it had just occurred to her that there would be no more such lunches.

Hillary nodded. 'I'm sorry. It sounds as if you were very friendly.'

'We were.'

'How did you meet?'

'At a funeral, of all things.' Caroline gave a grim laugh and turned her head to stare out of the rain-speckled window. 'A neighbour and close friend of my mother's. Flo also knew her from way back. We got talking, realized we only lived a few minutes' walk from each other, and she invited me over for tea the following week. I might not have gone, you know how it is, but it seemed rude. Anyway, I went, and we got talking, and we sort of clicked. Lots of people think that's strange – her being so much older, but that was never really an issue. Oh, over the years, I started doing bits and bobs for her – when she couldn't manage so well. You know how it is. But really, I'm not much of a good Samaritan. I don't help out charities, or spend time at soup kitchens or stuff like that. It was just for Flo.' She fiddled with a button on her jacket and frowned. 'I don't want you to get the impression I'm a goody two shoes. One of those frightful women who think they know what's best for the elderly and go around doing good works. That's not me at all. And it wasn't Flo, either. She was fiercely independent as a rule, but just lately she's been under the weather and simply couldn't do as much as she used to. She hated having to ask, so I made sure I asked her first if there was something she needed.'

Hillary nodded. 'I see,' she said. 'Can you tell me if Mrs

Jenkins picked up her pension yesterday? She'd have to get it in town somewhere, yes?'

'Yes, the post office on Sheep Street. It's situated at the back of that big newsagents just up from the Penny Black pub. And yes, she did get it. I drove her down that morning, then back again in my lunch hour. She liked to wander around the charity shops and have a cup of tea and a bun in Nash's.'

'Do you know what she did with it? Her pension money, I mean?' Hillary asked, and the other woman looked at her blankly.

'Good Lord, no. I suppose she kept it in her handbag. Or she might have hidden it somewhere I suppose. I don't really know. We didn't discuss money much. Sometimes, if I'd take her to somewhere like Oxford or Banbury, she'd try to insist on paying me some petrol money, but I'd always turn her down. Say I had to go into town anyway, something like that.'

Hillary nodded. 'And this morning. You walked to her door and knocked, same as usual?'

'Yes. But nobody answered, and the curtains were all drawn. The woman across the street ... oh I do wish I could remember her name, it's been on the tip of my tongue all morning. I can't think why ... Well, she was just collecting her milk. We talked for a bit, but she hadn't seen Flo that morning, and I was getting a bit worried, so I used my key to go in.'

'You have a key then? May I have it, Mrs Weekes? I need to log it into evidence.'

'Oh, yes of course. My bag ...' She looked around, and Hillary pointed to the bag on the floor beside the sofa. 'Oh thanks. Right. It's this one.' She fiddled with a fairly bulky set of keys, hanging from a black cat key ring. 'Here.' Finally she handed over a silver-coloured Yale. Hillary carefully retrieved an evidence bag from her pocket, slipped the key inside and sealed it, then peeled off a label from a roll kept in her handbag, noted the time and details, and slipped the whole lot back.

'Can you remember when Mrs Jenkins first gave you her key?'

'Oh, nearly a year ago now. It made sense, I suppose. Sometimes she'd be out and I'd have shopping for her that I couldn't leave on the doorstep. Sometimes she'd phone from bingo and ask me to let her cat in, or she'd go off on one of those old folks weekends to Paignton and ask me to feed it. It was just easier to have a key.'

'Right.' Hillary made a note in her book to see to the cat. If a neighbour or friend didn't want it, she'd have to get the new boy to take it to an animal shelter. There'd been no sign of it that morning, though. Probably all the people and activity had kept it away. 'And this morning...?' she prompted, and Caroline's face tightened.

'Yes. Right, this morning.' She rubbed her palms nervously against the tops of her knees.

She didn't really want to go there, Hillary realized, but it had to be done.

'Like I said, there was no answer, so I used the key. I went into the hall, but I couldn't hear her moving about upstairs. I thought she might have overslept see. I went into the lounge. I was surprised to see the telly on. And the lights were on, but the curtains were drawn. And then I saw her, or rather, the top of her head, showing over the chair. And I walked forward a little, thinking she'd nodded off and saw ... well, that thing sticking out of her chest. And she was so still and pale. I just knew she was dead.' She was taking deep, quick breaths now, fighting back tears and rising hysteria.

'Did you touch anything, Mrs Weekes?' Hillary asked gently, calmly, trying to slow her down.

Caroline Weekes shuddered in another breath, and wiped her palms frantically against her knees. 'No. No, I don't think so. I remember walking outside, and thinking how nice and cool it was. And phoning. And waiting.'

Hillary nodded. 'Did you notice anything odd or out of place in the room?'

Caroline frowned, looking puzzled. 'No. I don't think so. I didn't really notice. All I could see was Flo.'

'And earlier, when you approached her house. Did you see anyone hanging around, or a car you hadn't seen before, parked close by, or pulling away from the kerb?'

Caroline shook her head.

Hillary hadn't really expected anything else – it was beginning to look more and more as if the old woman had been killed last night. But the routine questions were having the effect of calming the witness down. 'Had Flo mentioned anyone harassing her lately?'

'No. Well, only that grandson of hers, but he was always scrounging off her. Nothing more than usual.'

'And she seemed much the same as ever, this last week or so?' Hillary asked.

'Yes. She was looking forward to her birthday party for instance. Nothing fancy, she was just going to invite all her old friends around. I was going to bake her the usual chocolate cake. She always liked my chocolate cake. Everyone was to bring a bottle of booze with them, and she and Walter next door would make sandwiches and heat up sausage rolls, that sort of thing. She did it every year.'

Hillary nodded. This confirmed Walter Keane's assessment of Flo Jenkins. It was looking more and more unlikely that the victim had been aware of any danger. Had she simply been killed for her pension money? It seemed a bit extreme. But stranger things had happened. She'd certainly have to interview this grandson of hers soon.

Caroline Weekes closed her eyes for a moment and then had to force them open. Soon, she'd be asleep. Hillary had seen that before. Emotional exhaustion had a way of catching up with you.

'Well, that's all for now, Mrs Weekes. I'll just have a

quick word with the WPC. She'll stay for a little while longer. Has she called anyone for you?'

'Yes, my mother. She lives in Cowley. She'll be here soon.'

'Good. I'll probably have to talk with you again, as things come up. Perhaps, when you're feeling better, you can have a think about any items of value you noticed in Flo's house and make me a list. We haven't ruled out robbery as a motive yet.'

'Oh. Well, I'm not sure I'll be much good at that,' Caroline demurred, flushing slightly. 'I'm not the sort of person who notices things like that. I mean, what people have. Or wear. That kind of thing.' And then, as Hillary glanced around the glamorous room, she laughed. 'Oh, all this is down to my husband. He has taste,' she said the final words as if it was a virtue on a par with courage or chastity.

Hillary nodded. 'Well, if you could do your best,' she encouraged, and got up. Out in the kitchen, she accepted a now nearly cold cup of tea, and drank it off in a few gulps, reminding the WPC to bag and tag the clothes Caroline was wearing, and send them to the evidence officer. 'Oh, and take a set of her prints. At this point we only need them for elimination purposes.' But you never knew. If Caroline Weekes' dabs turned up on the murder weapon, she might be able to wrap this case up in record time. But something told her it wasn't going to be that easy. In the meantime, it was back to number 18 Holburn Crescent.

Back at Kidlington HQ, a young man dressed in uniform watched as one of the civilian admin workers pushed the mail trolley down the corridor and paused outside the common room. It was mostly deserted and when she went inside to help herself to a quick cup of coffee, he moved carefully and fast, slipping a long, plain brown envelope under a pile of internal mail. He did it without breaking his stride, and once past the trolley, he began to whistle lightly as he crossed a small hall area, and headed for the stairs.

He was smiling as he headed down towards Records. The blonde baby doll was going to appreciate his latest offering, he was sure.

Hillary wasn't all that surprised to find most of her team standing outside Flo's garden gate. Janine was the first to spot her and the new boy stiffened and turned as she said curtly, 'Boss.'

Frank Ross, who was just making his way towards them, drew level and gave Keith Barrington a flat stare.

'I've finished the inventory,' Janine was saying. 'Someone could have lifted a music centre, there seems to be a space where something like that might have stood. There's nothing of obvious value left in the house save for the telly. But it could be the old dear was just hard up.'

'Right, Frank. Introduce yourself to the old man next door, Walter Keane. He knew the vic well. Sit with him and coax out a list of Flo Jenkins' worldly goods, would you? I've asked Caroline Weekes to do the same, but I'm not holding out much hope on her.'

'Guv,' Ross said, not moving. 'This the new bloke then?'

Hillary sighed. 'Keith Barrington, Sergeant Frank Ross.'

Ross grinned savagely. 'Better not pop off on me, sunshine. I'm not some nancy pansy city boy. Take a swing for me and I'll be marching on your goolies before you know what's hit you.' It went very quiet.

Into the silence, Hillary said drily, 'That's Sergeant Ross' way of welcoming you to the team, Keith.'

Janine snorted a laugh, and Hillary pointed to the house next door. 'Work, Frank. And don't …' before she could say anything more her mobile rang. She sighed heavily and reached for it. 'DI Greene.' she snapped, then blinked. 'Yes, sir.'

Janine rolled her eyes. 'Must be Donleavy,' she whispered sotto voce to Barrington. 'Our chief super. She never uses that tone when talking to Mel. She and the super are old friends from way back. It was his life she saved when she got her gong.'

Hillary's face became tight, making Janine break off the history lesson. 'Hello, something's up,' she muttered.

'I understand that, sir, but I've just started a murder investigation. I've only been on scene less than four hours ...' She bit the rest off, listened, sighed and said, 'Yes, sir, I'll return right away. I'll be with you in half an hour.' She listened for a few more seconds, said tersely, 'Sir,' and hung up.

'Trouble back home, guv?' Ross said, just a shade nervously, Barrington thought.

'Don't know,' Hillary said dully. 'Damn. OK, well, Janine, you can oversee everything while I'm gone. Before I scoot off, anything interesting from house-to-house?'

'Nothing that won't keep, guv,' Barrington said. Ross didn't bother to reply. Hillary got into her car, frowning, and headed back to HQ.

Donleavy's civilian secretary smiled at her sympathetically as she buzzed her through, and Hillary went into Marcus Donleavy's office with just a niggling tinge of dread. Getting called back to HQ right at the start of a major inquiry was unusual.

Donleavy, a silver-haired, silver-eyed man, was today dressed in slate grey, with a mint green tie. He indicated the chair in front of his desk and watched her sit. 'Hillary. Straight to the point. I've got some unpleasant news. I've just been informed that Superintendent Jerome Raleigh has been sighted in Malta.'

Hillary, caught totally unawares, felt her stomach fall through the chair and hit the floor.

Donleavy watched the colour fade from her face, and nodded briskly. 'Apparently, a DI from Vice is on holiday over there. He's not a hundred per cent sure it's him, but he called his guv'nor for advice, and they've called me. As you know, the Raleigh affair is still a bit up in the air.' Hillary had to smile. That was one way of putting it. 'Officially, of course, he's not a wanted man,' Donleavy carried on curtly. 'No warrant was ever issued for his arrest, although the inquiry committee set up to investigate the Fletcher shooting might very well want to talk to him. I'm not sure I can sit on this.'

Hillary sighed grimly. Back in the summer, Luke Fletcher, a drug dealer and suspected murderer, had been shot dead in a joint raid by Vice and her team, lead by Superintendent Raleigh. As a result, some very searching questions had been raised. A side issue was her own shooting, and the award of a medal for bravery. But the real poser had been why Raleigh had done a runner shortly afterwards. For, just as the committee was about to close the case, with no charges pending, Raleigh had just upped and vanished.

Only Hillary knew for sure why. And the anonymous report she'd written and left on Donleavy's desk meant that he knew more than he wanted to as well. But not even Donleavy knew the *whole* story. He knew nothing about Ronnie Greene's dirty money, for a start. Now, just when it seemed that old ghosts had been laid to rest, one of them might be rising from the dead to bite them in the arse.

And neither one of them was happy about it.

'Sir,' Hillary said neutrally, making Donleavy's lips thin impatiently.

'If it *is* Raleigh, and the committee wants to interview him, any idea what he's going to say?' he barked. He was almost certain that Hillary knew far more than she was saying about Raleigh's abrupt resignation, but he wasn't at all sure that he wanted to know what it was.

'No sir,' she said truthfully. 'But ...' She hesitated, then said carefully, 'But I doubt he'll cooperate.' There were several million reasons why Raleigh wouldn't be eager to talk to his old buddies at Thames Valley. 'I don't think we have much to worry about.' Surely the wily Raleigh would just disappear again. He was so good at that, after all.

Marcus Donleavy slowly leaned back in his chair. He'd always rated Hillary Greene. He had trust in her brains and gut instinct, and if she seemed to think there was no danger, it was good enough for him. Well, almost. 'I have to pass this information on this afternoon,' he warned her flatly. 'I'm sitting with the assistant constable on the recruitment committee. As you know, he was in overall command of the inquiry. There's no way I can keep it back from him.'

Hillary nodded grimly. Well, if they did pinch Raleigh and make him talk, there was very little she could do about it. And at least, she thought cheerfully as she left Donleavy's office a few moments later, there was nothing that led back to her. And why the hell should it? She'd done nothing wrong.

Even so. Raleigh could really drop her in the shit.

When she got back to the office, Janine was sitting at her desk, hunched over the computer. Hillary caught sight of the Births, Deaths and Marriages Register on her screen as she passed by, so she was probably putting together a profile of their vic.

As she took a seat, Janine shot her a glance, but one look at Hillary's closed face told her that she was not about to explain her meeting with the top brass, so she turned back to what she was doing.

The two women worked separately in silence for half an hour. Then Hillary's phone rang. 'DI Greene. Steven, hello. You extracted it?' She listened carefully to the police surgeon's description of the murder weapon, making notes in her book as she did so.

'It's like I thought,' Steven Partridge said from his desk at the morgue. 'It's a long, very narrow, extremely sharp blade, almost certainly foreign in manufacture. Probably meant as a paperknife. The damned thing's lethal – both edges as sharp as my mother-in-law's tongue. Can't see any hall-marks on it, no 'Made in Spain' or what have you. It's on its way to you as I speak.'

Hillary grunted her thanks, noting the arrival of the after-noon internal mail. She nodded a vague thanks as the secretary left a pile on her desk, and watched idly as she did the same for Janine. 'Any chance of bumping her autopsy to the head of the queue, doc?'

'Not much. I'll see what I can do.'

'Thanks.'

As she hung up, she saw Janine rifle through her mail and then go very still. From where she was sitting, Hillary saw her extract a long brown envelope that was addressed to her in distinctive green ink.

Janine felt her flesh begin to crawl, and the niggling, now familiar sense of paranoia creep over her. Another one, so soon after the last. She glanced instinctively around, then froze as she saw Hillary Greene watching her. Her face flamed briefly with colour and she shoved the envelope quickly into her In tray, then began to open the rest.

Hillary picked up the phone, watching Janine thought-fully as she speed-dialled Frank's number. 'Frank, it's me. You still with Walter Keane? Good, see if he remembers Flo Jenkins having a narrow, sharp paperknife amongst her things. It's important,' she added sharply. 'Thanks.'

If the killer had brought the weapon with him or her, then they were looking at premeditated murder. And if they could trace the weapon, they had a chance at tracing the killer.

'Janine, I don't trust this paperknife business to Frank. When you've finished, go back and talk to the woman across the street, see if she's ever seen this paperknife in our victim's possession. If not, try and get from her the names of people who knew Flo best and ask them about it.'

Janine sighed heavily. 'Right, boss, I'll go now. This lot'll take a few minutes to print out anyway.' She slung on her coat and walked to the door. The moment she was gone, Hillary got up and went to her sergeant's In tray. There she

extracted the long brown envelope, and tapped it thoughtfully against her palm.

Then she carefully opened it.

chapter four

Hillary slowly pulled the folded piece of white paper out of the envelope, conscience tickling the back of her mind like an old parrot feather. She didn't make a habit of reading other people's mail, and when she did, she usually had a signed warrant enabling and entitling her to do so. To read a co-worker's private correspondence was as far removed from that as it was possible to get. Nevertheless, Hillary was used to relying on her gut. In her job you used everything you had – intelligence, experience, luck, grim determination, the lot. Right now, her instinct was screaming at her that Janine Tyler was in some sort of trouble. And Janine Tyler, until the end of next week at least, was her responsibility.

Gingerly she turned the piece of paper over and unfolded it. As she did so, it fleetingly occurred to her that she could have read the signals wrong. What if Janine was having an affair? What if she'd been acting like a cat on hot bricks because she was scared Hillary or Mel would find out? What if this was a bloody love letter, for Pete's sake? Inside, Hillary began to squirm, and before she could talk herself out of it she opened the paper fully out and gave it a quick glance. If it was handwritten, and the salutation read, 'Darling sugarbabe,' or something equally appalling, she'd put it back quickly, and would read no further.

One glance however was enough to put all such thoughts

right of out her head. The letter had been printed from a computer, was totally in block capitals, and was about as affectionate as a stick of dynamite.

Grimly, Hillary read it.

HELLO BITCH/BLONDE,
HAVEN'T FORGOTTEN ME HAVE YOU? HOPE YOU
ENJOYED THE FLOWERS I SENT THE OTHER DAY. DEAD
ROSES ARE SO HARD TO FIND NOWADAYS. I HAD TO BUY
THEM ALL NEW AND RED AND SUCCULENT AND LEAVE
THEM OUT IN THE FROST TO GET THAT PARTICULAR
SLIMY BLACK FILM ON THEM.

SO, THE WEDDING DAY'S GETTING CLOSER HUH?
LOOKING FORWARD TO GIVING MALLOW A MELLOW
FEELING? OF COURSE, YOU'VE BEEN DOING THAT FOR
SOME TIME NOW THOUGH, HAVEN'T YOU? NO OTHER
WAY YOU'D GET PROMOTION OTHERWISE. HOPE YOU'VE
GOT SOMETHING EXTRA SPECIAL PLANNED FOR YOUR
WEDDING NIGHT, OR THE POOR OLD SUPER WILL FEEL
DISAPPOINTED.

BUT DON'T WORRY, I KNOW A WHORE. I ASKED HER
FOR SOME TRICKS THAT COULD HELP TEASE A JADED
OLD SUPER. SO YOU COULD ALWAYS TRY THIS ...

At this point, the wording became very graphic and descriptive, and Hillary raised her eyebrows as she read the suggestions. 'Very imaginative,' she murmured to herself, sitting back down in her chair and placing the paper carefully on her table.

Reaching into her drawer, she drew out from the very back a dusty red tin case. She couldn't remember the last time she'd used it, but it had to have been back in her uniform days out of Headington. She opened it and eyed the fat, soft brushes, the magnifying glass and tin of fingerprint powder and shook her head. Nowadays the lab did all this, and coppers had no need of them. Not even in her young days at the very beginning of her career. But an old sarge had handed it down to her on his retirement, plus a few lessons in how to use it. 'Never know when it might come in handy,' he'd said, grinning widely. At the time she'd been too young and naïve to wonder what he'd been on about. She'd kept it more for sentimental reasons than anything else. Now she blessed his foresight.

Feeling rusty at this kind of thing, she set tentatively to work, but wasn't really surprised to find, a few minutes later, that the paper was clean of all dabs, save her own. Whoever their boy was, he knew enough to wear gloves. Which was hardly surprising.

Because it had to be one of their own.

The envelope, she'd noticed, had no stamp, which meant it was generated internally. Now there were all sorts of civilians who worked out of HQ of course, from admin staff, to canteen workers, cleaners, not to mention the contracted help – window cleaners, sewage and drainage experts, hell, even the man who came and mended the office equipment, or delivered the water bottles used in the public areas. But how would any of them know how the internal mail was delivered? Answer, they wouldn't.

No, this had bluebottle written all over it. Whoever had written it had made no attempt to misspell it or be other than fairly grammatically correct. And there was no mistaking the frustrated venom over that crack about Janine not being able to get promotion except by sleeping with the boss.

She'd bet a month's salary that this had been written by some Jack-the-lad in uniform, who spent his nights fantasizing over soft porn, and his days craning his neck to catch a glimpse of the pretty blonde sergeant.

Hillary sighed and put her ancient finger-printing equipment away, then read the rest of the note, skipping over the graphic bits, which had become boring and repetitive, to the ending.

THINK YOU'RE SO CLEVER, DON'T YOU BITCH,
MARRYING THE BOSS, WEARING CIVVIES, LORDING IT
OVER YOUR BETTERS LIKE THE QUEEN BEE. BUT WE ALL
KNOW WHAT YOU ARE. AND YOU'LL GET YOURS, WHEN
THAT PRETTY BACK OF YOURS IS TURNED.
   I'LL BE WATCHING AND WAITING.

It was signed, of all things, LOVERBOY.

Hillary slowly blew all trace evidence of fingerprint dust
from it, put it back in the envelope, resealed it and returned
it to Janine's tray. Then she ran a tired hand over her face.
As if she didn't have enough to contend with as it was.
Now this. Well, it would have to be nipped in the bud
pretty quick. Letting a sick mind like this one run free and
getting away with a powerplay was just asking for trouble.
No, he'd have to go. And she had a pretty good idea how
to go about it.

She wasn't surprised that Janine hadn't confided in her, or
taken any steps to make it official. A woman police officer
being stalked in her own nick wouldn't please the brass, and
there would inevitably be the immature dicks who would
snigger at her behind her back. And with her wedding
coming up, the last thing Janine would want was to look
weak or in need of 'hubby's' help. No doubt that was what
the dirty little bastard who'd written it was relying on. Well,
he was in for one nasty surprise!

Keith Barrington returned to HQ, his stomach rumbling,
but decided to give the canteen a miss. Lunch hour was long
gone, anyway. Instead he raided the vending machine on the
second floor and munched on a Mars bar on his way up to
the main office.

Only Hillary Greene was at her desk when he peeked
through the big glass doors. He waited outside until he'd
finished the chocolate, then threw the wrapper in a bin and,

wiping his mouth with the back of his hand to remove any evidence, walked across to join her.

Hillary watched him approach, waited until he had sat down, and said briefly, 'Anything?'

'Guv.' He opened his notebook and quickly scanned his notes. 'I've got two people who saw someone walk up Mrs Jenkins' garden path around seven last night. I can't pin either of them down to more than that. One, the man who lives opposite and two doors down, Mr Lionel Manfred, was leaving for his night shift and saw someone, he thought a young lad, approach the old lady's door. He was driving past at the time, though and didn't see our victim open the door to him. Nor did he recall seeing any unusual vehicle parked on the road. His description is vague – it was dark, he wasn't paying attention. He thought the visitor might have been wearing a cap. Not a big bulking chap, maybe five foot eight or nine. Mr Manfred also thought he might have been carrying something. He had the vague impression of something white being held in his hand, but can't be sure. Maybe a shopping bag, maybe not.' He paused, turned the page and nodded.

'The second witness saw more or less the same thing, only he was coming back from work. He saw an average built, youthful figure walking back down the path. He can't be more specific about time either. Apparently he can get home from work anytime between 6.30 and 7.30 depending on traffic and hold-ups on the motorway. He works in Brum. That's it.'

Hillary sighed. 'We might have to put out an appeal on the local radio, then. If whoever it was had a legitimate reason for being there, they might come forward. On the other hand, if he's our man, he'll be alerted that he was seen. I'll have to give it some thought. Anything else you picked up on the vic herself?'

'No guv, everybody liked her. She wasn't one of those cantankerous sorts who put people's backs up, apparently.

Lived there for donkey's years, never complained about anyone or anything. Salt of the earth.'

Hillary sighed again. 'It's looking more and more like robbery was the motive.'

And yet, what kind of burglar or home mugger actually stabbed a victim through the heart with an ornamental paperknife? It was overkill to such an extent that it worried her. Also, the room had been too tidy. Flo hadn't put up even a token struggle. Surely if a youth, or even gang of youths had forced their way in, or even conned their way in, there'd be more evidence of their presence in the victim's home?

'You don't like robbery, guv?' Barrington said cautiously, and Hillary glanced at him. So, he was reading her was he? Well, why not? She'd have done the same in his place.

'It doesn't smell right to me,' she said. It was, after all, part of her job to train this young man, to teach him to think, to use his eyes and reason – if he was to be an asset, and not a liability. 'I've seen more than my fair share of the elderly who get mugged, beaten, robbed even raped,' she went on. 'But this is just too ... neat. She was sat in her chair, looking as if she was asleep. The doc tells me there was only the one blow, and no signs of a struggle or defence wounds. Does that sound like many muggings or robberies you've come across?'

Barrington shook his head. 'No. It didn't strike me that way either.'

Hillary nodded. So the new boy knew how to read a scene, and had at least enough experience to be confident in his own assessment. That was good. It was more than Frank Ross tended to bother with nowadays. 'It has all the makings of a deliberate killing. And yet, why would anyone want to kill a harmless old lady who seemingly didn't have an enemy in the world? It doesn't make sense yet.' She shrugged. 'OK, we ...' she broke off as she spotted Frank Ross weaving his way through the desks, grunting at those who bothered to greet him. Not many did.

'Guv.' He sat down, smelling faintly of beer. 'You were bang on the nose with that old geezer next door. Walter Keane reckons our description of the murder weapon fits exactly the paperknife Flo Jenkins kept in a vase on her mantelpiece. Apparently her daughter bought it for her on her last holiday to Spain. Flo cut her fingers badly on it once, and never used it again. Reckoned it was lethal, but she didn't want to chuck it, on account of it was her dead daughter who gave it to her.' Frank sniffed heavily and unbuttoned his jacket, letting his beer belly rest more comfortably on top of his desk. 'Reading between the lines, I got the impression that Liza, that's the dead daughter, never did much for her old mum, let alone buy her pressies, so the paperknife was of real sentimental value,' he finished, flapping his notebook shut.

Hillary was already reaching for her copies of the crime scene photos that had come in a half hour ago. Quickly she sorted through them, paused at the ones showing the mantelpiece, then pushed them over to Keith.

The mantelpiece did indeed have what looked like a black-painted, papier mâché vase standing on it, which housed some pens and pencils and what might have been a back-scratcher.

But no paper knife.

'So the killer didn't bring a weapon,' Barrington said, and would have said something more, if Ross hadn't interrupted.

'No shit, Sherlock. This might not be the big city, but us country bumpkins don't need the bloody obvious pointed out to us by detective constables.'

Hillary sighed. There was no way she could fight Barrington's battles for him, but she shot Frank a dirty look. 'OK, Frank, I want you to start the rounds of your snouts. Find out whose turf Holburn Crescent covers. See if you can find out if there's anything on the street about number 18 being turned over recently. Roust the local junkies, chase down anything they might have pawned today. You know the drill.'

Frank sighed heavily and rose ponderously to his feet. 'That's what real police work's about,' he sneered to Barrington, who looked back at him blank faced and unimpressed.

'Frank, today,' Hillary growled, knowing he was about to launch into the usual lecture about how he was underappreciated.

Ross snorted and walked off, in a reasonably straight line. As he went, Hillary reached for the preliminary forensic reports. They didn't make for very happy reading. Oh, there was lots of trace, but there always is when a crime scene happens to be in the victim's own home. There were, for instance, fingerprints galore, but she had a hunch that all of them would turn out to belong to either the vic, Caroline Weekes, Walter Keane, or a host of other people who had a legitimate reason to be there – home help, if the victim had qualified for it, meter reader, postman, Uncle Tom Cobley and all.

Similarly there were fibres, hair samples, tiny amounts of blood trace and DNA to spare, probably. But unless they could isolate something specific that had no place being there, and then matched it up to a definite suspect, there was nothing to help them.

Hillary soldiered through it, but with dwindling hope. Nowadays, the public watched those forensic crime scene programmes and thought cases could solve themselves, simply on the evidence. If only!

Much as she hated to say it, Frank Ross and his knowledge of the resident low-lifes had probably the best chance of cracking open this case. Unless it had been a planned, deliberate murder.

She leaned slowly back in her chair, her eyes narrowing. Unless someone had gone to 18 Holburn Crescent specifically to kill Florence Jenkins. Now if that was the case, there had to be a reason. And once you found the motive, the chances were good that you'd be able to find the killer. But she was back to that same old question. Who would have reason to kill an old lady?

'Keith, I want you to check the financial angle,' she said abruptly. 'Who knows, perhaps our vic has got thousands squirrelled away somewhere. She wouldn't be the first old codger to live like a pauper but have thousands stashed away under the floor boards.'

'Guv.' Barrington swivelled his chair around, rode it to his own desk a few feet away, and reached for the computer keyboard. Time was, he'd have had to wear out his shoe leather, and he might still have to make a personal visit to the vic's bank, armed with a warrant.

Hillary continued to sit and stare vaguely ahead of her, her mind racing. With the money angle being checked out, what other reasons could there be for Flo's murder? Sex? Hardly. Unless she was a flirtatious tease, and had pushed Walter Keane too far. Hillary smiled grimly at the image, and moved on to the other classics.

Revenge? Could Flo Jenkins have done something to somebody that had so pissed them off that they'd resorted to murder? On the face of it, it seemed very unlikely – there was so little a frail old lady could do to anyone. Blackmail wouldn't be beyond her of course. But blackmail had a certain smell about it that Hillary was sure she would have picked up on before now.

Flo might, of course, have done something long, long ago, that was only now catching up with her. But that was venturing way too far into Agatha Christie territory. In reality, the blast from the past coming back to wreak havoc very rarely happened.

Not revenge then. Probably not money, and almost certainly not love or sex. What did that leave?

Restlessly, she went back to reading the list of house contents, and paused, frowning, over Janine's carefully typed list of Flo Jenkins' medicine cabinet. Along with the usual Milk of Magnesia tablets, aspirin, and various creams promising to relieve the usual aching muscles and joints that tormented the elderly, were several long-sounding, unfamiliar names that raised her eyebrows.

She knew, from her own mother, that seventy-somethings could be struck down with all sorts of things requiring no end of pills. Diabetes, thyroid problems, angina, high blood pressure. Even so ...

She was vaguely aware that Janine had returned to her desk as she picked up the phone and dialled the morgue. 'Hello. Doctor Steven Partridge please. DI Greene. Yes, I'll wait.'

She leaned back in her chair, watching Janine carefully, but the blonde woman made no move towards her in tray. Seeing her boss on the phone, she simply slung off her coat, settled herself in front of the computer, and began to type up her case notes, breaking off now and then to enter things of significance into the 'Murder Book'. This was a folder that she was usually responsible for, which detailed every significant fact about the case as it became available, and that any member of the team could consult. It was a way of keeping everyone up to speed, without constantly reporting and repeating information.

'Hello?' Steven Partridge said in Hillary's ear, and she sat up straight in her chair.

'Doc, got a pencil? I've got a list of drugs our vic was taking and I wondered if they meant anything to you. They don't look run of the mill to me.' So saying, she rattled them off, more often than not simply spelling them out rather than trying to pronounce them. When she'd finished, Steven Partridge whistled thoughtfully down the line.

'Well, I can tell you straight off, our poor old dead gal had something seriously wrong with her. One of those is a serious painkiller.' He mentioned one of the more easy ones to say, and carried on. 'The other two can be used for a variety of conditions, none of them good.'

'The painkillers,' Hillary said sharply. 'Worth much on the open market?'

'Oh, there'd be a market for them, all right. Mix them with some downers, you'd be zonked for up to forty-eight hours.'

'I'll have to get on to her GP then,' Hillary mused, squinting at the list. 'It looks as if the bottle she had was fairly full, but if she'd been prescribed more than one bottle, we could be looking at a junkie hit.'

'I doubt the GP would have prescribed too many in one batch,' Steven cautioned her.

'Oh,' Hillary said, with instant understanding. 'And the other stuff? Much market for them would you say?'

'Not so much.'

'OK, thanks, doc. Have I tempted you to move her up your schedule any?'

Partridge laughed. 'You don't get me that way. I've still got a death by drowning, a probable suicide by carbon monoxide poisoning, and two RTAs to get through yet.'

Muttering to herself, Hillary hung up, then glanced at Janine. 'Yes?'

'Old lady across the street, confirms Flo Jenkins had a paperknife that fits the description, boss,' Janine said. 'Thinks it was dangerous. Apparently our vic cut herself badly on it once.'

Hillary nodded. It bore out what Walter Keane had said. 'So, either the killer didn't go there with murder in mind, or the killer knew about the paperknife and intended all along to use it. It was no secret how sharp it was, apparently. And it would be a smart move. How many times have we nailed someone by pinning the murder weapon to them?'

Janine nodded. 'From what the old gal had to say, Flo Jenkins didn't have two ha'pennies to rub together, boss. Telly was rented, and the only sound system she had was a radio and ancient tape recorder. Found that in the cupboard under the window in the living room. All the appliances were old and well used. Cooker was probably twenty years old if it was a day. According to the neighbour, Flo's grandson used up any money left over from her old-age pension. Although she did say Flo was determined to hold on to her money this month in order to do herself proud on her birthday, and have a nice Christmas.'

'Right. And perhaps that didn't sit well with ... what's his name...?' she reached for her notes, but Barrington was there first.

'Dylan Hodge, guv,' he said, from memory.

Hillary nodded, not missing it, but not about to start lavishing praise just yet. 'Right, Hodge. If he's used to relying on granny as a banker, he might have gone round for his usual handout, and not been pleased to be sent away with nothing. Her pension money was not in her handbag, so it must have gone somewhere. If she was determined to spend it on herself for a change, she might have felt the need to hide it somewhere. Keith, when SOCO give the all-clear I want you to turn that house upside down. Little old ladies can find clever hiding places sometimes. Think of it as a test for you ingenuity.'

'Guv,' Keith said.

Just then, Paul Danvers came out of his office, saw Hillary was at her desk, and headed over. She gave him a quick, precise and full report of her case so far. She left nothing of importance out, and managed to convey, without being obvious, that everyone was pulling their weight.

Maybe, for once, even Ross.

'You'll be pulling this boy Hodge in then?' Danvers asked, and Hillary nodded.

'First we've got to find him. I don't think we've got an address. It'll probably be tomorrow before uniform roust him out of whatever squat he's found. But it won't do him any harm to have a day free and clear. Maybe find a score.

That way, he might be in a mood for a nice chat about his granny,' she said, grinning savagely. He wouldn't be the first junkie, high from his place in nirvana, to blissfully admit to murder.

'OK. Reason I called over was to invite everyone out for an early Christmas drink. Maybe tomorrow, or day after, depending on how free you are. What with Janine leaving us, and our new recruit just coming in, it seemed like a good time for a social get together.'

Hillary hid a sigh. 'Sounds nice, sir. I'm sure we can all make it.' She glanced at Janine, who grinned, and Keith Barrington, who looked a shade nervous. 'Frank might be too busy, though.'

'Hell yes,' Danvers said, with feeling. 'Oh, and feel free to bring a date, if you want. I've just split from my partner, unfortunately, but Janine, if you want to bring Mel, or Barrington, if you've got a girl, feel free.'

'Only just moved here, guv,' Barrington murmured, and Danvers nodded and looked casually across at Hillary.

Hillary smiled briefly, and said nothing.

Danvers, after a moment, nodded and went back to his cubby hole. Janine shot Hillary an admiring look, but had to wonder why she was giving him such a hard time. Danvers was single, good-looking, and a rank above her. What was holding her back? She was free and single. With a mental shrug, Janine turned back to her desk, shot a tight, hard look at her In tray, then reached for the printouts waiting for her, from her background research into their victim. She'd collate them for Hillary then head off for home. Maybe she'd cook Mel something special. She'd be Mrs Mallow in a few days' time, after all. But somehow, she was finding it hard to feel the old excitement.

She studiously avoided her In tray, and reached for the stapler.

*

It was nearly eight o'clock that night before Hillary finally put away the last of the reports and stretched out in her chair. Danvers had just left, and her team had long gone – Barrington being careful to be the last of them to leave.

At some point she was going to have to ask him flat out why he'd lost his cool and decked his sergeant. But that could wait. One problem at a time.

She put on her coat and walked out into a windy, wet night. On the main road, the council had already put up the Christmas light decorations, and they cast a cheerful, multi-coloured hue in the background. The rain had come back with a vengeance however, so she dashed to her car, and once inside, delved into her handbag for her oldest filofax. The name she was looking for went back many years now. Finding the number she wanted at last, she punched in the buttons, hoping the man hadn't moved. Or died.

'Hello, Titchmarsh residence,' the precise female voice took Hillary by surprise for a moment, before she remembered that 'Mitch' Titchmarsh's missus was supposed to be from the upper crust. An old desk sergeant had once told her that she'd been a primary school teacher in Windsor before she'd married Mitch from Bunko, and living so close to the royal family had given her airs.

Now she bit back a grin as she said cheerfully, 'Is Mitch there please?'

There was moment of painful silence, and then the voice said, 'Certainly, Thomas is here. I'll just get him.'

Thomas. So that was Mitch's real name. The legendary Mitch the Titch. Tom Titch. Well, well.

'Hello?' the voice asked cautiously, and Hillary felt herself grin.

'Don't worry, Mitch, this isn't some old lag with a grudge.'

'Hillary?'

'Thought you might have forgotten me.'

'Not you, you're unforgettable, girl. Still got all those

65

curves? I used to watch you go by in that tight little uniform and salivate.'

'Pervert! But I've got even more curves than ever nowadays. I need to go on a diet.'

'Don't you bloody dare!' And then, some of the laughter dying out of his voice, he said craftily, 'You need something, gal?'

Hillary sighed. 'Couldn't I just be ringing up an old pal, a departmental legend no less, just for the hell of it?'

'Course you could,' Mitch Titchmarsh said stoutly. Then added, 'But I bet you ain't.'

Hillary nodded in the dark of her car. 'No,' she said flatly. 'I've got a problem, Mitch. A particularly nasty, dirty problem. I might need your help. The kind only you can provide. Know what I mean?'

There was silence for a moment, then he said thoughtfully, 'OK. Want to meet for lunch? You remember the old pub?'

'That fleapit? Didn't public health and safety close it down long ago?'

Mitch gurgled with laughter. 'Hell yes. But it got resurrected. It's respectable now. Well, almost.'

'Can you make it tomorrow?' Hillary asked anxiously.

'For you, darlin', anything.'

'Don't tell your wife that,' Hillary shot back. 'Tomorrow lunchtime then. Not sure when I can get away – I just caught a bad one. Old lady stabbed to death. You know what the first forty-eight hours are like.'

Mitch did. 'So it'll mean I have to hang around the pub for hours waiting for you to show. Might have to have a game of darts, a pub pie, watch the football on telly. Poor me.'

Hillary laughed, said goodnight, and hung up. Then she glanced thoughtfully at the big, well-lit HQ building behind her. Maybe their stalker had gone home for the night, or maybe he was working the night shift. Perhaps he was laid up in a lay-by somewhere with a speed gun, or parked outside a pub with a breathalyser unit.

He may not know it, but wherever he was, Hillary had just taken herself a big step closer to nailing him.

chapter five

Hillary awoke slowly the next morning, aware at once that something was wrong.

She opened her eyes warily, and stared at a ceiling. A large, white ceiling, that had recently been Artexed. She stared, bemused, at the fan-shaped pattern over her head, and slowly closed her eyes. Ahh, she wasn't on the *Mollern*, her narrow boat and home for the past five years. There was no reassuring swaying motion caused by the high wind raging outside. There was none of the silence that came from living in a hamlet in the middle of the countryside in the depths of winter.

Instead she could hear a council rubbish collection lorry outside, giving its usual and annoying bip-bip-bip as it backed up, and a corresponding flashing orange light intermittently lit up the wallpaper on the far wall.

She was curled up on a double bed, which was far more space than she was used to, even with another body pressing next to her own. Slowly, she yawned and stretched, her cold toes making contact with a warm, hirsute calf, and she heard the man beside her draw in his breath sharply. 'Bloody hell, Hill, why don't you wear socks?'

Hillary gurgled with laughter, pressing her nose into a lavender-scented pillow case. 'How very romantic,' she said drily. 'You want me to buy those fluffy powder-blue bedsocks little old ladies favour? Maybe I should buy one of those big, tent-like flannelette night dresses to go with them

– the kind with bow ribbons under the chin. You'll be taking a hot water bottle to bed next.'

'Oh very funny,' Detective Inspector Mike Regis grunted, rolling onto one side, bending his elbow to lever himself up, and resting his chin in the cup of one hand, the better to look at her. 'Mornin' gorgeous.'

Hillary sighed. She doubted she looked gorgeous. Her hair was probably tangled, she hadn't got on a scrap of make-up, and she still felt absurdly self-conscious.

Even though they'd been seeing each other for nearly two months now, she rarely spent the night at his place, and it still made her feel slightly uneasy to do so. Regis, recently divorced, lived in a decent-sized flat, converted out of a large, 1930s villa-type house in Botley, one of Oxford's many suburbs. It was clean and spacious, and pleasant enough, but it had no personality. She much preferred her boat. And her old, single lifestyle. Mind you, there *were* certain compensations to being part of a couple again.

She settled herself more comfortably against the pillows, and eyed Regis thoughtfully. He was not most people's idea of a handsome hunk, being just a little on the short side, with thinning dark brown hair and, at the moment, a five o'clock shadow that could rasp the skin off a rabbit hide. But his eyes were spectacular, Hillary thought, a shade of emerald green that sizzled with intelligence, or, at the moment anyway, good old-fashioned lust.

He worked out of Vice, his home station being in St Aldates, in Oxford itself. They'd met on her first murder case where she'd been acting SIO, and their paths had crossed once or twice since. Their attraction had been immediate and unmistakable, each recognizing in the other someone who thought as they did. Their views on the job, criminals, the justice system, and life in particular gelled very nicely. But he'd been married, and Hillary, having survived the marriage from hell with Ronnie Greene, had had no intention of being 'the other woman'.

But with his divorce finalized, Mike Regis had become a very different proposition. He was good company, liked more or less the same music as herself, had her taste in theatre, films, the arts and – some of her preferences in literature. Hillary, being an OEC (Oxford-educated cop) had graduated from a non-affiliated college with a degree in Literature, and if the man in her life couldn't truly appreciate Jane Austen, well, it was hardly an obstacle that couldn't be overcome.

Nevertheless, as rosy as things seemed, she was aware of clouds on the horizon.

The last two months had been great, much better, in fact, than she'd anticipated. When Regis had asked her out to dinner two months ago, she'd been celibate for nearly three years. The death of her estranged husband, and the fall-out from it, had put her off men, she'd thought, almost certainly for good. It had taken a fair bit of nerve for her to accept the offer, and even more nerve, a week later, to repeat the date, and accept his offer to stay the night.

But Regis wasn't without experience, or tact, and her fears and nervousness had quickly dissipated. And so far, their affair had been both tender, satisfying and a huge boon to her ego. But there was no getting around certain problems. As a rule, the brass didn't particularly like marriages within the force, and their disapproval of Mel and Janine was just a case in point. Of course, Mike and herself weren't on the same squad, or even worked out of the same nick. Even so. They hadn't actually discussed it as such, but both of them had been careful to keep their relationship discreet. They weren't exactly secretive, but they never went to a pub or restaurant that was known as a cop hangout, for instance. And they were careful with their phone calls, never putting through a personal call whilst at work.

So far it seemed to be working, and nobody had yet twigged, but it could only be a matter of time. So far as she was aware, the only one who knew about them was Colin

Tanner, Mike's DS for the last noughty-nought years. They'd worked together for so long, and knew each other's strengths and weaknesses so well that rumour had it they were telepathically linked. She knew for a fact that neither of them seriously considered working with anyone else. Tanner was married, she'd learned, since picking up with Regis, and had a disabled daughter. He had no real ambition for promotion, but their arrest and conviction rate at Vice was so high, neither of them had any worries on the work front.

It wouldn't be such a disaster, Hillary supposed, when the rest of HQ finally twigged that Hillary had got herself a man. But then there was the problem of Paul Danvers.

Hillary hadn't missed the way he'd invited them all out for a drink, using it as a way of finding out her current status. How long before he found out about them? And how would he take it?

'You're frowning,' Mike chided, running a finger across her forehead.

Hillary sighed. 'You'd frown too if your boss fancied you.'

'I certainly would. My super is a twenty-stone ex-rugger play from Newport Pagnell called Kneebreaker Burgess. He's sweet, but he's got two cauliflower ears, and his nose has been broken so often it sort of sits to one side of his face like a dowager duchess sitting side saddle. Definitely not my type.'

Hillary was still laughing as she swung her legs out of bed and slowly sat up, yawning down at her watch. She had plenty of time, but she wanted to get in early.

Regis ran a hand tenderly up her back. 'You really worried about Danvers?' he asked quietly. Life, he knew, could get really complicated, really fast, for female officers who fell foul of Casanova superior officers.

Hillary sighed. 'No, not really. I think he came down from Yorkshire to Thames Valley for his promotion prospects all right, but, I think he also came down partly to see me again. I'm not convinced his getting Mel's old job as my direct boss was as much of a coincidence as he'd have me believe. And he dropped some very broad hints yesterday that he'd just split from that barrister woman he was seeing.'

Now it was Regis' turn to frown. Ever since he'd first met Hillary, he'd known they'd be good together. They had just clicked. She was smart, courageous, practical, experienced, and capable. As a police officer, he'd admired her at once. As a woman she had curves that a man could admire, gorgeous nut-coloured hair and the dark chocolate melting eyes that made a man go gooey inside. She was straightforward and yet warm-hearted, and he felt that she was somebody he could trust in both his professional and his private life. Which was such a rare thing, he was determined to protect it.

Things had been a bit rocky between them for a while, after she'd learned he was still married and had told him to go paddle his canoe. But his marriage had been on the rocks long before he met her, and he hadn't let her rejection hurt his pride.

He knew she hadn't been exactly over eager about starting their affair, and he didn't need a degree in psychology to know why. Her marriage to that bent bastard Ronnie Greene had really screwed her up. Greene's penchant for blondes with loose knickers wasn't exactly a secret, even when he'd been alive.

He'd seen the worry in her eyes, even as he'd picked her up for that first date – dinner at the Trout in Wolvercote, followed by a production of an Ibsen play at the Playhouse. The play, it had to be said, had gone over his head, but Hillary had obviously enjoyed it. He'd chosen it, knowing she'd taken a literature degree, and he'd been glad she'd had a good time. Even so, relaxed as she'd been, she'd tensed up yet again when it came time for the goodnight kiss. He'd handled it well, putting no pressure on her, and keeping it light, and was relieved when she'd agreed to another date.

It had taken patience and understanding on both their parts, to get where they were now – comfortable in their own skins, and each other's beds. And it rankled deeply that her DCI was trying to put a spoke in the wheels.

'You could always ask for a transfer,' he said, but without much hope.

Hillary, reaching for her navy blue skirt, slipped it under her feet and glanced at him over her shoulder. 'No way. I worked hard to get into CID. Besides, I've just landed my sixth murder inquiry. What do you think? I'm going to transfer to the sex crimes unit, or the fraud squad now? No way.'

'I know,' Regis sighed. Hillary was right. She was made for CID. 'But you can't let Danvers twist your arm either. Just tell him to sod off. Mel will cover your back, right, if he tries anything on?'

'Of course he will.' But her heart fell at the thought of going down that route. So far in her career, she'd managed to avoid filing any sexual harassment suits. No matter what the civil and equal rights pundits said, it was still counted as a black mark against you. *Women not being able to take care of themselves.* That was still the attitude, and it stank. But Hillary was nothing if not a realist. 'Look let's not get ahead of ourselves, all right? It's probably nothing. Danvers seems to be a decent enough bloke.'

Regis slowly leaned back against the pillow, folding his arms behind his head. 'Sure,' he said casually.

Hillary slipped into her bra, pulling on yesterday's white blouse, giving it a cautious sniff as she did so. She'd have to go back to the boat to change.

Regis, catching her out, smiled and said, even more casually, 'You know, you could always leave a few things here. There's certainly plenty of wardrobe space.' As a single male, he felt that he tended to rattle around the large flat like a pea in a pod. Not that he wasn't lucky to have such a place. Oxford being Oxford, affordable accommodation was at a premium. He could only afford this place because he got the rent cheap – most landlords liked to have a senior police officer on their premises. It tended to give burglars and car thieves pause for thought.

Hillary got up and slipped into her shoes. She shot Mike a brief smile as she picked up her jacket. 'We'll see,' she hedged, and blew him a kiss.

Outside, she took a deep breath of fresh air, shivering as the strong, near-gale force wind whipped around her as she walked to her car.

She hadn't missed the flash of disappointment that crossed his face when she hadn't leaped at his offer of storage room. But leaving a change of clothes at Regis' place was tantamount to taking the first step to moving in, and she wasn't ready for that just yet. Not nearly ready.

At the back of her mind was a distinct warning note. Just why had it felt 'wrong' to wake up at Regis' flat? Was it just the grumpy reaction of a home body who'd been lured off her home patch? Or was it something more fundamental? What would a shrink make of it?

Hillary sighed, unwilling to go into it now. With the Flo Jenkins case looming large on her mind, now was not the time to start contemplating her navel.

To her relief, Puff the Tragic Wagon started first time, and she had no trouble getting to Thrupp, since the rush hour had barely started. As she walked along the muddy towpath towards her grey, white, black and gold painted narrowboat, she glanced sadly at the gap next to her boat. Nancy Walker, on *Willowsands*, had been her next-door neighbour for nearly four years, and she missed her. Of course, the barge community was always on the move – by its very nature, it tended to be transitory. But Nancy had left nearly five months ago to chug her steady way up to Stratford-upon-Avon and Hillary felt her absence. A fifty-something, who liked to hunt the shoals of young men who congregated around any university town like a predatory hammerhead shark, Nancy had wanted to try her luck with the wannabe actors in Shakespeare's home town.

Now why couldn't *she* have that casual, fun, attitude to men, sex, and the whole emotional mess that was the dating game?

With a sigh she let herself onto the boat, noting that her other next-door neighbour, moored off her prow, had already put tinsel up in the windows.

Early as she was in to work, the first thing Hillary saw as she got to her desk, was Janine's blonde head bent over her paperwork. She was updating the Murder Book, Hillary noticed, and on her computer VDU was a neatly typed report awaiting printing. Her In tray was studiously empty.

Janine glanced up as Hillary slung her bag under the desk and sat down. 'Boss, Jenkins' bio,' she said without preamble, holding out a beige folder.

Hillary grunted, wishing she'd had a second cup of coffee, and reached for it, blinking.

Sensing the lack of caffeine that her superior seemed to need to jump-start her day, Janine rattled off the salient highlights to save her having to read it. 'Flo Jenkins, seventy-six, born 9 December. Her birthday would have been in just three days' time.'

Hillary nodded. 'Yes, I remember. Everyone who knew her commented on how much she was looking forward to it. That and Christmas.'

'One child, Elizabeth, generally known as Liza, now deceased. One husband, also deceased. One of them must have been a bit of a romantic, because they got married on Valentine's Day, 1949.'

Hillary smiled. 'Most popular day for winter marriages, or so I'm told.'

'No record, no driving licence – never learned, apparently. The grandson we know about. Oh, by the way, uniform called, they've got a lead on his whereabouts – almost derelict 'vacation' cottage near Fewcott. Or was it Ardley. One of those villages that cluster around Bicester anyway.'

'Good. I hope you told them to bring him in if they lay hands on him?' Hillary prompted.

'Yep,' Janine said, still thinking over the victim's biography. 'Husband was a bit of a weakling after the war – some old injury. Did light work, never amounted to much or earned much. Died back in the late seventies. Flo did mostly char work to make ends meet. Was in the WAAFS after the war, stationed at Upper Heyford. She was born in Leicester. No family left to speak of, apart from an older sister, in a nursing home up that way. She's been informed of her sister's death, but I'm not sure if she's up to arranging for the funeral. The nursing sister I spoke to said it would probably be a bit beyond her.'

Hillary shook her head. 'It'll either be down to the grandson then, or maybe the neighbours. I'll have a word with Caroline Weekes about it. She seems the competent sort. But there's no rush on any of that just yet.' She glanced up as Keith Barrington pushed through the door. It wasn't yet 8.15, and she could tell by the way he gave them a double take that he'd expected to be first in. She smiled briefly at him as he got to them, then waved her empty mug in the air. 'Wouldn't mind a refill, constable.' There were a couple of coffee-making machines littered about the huge work space, and Barrington took her mug without a word and set off in search of a percolator.

Hillary tackled her mail, first the actual stuff that consisted of paper and real envelopes, then the stuff that came through the ether to her email address. At some point Frank Ross checked in, then checked out again, muttering about leads. Hillary initialled some reports on her other cases, and drank her coffee. When she'd finished, she reached for her notebook and checked her to-do lists. Just as she was flipping the last page, her phone rang.

'DI Greene?' a gruff voice said. 'Desk sergeant here. Uniforms have brought in a suspect on the Jenkins case. They say you're expecting him?'

'Dylan Hodge?'

'Yes ma'am.'

'Right. Which interview room's he in?'

'Six.'

'Thanks. I'll be down in a minute.' She hung up, and caught both her sergeant and DC Barrington watching her hopefully. 'They've found Hodge,' she said somewhat unnecessarily. She hesitated a moment, knowing that Janine had seniority and must want in on the interview. But Barrington probably needed the practice more. 'Keith, with me. Janine, I want you to go back to Holburn Crescent. Fill in any holes the house-to-house missed. Also, I want you to do a thorough background check on Caroline Weekes. Chivvy up SOCO, and see if Doc Partridge can give us a definite time for the autopsy. I don't doubt the cause of death, but I've got a feeling there's going to be something interesting besides that.'

'Boss,' Janine said flatly. She'd have liked to be in on the interview with the grandson. Chances were, the toerag had done it, and once upon a time, she'd have made her feelings clear. But what with the wedding coming up in just a few days, and with everything else on her mind, it hardly seemed worth the effort somehow. Besides, she'd be in Witney soon.

A new start.

It seemed, suddenly, more of a blessing than a set-back.

She gathered her stuff together and walked out to the car park, cursing as the high winds caught at her long black coat and whipped her long blonde hair around her eyes. She was just pulling the strands back from her face when she reached her car, which was perhaps why she didn't realize the problem sooner. As it was, she opened the door and got in, then cursed, as the car felt distinctly spongy and oddly low-slung beneath her.

She struggled out, again battling with her hair and the wind, and stared at her front left tyre. It was as flat as a pancake. Great. She turned, about to walk to the boot for her spare, and instead stared in dismay at her left rear tyre. It too was flat.

Numbly, she walked around to the other side of the gleaming red mini, her pride and joy. All four tyres had been slashed.

With a yell of rage, she turned and glared around the car park. But the high winds weren't encouraging anybody to linger, and it was deserted. No roaming gangs of uniforms, entering or leaving, no fag-addicted DCs grouped around the horse chestnut trees having a crafty one. No doubt that was why the stalker had chosen this morning to get out his flick knife. She'd even helped the bastard out by parking about as far away from the nearest CCTV camera in the bloody car park as she could get.

'Shit, shit, shit!' she yelled, and leaning against the top of the mini, felt hard, hot tears clog her throat. Damn it! She wanted to stomp inside and harangue the desk sergeant, set a fire under Traffic's arse, wail and rant and rage to Mel. Demand to know where somebody's car was safe, if it wasn't effing safe in the effing Thames Valley effing Police Force's HQ car park.

She did none of those things of course. Instead she forced herself to calm down and call a local tyre and exhaust company. She shamelessly used her status as a police officer to get someone down there right away and watched, impotently, as an acne-beleaguered youth, trying hard to hide the grin on his face, changed her tyres. He eyed her up as he handed over the bill for what she considered to be an outrageous, three-figure amount, and two minutes later, she roared off far too fast up Kidlington's main road.

All it needed now was for her to get a speeding ticket. She tried to laugh at the thought, to get back some sense of equilibrium. But all the way to Bicester, Janine was aware of fighting off scalding tears of humiliation, pain and exhaustion.

As Keith Barrington followed his boss down the stairs, he felt the familiar tingle that always came whenever he was about to confront a suspect. And, in this case, maybe even their prime suspect.

He was glad, and a little surprised, that Hillary Greene had asked him to sit in on it. He knew Janine Tyler was the logical choice. Perhaps Hillary was already gradually sidelining her, since she was about to leave. It made sense – the Jenkins case might still be ongoing by the end of next week, when Janine left for her new posting, and she'd need to have one member of her team up to speed on everything. And it was beginning to look more and more as if Frank Ross, although technically holding the rank of sergeant, wasn't a serious player. For the first time, Barrington began to feel a real sense of optimism about this new posting.

When Hillary pushed open the door to interview room six, a uniformed PC nodded, then stared stoically ahead again. Seated in front of a plain wooden table, nervously shifting about on his chair, was a young man.

From his record, Keith knew he was twenty-four years of age, but his body was so stick-like, his face so gaunt and with the skin stretched taut over his skull, he could equally have been a teenager or an old man. He looked, Barrington thought uneasily, like one of those survivors of a concentration camp he'd seen in history books at school.

He was dressed in filthy jeans and a T-shirt so big and loose it threatened to literally drop off his skinny shoulders. It bore an old Def Leopard montage, so worn away it resembled an abstract painting – the sort a seriously mentally disturbed David Hockney might have painted.

Hillary drew out a chair and sat down, waiting until Keith had done the same, then nodded at the tape recorder.

Keith obligingly went through the ritual, stating the time and date, the names of those present, and that Mr Dylan Hodge had voluntarily stated that he did not request the presence of a solicitor. Hillary knew that the junkie couldn't afford one, and was probably either too high, or too far gone on withdrawal systems to realize he probably needed one.

His thin arms bore scabs on both wrists, and no doubt, would bear similar scabs on both the insides of his elbows and the tops of his shoulders. He probably had old needle tracks in his groin and between his toes as well.

She opened her case and pulled out his file. She read it in silence for a moment, whilst the young man opposite her watched, his eyes constantly shifting about the room. He seemed to be most worried about the silent, uniformed police officer standing by the door.

'Says here you trained to be a television repair man, Dylan,' Hillary began gently. 'You even held down a job for nearly ten months. Then you were caught stealing from a customer.'

Dylan Hodge shrugged his shoulders. 'It was a mistake. Didn't get sent down for it, did I?' he added triumphantly, casting a belligerent look at the uniformed constable who was staring blankly at the wall about a foot above his head.

Hodge had greasy brown hair that lay flat against his skull, and the pupils of his eyes were so dilated it was hard to tell what colour they were.

Hillary turned a page on the dossier, and said, her voice totally without emotion, 'I see a few months later you were back before the same judge for car theft. You got eighteen months for that.'

Hodge shrugged. 'A mistake again,' he muttered. 'Thought it was the girlfriend's dad's car, didn't I?'

Hillary sighed and pushed the dossier away. 'Let's face it, Mr Hodge. You're a drug addict. Your girlfriend is a drug addict. You live in a squat. You scrounge off your only relative, you thieve and you con and you'd do anything for your next fix. How long has it been since you had a hit?' she asked curiously.

Hodge sneered at her. 'On the methadone, ain't I? Can't get me on nothing like that.'

Hillary smiled. 'I'm not trying to get you on nothing like that, Mr Hodge,' she said, very softly.

Dylan Hodge suddenly went very still in his seat. For the first time he glanced at Keith. Then he frowned. 'Here, you're not Vice,' he said. His tone of voice made it an accusation.

Hillary smiled. 'I never said I was, Mr Hodge. We want to talk about your grandmother.'

Dylan Hodge blinked. Something – a look that could have meant anything – crossed his face. Part of it seemed to be the recall of a memory. What might have been fear or apprehension made up another part. But his fried, junkie brain didn't seem able to unscramble it, and after a second, it was gone, leaving behind his habitual sneer. 'Gran. Yeah, what about her?'

'She's dead, Mr Hodge,' Hillary said matter-of-factly.

Dylan Hodge began to scratch at the scabs on his wrist. Hillary watched the top of his bent head, and thought she saw the sly, darting movement of lice.

'Mrs Florence Jenkins is your grandmother, Mr Hodge?' she prompted.

'Yeah.'

'She lived at 18 Holburn Crescent, in Bicester?'

'Yeah.'

'When was the last time you saw her?'

'Dunno. I'm not much good with time.'

This Hillary could well believe. To the likes of Hodge, ten minutes could feel like ten months, or last year could seem like a minute ago. 'You didn't come near her place yesterday,' Hillary began patiently. 'What about the night before?'

Hodge could certainly fit the very vague description the witnesses had given for the man who'd called at the victim's house on the night of her murder. A not-bulky figure in a cap.

'Do you own a cap, Mr Hodge?' she asked and Dylan, having picked one scab until it began to ooze, turned to another. Hillary let him get on with it, fighting the urge to lean across and rest her fingers on top of his, stopping the frantic scrabbling. But she knew better than to give him any excuse to start screaming police brutality. She wasn't about to lay so much as a finger on him.

'Dunno. Might do. There's clothes at the squat. We share. Donny's got a bloody good donkey jacket.'

'I'm surprised someone hasn't stolen it,' Hillary said drily. 'Must be worth the cost of a few good fixes.'

Dylan grinned. 'Oh yeah. I forgot. Donny's gone. Took his jacket with him. Or is he inside? Not sure.' His eyes, already vague, almost crossed. How long before he simply passed out?

'The night before last, Mr Hodge, did you visit your grandmother?' Hillary said loudly, allowing an edge of impatience to lance her voice now.

Instantly the sneer was back. 'No I didn't, see. And you can't prove I did.'

And neither could they, Hillary conceded glumly. Yet ... 'You don't seem very upset that your grandmother is dead, Mr Hodge,' she said.

'Yeah. Well, she was old, wasn't she. Really old. And she was always complaining about being ill. I suppose she was. The old die, don't they?'

Hillary stared at him without speaking.

'I mean, she had these pains and all,' Hodge said, not liking the silence.

Hillary continued to stare silently at him, hoping to get more.

'Look, I'm off,' Hodge said, standing up so suddenly that

the chair crashed to the floor behind him. The uniformed officer, startled, took an instinctive step forward, and Hodge reared back.

Hillary quickly held out a hand. 'It's all right, Mr Hodge. You're free to go. For the moment.'

It was pointless, Hillary knew from experience, to talk to them when they'd got to this stage. A mixture of bravado and repetition was all she'd get from him now. Better to try another time – catch him on a high if she was lucky. Besides, with no evidence to link him to the crime, she had no cause to hold him.

Hodge charged for the door clumsily. Hillary watched him go, then turned to Keith. 'Get out to that squat before he does. I dare say they'll all be suffering from severe amnesia, but see what you can find out about his movements the day of the murder. Then take his mug shot to your witnesses – but I doubt you'll get a positive ID.'

'Guv.'

Hillary glanced at her watch, saw that it was gone twelve, and collected her bag.

She had a lunch date with a legend.

J

chapter six

In spite of the no-smoking signs and laws, the room was hazy when Hillary walked into the public bar, enough to make her gag, since she was somewhat allergic to cigarette smoke. She coughed into her hand and looked around the crowded bar room, eyes watering slightly, and saw a hand go up in the far corner.

When she made her way over, one toothless octogenarian playing dominoes with someone even older, gave her a wolf whistle from the far corner. She was still grinning when she sat down opposite Mitch Titchmarsh, and shrugged off her coat.

'What you having?'

'Just orange juice, thanks,' Hillary said, ignoring Mitch's grimace of sympathy. He made no attempt to talk her into something stronger, however, but nodded and wandered over to the bar. The fact that he recognized her need to keep a clear head whilst heading up an investigation, made her feel a little bit better about the favour she was going to ask him. Mitch might have been retired for over five years now, but he was still a copper through and through. Once a professional, always a professional.

She thanked him again as he placed her drink in front of her, and glanced at the blackboard menu. 'The ploughman's any good here?'

'Hell no.'

'I'll give it a miss then. Cheers.' She took a sip of her

drink, and glanced surreptitiously at her watch. Mitch caught it, and smiled.

'Case hotting up?'

Hillary sighed. 'Not really. We're still in the collating phrase. You know how it is.'

Mitch did. 'No obvious suspect then?' He knew, as did most people who took up law enforcement, that nine times out of ten, the culprit in any case was fairly obvious – unlike television dramas would have you believe. The husband who'd battered his wife just a bit too hard this time. The long-feuding neighbours where one of them had taken hostilities a shade too far. The hit-and-run driver with a series of convictions for drink driving behind him.

It was when things weren't obvious that the need for painstaking detail came into its own.

Hillary thought fleetingly of Dylan Hodge and shrugged. Did he count as an obvious suspect? Her gut wasn't yet convinced. 'I'm not sure.'

Mitch grunted. 'An old lady you said?' He shook his big, shaggy head sadly. His own mother had lived until she'd reached her nineties.

Mitch Titchmarsh had joined the police force on his eighteenth birthday. Big, burly, tough as old boots even then, he'd quickly become known as the man you wanted to have guarding your back in a tight spot. He'd served his time on the football fields, fending off hooligans, and on front lines during violent pickets. He'd married young, to a woman who produced a baby boy once a year. By the time he was forty, he had nine sons, and, during the course of the next twenty or so years, all but one had joined the force. Some had climbed the ladder, the brightest and most ambitious now being a DCI out Banbury way. The vast majority, however, had opted, like their father, to stick at the rank of sergeant.

But Mitch had always had brains as well as brawn, and his arrest rate during his stint at HQ had been second to none, earning him kudos and respect from all ranks. He was helped, no doubt, by the fact that he was the son of a car factory worker out of Cowley, who'd been born and raised in a hard, working-class neighbourhood, and retained many friends and snitches, who kept him well informed. Even when university graduates started joining the force, and computers, profiling, forensics and PR began to take the place of foot-soldiering, Mitch's arrest and conviction rate continued to rise.

He was also a larger than life character, a known womanizer, with just a slightly dodgy reputation for scaring villains that had turned him into an object of hero worship for generations of uniforms. His gang of sons still kept him well up to date about goings on in his old patch, and Hillary wouldn't be at all surprised if he knew almost as much about what went on as she did.

'Your Roger did well the other week. Ram-raiders, wasn't it?' she said, taking a long drink of her nearly warm orange juice.

Mitch's big, florid red face flushed even more roseate with pride. 'He's a born thief-taker that one,' he admitted gruffly.

'And how're Maurice's scars doing?'

Mitch guffawed. 'He always did have an ugly mug. A bit of a white line down the side of the jaw ain't going to make no difference. His wife still loves him.' Maurice, one of his younger sons, had got on the wrong end of a drug dealer's flick knife last year.

Mitch quaffed nearly half a pint from his pint glass of Hook Norton ale, and then slowly put it down. 'Right, that's the pleasantries out the way. What can I do for you, gal?'

Hillary grinned. Mitch had been one of the first of the old guard to accept her as a player, all those many moons ago. He'd first noticed her when she'd still been in uniform, of course. That thick nut-brown hair and attractive figure had instantly caught his attention. Naturally, he'd tried it on and been firmly rebuffed, but hadn't taken it personally. And when she'd finally made it into CID, he'd been as proud as a peacock, almost as if he'd had something to do with it. When others had grumbled and moaned about her promotion, he'd cut them off at the knees, and had crowed every time she'd had a success. Even her disastrous marriage to Ronnie Greene hadn't lessened his respect for her.

For her part, she knew that having Mitch in her corner had gained her acceptance far sooner than it might have done, and she'd always had a soft spot for him, steering him a few good leads whenever they came her way when she thought he could make better use of them. Those days now seemed long ago and far away.

Now she shrugged. 'I need a favour.'

Mitch grinned. 'It didn't take an Einstein to figure that out.' He leaned back in his chair, a big bear of a man with the makings of a beer gut, dressed in old grey slacks and a lumberjack's red and black check jacket. 'Didn't ever think the day would come when you'd need one, mind,' he mused, his somewhat watery grey eyes watching her closely. 'You always were able to look after yourself.' The way he said it made it sound like more of a question.

Hillary nodded. 'It's not me who's in trouble, but my sergeant.'

Mitch snorted. 'You can't mean Frank Ross? If that git's in deep shit, let him drown.'

Hillary smiled. 'Janine Tyler,' she corrected. 'Heard of her?'

Mitch had, of course. It was inconceivable that he hadn't. 'Pretty blonde bit, getting married to Mellow Mallow, your old pal?'

'That's her. She's attracted an admirer. The kind who leaves nasty notes and nasty gifts.'

The smile was gone instantly from Mitch's face. A deep

frown wrinkled his brow, for, quick as ever, he'd already figured out the sub-text. 'One of our own, you mean?' he said grimly.

As pater familias to all the young and not so young lads in blue, she could tell the thought disturbed him. 'It's not one hundred per cent certain,' Hillary said. 'But I can't see it being a civilian. I think her up-coming marriage to Mel sparked it off.'

Mitch nodded. 'Someone thinks she's slept her way to the top and doesn't like it.' He took a swig of beer, then asked, curious, 'Did she?'

Hillary paused in the act of reaching for her own glass, thought about it for a moment, and said at last, 'No. Not really. Janine's bright, ambitious and tough. But she's also got her head screwed on right, and isn't above twisting Mel around her finger to get ahead. But there's no doubt in my mind she'll be inspector one day, maybe even Super. With or without Mel.'

Mitch nodded. 'Fair enough.' He himself had never wanted to achieve high rank. Working the streets, taking thieves, beating the crap out of wife beaters and kiddie predators. That was his forte. But he was wise enough to know that the force needed all sorts, and was never quick to judge. And Hillary Greene, of all people, coming to him for help, was distinctly flattering. 'I followed all your murder cases by the way,' Mitch said. 'Well done, gal. I'm proud of you. Never lost one yet, right?'

Hillary smiled, somewhat wryly. 'Not so far. And thanks. About Janine. The trouble is, I'm not in much of a position to help her.'

Mitch nodded, understanding her predicament at once. If it *was* a young, uniformed cop doing the stalking, a middle-aged, female CID officer asking questions and trying to snoop around would soon get given short shrift. Uniform knew how to look after its own. Even though Mitch knew Hillary's rep at HQ was gold, especially after her bravery award, any goodwill she had garnered would soon disappear when it became known what she was after.

'And Mel can't help?' Mitch mused. The same scenario applied.

'I doubt she's even told him,' Hillary said. 'She hasn't even told me.'

'Eh? How do you know about it then?' Mitch said, then grinned savagely. 'Sorry. Forget I asked. Must be getting old.'

'You see her problem though?' Hillary persisted. Mitch might not relish sorting out one of his own, but he did have an old-fashioned sense of honour when it came to standing behind someone in trouble, which was what she was counting on. Especially when they were getting right royally shafted. And Janine, female though she might be, and marrying a super though she was, was still getting shafted. 'She can't go the official complaint route, because it'll go on her record,' Hillary pointed out. 'And you know how effective it would be anyway.'

Mitch snorted. 'Fart and colander comes to mind.'

'Right,' Hillary concurred drily. Official complaints, when investigated, tended to do only two things; firstly, make everyone clam up and, secondly, spread resentment and general malcontent throughout the force. Hardly surprising, then, that they more often than not failed to find conclusive evidence one way or another, and only made things worse.

'She's got too much pride to ask hubby-to-be for help,' Hillary carried on, 'and since we're busy trying to find out who stuck a knife into a seventy-six year old woman, she hasn't exactly got time to spare to try and track him down herself.'

Mitch snorted. 'She couldn't if she tried. If it's some inadequate wanker in uniform she'll never ferret him out. His mates'll cover for him for a start.'

'Exactly.'

'You want me and the lads to winkle him out for you?' He didn't sound particularly enthusiastic, and she could understand why.

'I can't have her distracted now, Mitch,' Hillary said, her voice going hard. 'Until the end of next week, I need all her attention focused on the case. Frank Ross isn't exactly an SIO's answer to a dream, plus they've just landed me with this kid from London who decked his old sergeant. He seems OK, and is certainly bright enough, but I need Janine Tyler on top form right now. And Flo Jenkins deserves to have the people investigating her murder giving their one hundred per cent effort.'

Mitch's face hardened, as she knew it would. Part of any successful copper's repertoire was knowing which buttons to press – and Hillary was very good at it. 'Damn right she does,' Mitch muttered grimly. He finished his drink and sighed heavily. 'OK, count me in. I'll put out feelers right away.' Apart from having three of his sons working out of Kidlington HQ, he no doubt had plenty of others he could call on as well, and obviously wasn't expecting it to take long. 'Blokes who like to stalk women always give off the vibes. Somebody'll know who our chap is, and once they know I want to know, I'll have him. Oh, and gal, I know you just played me.'

Hillary smiled and reached for her juice. 'What else are friends for?' she asked, and Mitch Titchmarsh erupted into loud belly laughter, making several people in the pub look his way indulgently.

Caroline Weekes nodded her head, squeezing the handkerchief in her hands compulsively. 'Of course I'll see to the funeral. I know what Flo wanted, she talked about it often enough.'

They were sitting once more in her curiously elegant home, and Hillary had to fight the urge to check that her shoes hadn't left any marks on the immaculate flooring.

'She reserved a space with her husband in the church yard, so that won't be a problem,' Caroline went on, her dark, red-rimmed eyes staring down into her twisting hands. 'She never believed in cremation. Her generation doesn't, does it? I can have a little reception here afterwards.'

'That sounds fine,' Hillary said. She wasn't surprised to find Caroline Weekes had taken the day off work. Her nerves looked shredded. No doubt she had an understanding boss. Outside the window, she saw Janine Tyler walk up the road and turn into a house a few doors down.

'Your husband not at home?' Hillary asked.

'No. He has a rather high-powered job. Can't take time off work, like I can.'

'This is your second marriage, yes?' Hillary asked, having read up the notes on their principal witness before coming over to Bicester.

'That's right. The first one was a bit of a disaster. John's so different. So much more mature and dependable, even though he's younger than me. We're trying to have a baby,' she added, for the first time some animation coming into her voice.

Hillary smiled.

'You have children?' Caroline asked eagerly.

'I have a stepson,' Hillary said.

'I think it's really important to have kids, don't you?' Caroline Weekes rushed on, making Hillary wonder if she'd even heard what she said. 'With my first husband, they just never came along. When I married John, though, he was really keen to become a father. Said he didn't want to wait until he was in his fifties, like some of the executives at his firm. Said he'd be too old to play football with them.'

Hillary watched, fascinated, as the handkerchief being twisted and turned in Caroline's hand, threatened to actually tear.

'But when, after a few months, we still didn't fall pregnant, I had some tests done, and it seems there's a bit of a problem. But we'll be starting IVF treatment soon. It has a really good success rate,' Caroline said brightly. 'I thought Ruth, or maybe Hope, if it's a girl. Something simple but pretty. And John of course, if it's a boy. But we won't call him junior.' Her voice was too bright, too fast. Her smile too forced.

Hillary nodded. She's coming unravelled, she thought to herself. Any time now, her doctor's going to put her on Prozac. She didn't know what that would do for her prospects of IVF treatment, but it couldn't be good.

That was the thing about murder cases. It didn't only ruin the lives of the victim and the immediate family. It could have all sorts of dire ramifications for anyone on the periphery as well. Like a disease, it spread ever outwards, causing misery and disruption to people's lives.

Hillary hated killers.

'Have you thought of anything else that could help us, Mrs Weekes? Anything about Flo, or that morning you found her. Or the night before?'

Caroline Weekes shook her head helplessly. 'I'm sorry,' she said miserably. 'I've thought about it, the Lord knows. I lay awake all last night thinking about it. But there's nothing. Flo was a good woman. A nice woman. I miss her already.'

Hillary nodded and put away her notebook. This wasn't getting either of them anywhere.

Outside, Janine Tyler passed a young constable who was coming down the garden path of the house beside her, and nodded. Follow-up interviews were well under way, since witnesses sometimes came up with something new after they'd had a day or so to think about things. Normally this was a job for uniform, but it was one of Hillary Greene's quirks that she liked her team, and sometimes even herself, to take part. Tiresome as this was, more often than not it had paid off and Janine couldn't really object to doing her share.

Janine saw the young lad meet up with another older man in uniform, and froze when she heard them laugh. She turned sharply, expecting them to be looking at her, but neither was.

With her marriage to Mel only two days away, she was getting hypersensitive. There was no reason on earth to think that the two men were talking about her behind her back. Shit! This was getting ridiculous. The arsehole who'd slashed her tyres was really beginning to get to her.

She shook her head and moved on to the next house, but when nobody answered, and she came away, she looked at the two chatting constables closely. One of them could be him. She had no way of knowing. The sooner she was restationed at Witney the better she'd like it. She didn't let herself wonder what she'd do if the harassment continued even there.

It simply didn't bear thinking about.

Back at HQ again, Hillary found the new boy up to his ears in polythene bags. 'Those the contents of Flo's house?'

'Yes guv. At least, those that forensics and the evidence officer thought you might find interesting.'

Hillary nodded. Barrington was going through them, checking the itemizing and making notes. 'Give us a box, then,' she said, making him almost fall off his chair in surprise. No doubt he'd never known an SIO so hands-on and willing to do scut work. 'I like to get a feel for the victim,' she explained, as he reached for a box hesitantly, as if still unsure he'd heard what she said correctly. 'It helps,' she added softly. 'Something you might like to bear in mind.'

'Yes guv,' Barrington said, handing a large cardboard box over.

'Especially in cases like this one, where the motive isn't clear.' She poured out the slither of envelopes onto her desk. 'As you know, according to British law, a prosecution case doesn't have to produce motive in a murder enquiry. But I've never seen one yet that didn't. Juries need to know whydunnit, just as much as whodunnit.'

Barrington nodded. 'Right guv.'

Hillary spent the next hour looking at old postcards from friends called May, Danny, Milly and Jean, who seemed to favour the Spanish costas. She read old letters from years ago, kept because of news about family now long since dead, or for their feel-good notes of thanks or cheerful optimism. She saw from the sheaf of knitting patterns that Flo had once knitted her grandson SuperTed jumpers, or V-necked pullovers with a tractor or mini on them. She had kept an old button tin, and a sewing box that had seen better years. All the usual, sad, personal, precious detritus of a life now gone.

Hillary was leaning back, looking through an old photograph album when Frank Ross came in. 'Nobody burgled our vic's house, guv, I'll stake my life on it,' Ross said, pulling out his chair and sitting down heavily. 'But I reckon somebody's been selling a lot of gear this last day or two to our lad Hodge. Got a toerag who hangs out with a junkie runner for Benny Higgs to admit to snaffling some crack from Hodge last night.'

Hillary nodded. 'Find Higgs and lean on him hard. Bring him in if you have to.'

'Already got feelers out for him, guv,' Ross said, and began, in a desultory way, to sift through his mail.

She sighed, and turned back to the photo album. In some of the old, black and white ones, Flo Jenkins was almost unrecognizable as a young, svelte, rather pretty girl, with big brown curls and a cute, chipmunk-like face. Some of the people in the snapshots were repeated in different times, different places – a man and woman who were obviously her parents, a sister and brother-in-law maybe, growing older in years as the album progressed.

She turned a page and spotted a photograph that had

come loose from the old, yellowing Sellotape Flo had used to keep it in place. It wasn't a face she'd seen before that belonged to a young man, looking self-conscious in a darkish suit and tie. A quiff of wayward dark hair, and a shy smile, spoke of a much younger, innocent age. She turned it over, and had to squint to make out the line of faded blue ink handwritten on the back: 'R.G. 1945. *Walking wounded*?' It was probably in Flo's handwriting, although it was so faded it was hard to tell.

Who was RG? An old boyfriend maybe. And 1945 was right at the end of the war. The young man had probably only been old enough to serve in the last one or two years of it at least, but that had probably been long enough for it to leave its mark – hence the walking wounded reference. But why put the question mark after it? Didn't Florence know?

Hillary frowned at the photograph thoughtfully. It was probably nothing. But Flo had kept it and written that cryptic remark on the back.

'Frank, I want you to see if you can trace this man.' She handed over the photograph, and grimaced as Frank snorted. 'Yes, I know it's a long shot. No name, and he might be long dead.'

'Bloody waste of time, guv,' Frank moaned. 'I'm telling you, it's gonna be Hodge. Junkie bastard ripped off his grandma for the cost of a fix.'

'Keith, want to give it a go?' Hillary said, and wasn't surprised when Ross all but the threw the photograph his way. Normally Frank Ross wouldn't have trusted a newcomer with making his coffee, but he obviously considered this assignment so pointless that the boy from the Smoke couldn't possibly screw it up.

Keith caught the photograph and studied it thoughtfully. 'Looks like it was taken in front of a house. Maybe somebody would recognize it. Might be worth talking to the county council planning officer. They have records going back to then, I dare say.'

Ross snorted. 'If it was even taken in Bicester.' He poured cold water over the suggestion gleefully.

Hillary ignored Ross. 'Good idea,' she said. 'Give it some more thought – but chase it up only when you've got less urgent work to do. Think of it as an ongoing project.' She doubted as much as Frank that it would come to anything, but the case so far wasn't exactly swimming in clues that they could afford to overlook even a long shot. 'By the way, any luck with searching the house for Flo's pension money?' she added.

'No guv,' Barrington said. 'I'd swear there was nothing there. I found a hidey-hole in the airing cupboard, but it was for a small bottle of gin.'

Hillary laughed. 'I dare say, with all the pills she was on, her doctors had forbidden her any of the hard stuff. She probably kept it hidden so her grandson didn't get his hot little hands on it. Speaking of the devil,' Hillary said sharply, 'how did you get on at the squat?'

Barrington reached for his notebook, but didn't really need it to refresh his memory. The details were all clear in his head. 'When I got there, I found three people in residence. A woman, who gave her name as Phoebe Cole, someone called Rainman who refused to give a proper name, and another male known as Bas Q. Again refused to give a last name.'

Ross laughed. 'I'd have got it out of 'em. You're too damned soft. You won't last long on this squad, mate, if you can't get the job done.'

Hillary sighed very loudly. Ross shot her a sideways look and went back to reading his mail.

'Phoebe admitted to being Dylan's girlfriend. Claimed he was with her all that night "the old lady got it", to quote her verbatim.' Barrington went on as if Frank hadn't spoken. 'But since she didn't seem to know which night that even was, I don't think it means much, guv.'

Hillary rubbed a hand across her forehead. Damn, she was getting a headache. 'Go on.'

'Bas Q is an old bloke, a real derelict. It was hard getting a coherent sentence out of him.'

'And this Rainman character?'

'Bit more fly, guv,' Barrington said thoughtfully. 'According to him, he's been at the squat the last three nights running. Bit under the weather. Says how Phoebe and Dylan have the front upstairs bedroom and heard them "scuttling about like rats" late at night, but not a peep from either of them in the earlier part of the evening.'

'Out scoring, I expect,' Ross snorted. 'Or thieving, or mugging, or selling their arses to a discerning public. Gets dark quick this time of year. Gives them plenty of scope to get up to mischief.'

'Right, let's get Hodge back,' Hillary said. 'Really push him as to his whereabouts. The fact that he was in this morning, only to be pulled back so soon might catch him on the hop. Frank, I want you to do the pulling. Scare him a bit. Keith, I want a search warrant to search that squat. Ask Janine for details about the best way of going about it.'

Suddenly galvanized, the two men left the room. Hillary glanced at her watch. Just gone two. She could nip up to the canteen for a late lunch.

But better not.

Now she had even more reason to try and keep the weight off. She wasn't sure Mike Regis was the type who fancied love handles.

chapter seven

Benny Higgs wasn't hard to find, but he wasn't happy to be paying a visit to Thames Valley HQ. He was a small, smartly dressed, nervous-looking individual, with a shock of pure white hair and very blue eyes. If you went by looks alone, he should have been a busy dentist, a successful school teacher or even one of those shoe salesmen who can take one look at a little old lady's bunions and know exactly what pair would fit and be comfortable to wear to the shops.

As she sat across the table from him, Hillary could imagine even the most streetwise and hardened of urchins accepting a Werther's Original from him without a qualm. He simply didn't look, act, or talk like a small-time drug dealer.

Officially, of course, he ran a small office supplies warehouse located in Bicester's small industrial estate off the Launton Road. He was still whining about being taken out of his office even as Janine went through the motions for the tape. The fact that this was a full-blown interview, under caution, took a little of the wind from Benny's sails. But not much. After all, it wasn't as if this was the first time he'd had his collar felt.

'Mr Higgs,' Hillary said pleasantly. 'I'm Detective Inspector Greene. I'm currently in charge of the Florence Jenkins murder inquiry.' She let the last two words, unstressed though they were, speak for themselves, and saw him instantly pale. His nose was slightly red and broken-veined, either the sign of a drinker, or someone who liked to be outdoors a lot. Now it stood out as the only piece of colour on his face.

'Murder? I don't have anything to do with that sort of thing,' he spluttered indignantly, as if selling Ecstasy to ravers never resulted in the death of a teenager, or selling horse to a 28-year-old party girl who should know better, never led to death from disease, malnutrition, or overdose, six years down the line.

Hillary smiled grimly. 'But I believe a client of yours might be. Name of Dylan Hodge.'

The really quite beautiful blue eyes blinked at the mention of the name, and lily-white hands spread in an appeasing gesture. 'Mr Hodge? No, I know a Hodgkins – he ordered several hundred weight of copy paper from us just last week. But Dylan Hodge doesn't ring a bell.'

Hillary smiled again. 'I'm talking about your other clients, Mr Higgs. The kind who like buying powder.'

'Printing powder for photocopiers, you mean? No, I don't think so. But I can have my secretary check our back orders.'

Hillary sighed heavily, and beside her Janine tapped her pen on her notepad in a rat-a-tat gesture of impatience. No doubt she was thinking the same thing as herself. Everyday you had to go through the same old rigmarole. It would be nice and refreshing if once, just once, someone would put their hands up to it, and admit to being a money-grabbing, conscienceless chancer.

'I was talking about white powder, Mr Higgs,' Hillary corrected, her tone of voice never varying. 'You remember? You served eight years for supplying it not that long ago.'

Higgs flushed. 'That was a mistake. It was one of my staff who stashed that gear. I knew nothing about it.'

'Your fingerprints were found on the polythene covers, Mr Higgs,' Hillary said, then leaned forward, allowing a tight smile to stretch across her face. 'Look, let's cut out the song and dance, shall we? All I want to know, pure and simple, is if you sold Dylan Hodge more than his usual amount of junk in the last two days. Then you can walk. Understand?'

Higgs licked his lips and darted a glance at Janine, but there was no help there. The pretty blonde woman looked as if she was miles away. Hillary leaned back in her chair, and could almost hear the wheels turning in his head. Could it be true? Was it a trick? Could he be out of here, no harm, no foul, if he told them what they wanted to hear? Or was this a trick? 'I ain't falling for no entrapment,' he said sharply, and Hillary smiled ruefully.

'Do you even know the rules governing entrapment, Mr Higgs?' Hillary questioned, cocking her head to one side. 'Because I'm not sure I do.' She looked across to Janine. 'Do you, sergeant?'

'Can't say as I do, boss,' Janine said promptly on cue.

'As a copper, I know all about PACE and what have you, but even the lawyers twist themselves up into knots when it comes to what constitutes entrapment and what doesn't.' Hillary carried on in her same, flat, cordial manner. 'The Department of Public Prosecutions wet themselves when a case even smells of it. Isn't that right, sergeant?'

Janine grinned savagely. 'Won't touch it, boss,' she agreed.

'See, Benny,' Hillary said, leaning forward once more. 'We're working a killing here. We're not interested in faffing about. We've only got so much time, so much funding, so many days we can keep up a full squad, before the big bad budget starts to bite, and we get scaled down. Now, why would I want to go wasting any effort in trying to set up a small fry like you?'

Higgs didn't seem to take offence at being relegated to the small time. Instead a look of what passed for animal cunning spread over his face.

Hillary didn't hold her breath. Higgs got caught regularly, and wasn't exactly known for his genius. She doubted that whatever cunning plan he'd just come up with would seriously worry anyone.

'Let's talk hypothetically then,' Higgs said, and beside her Janine snorted.

Hillary nodded wearily. Anything to get the ball rolling. 'All right, let's.'

'Let's say I knew what you were talking about. Let's say I know this chap called Hodge. Just for the sake of argument, like.' He cast a beautiful blue eye at the silently turning tape. 'I'm not admitting I do, mind.'

Hillary flapped her hand in a yeah-yeah-yeah, get-on-with-it gesture.

'Let's say he likes some uppers. Mostly a bit of crack, when he's flush. Nothing big time. Know what I mean?'

Hillary nodded encouragement.

'And two nights ago, about 10, 10.30, say, he approaches one of my ... er ... members of staff, who happened to be working late in the office ...' He paused, because now he'd realized he was well off into the realms of fantasy land.

Hillary rolled her eyes. For 'member of staff' she read one of his army of juvenile runners, and for 'working late in the office' she knew he meant where one of his pushers hung out nearby teenage hang-outs. A pub that was currently 'in'. A café that had become that month's flavour of the moment. Cinemas, schools, anywhere where the young and vulnerable with money to spend could be shang-haied. 'OK, OK.' Hillary sighed heavily. 'Let's just say, hypothetically speaking, Mr Hodge found himself in desperate need of some staples, pens, and a cartridge or two of ink pellets. Did he buy more than his usual quota two nights ago?'

'Oh yes,' Benny admitted, almost amiably now. 'Much more than usual. I, that is, my member of staff was quite surprised.'

'How much more did he spend?' Hillary asked abruptly.

'Well now, his, er, stationery bill, usually came to some-thing like twenty, twenty-five pounds. This time he spent more than double that.'

Janine scribbled something down in her notebook, and Benny Higgs suddenly looked nervous again.

'I don't suppose he said how he came to be so flush?' Hillary asked, without much hope.

Benny shrugged, suppressing a laugh. 'People don't tend to talk much.'

Hillary guessed that was something of an understate-ment. You don't buy drugs whilst standing on a cold December street corner, and then hang around swapping anecdotes. She didn't bother to ask if Benny still had the ten or twenty pound notes that Dylan Hodge had used to pay for his skank. Even if he could remember exactly which ones were which, there was no way the Post Office would have kept records of the serial numbers on notes handed out to old-age pensioners. Why would they?

Which meant they had nothing by way of solid proof. Common sense said that Dylan Hodge had almost certainly used his grandmother's entire pension to feed his habit, but common sense had surprisingly little place in a court of British law.

'All right, Mr Higgs. Thank you for your co-operation,' Hillary said. This case was turning into something of a bugger. She couldn't remember the last time she'd worked a serious inquiry that turned up so little by way of forensic evidence to help them out.

'I can go?' Benny sounded quite surprised, almost as if he'd resigned himself to being a victim of entrapment after all.

'Yes,' Hillary said sourly. 'You can go.'

She watched the good-looking, well-dressed man leave, and vowed to have a word with Mike about him the next time they met up. As a man with pull in Vice, he could sign off on a watch-and-grab offensive. Higgs might be small time, but he got her goat. It was about time he was back in jail, where he belonged.

She sighed, and glanced across at Janine. 'Looks more and more as if our boy Dylan was spending his granny's pension money.'

Janine nodded. 'But according to our wits, Flo was determined to hang on to it for once and have a good birthday bash with it.'

Hillary nodded, but didn't speak. Surprised, Janine pressed on, 'So Dylan goes round there, is spotted by Barrington's witnesses, and cuts up rough when granny, for once, won't cough up the dough. He must know about the paperknife, is probably either high or coming on with the DTs, whichever, and loses his head. Stabs her, grabs the cash, and legs it. Goes straight to his nearest candy man and buys some goodies. It all fits, boss.'

Hillary sighed. Yeah it all fit. So why wasn't she more happy about it? She was old enough, and wise enough, not to look a gift horse in the mouth. And ninety-nine times out of a hundred, the obvious answer was the right one. So was she just being dog-in-the-manger because she didn't want to sign off on her murder case so easily?

'You don't like it,' Janine said flatly, and Hillary stirred.

'I wouldn't say that,' she said cautiously. 'We need to get Hodge in and really press him. But there were no fingerprints on the handle of the knife. If Hodge was so off his head that he flipped and stabbed Flo, we can't then turn around and say he suddenly got clear-headed enough to wipe his prints off the handle. Junkies, as a rule, don't think that clearly.'

'So he always meant to do it.' Janine played devil's advocate without really thinking about it. 'He wasn't that high, or wasn't hurting too bad, and did it in cold blood.'

'Why though?' Hillary shot back, enjoying, as always, bouncing her ideas off her subordinates. It always helped clear her mind. 'He was killing the goose that laid the golden eggs.'

Janine shrugged. 'Maybe he was tired of getting the cash in dribs and drabs. Perhaps, as his nearest and dearest, Flo had always promised to leave him everything in her will?'

Hillary laughed. 'What's everything? The house is rented, she doesn't own a car, her electrical appliances could have come off the ark. Her furniture wouldn't make fifty quid at a car boot sale. And I've seen her bank balance. It wouldn't keep Hodge high for more than a week. No. There's the smell of something else going on here. I just can't seem to get a handle on it.'

Janine shrugged. She'd seen Hillary pull enough rabbits out of the hat in her time to ever bet against her being right. 'Well, we'll have a better idea once we have another go at Hodge,' she said philosophically.

But that, as it turned out, wasn't going to be so easy. Back in the office, Keith gave her a message from Frank. Hodge wasn't at the squat and nobody, including his girlfriend, knew where he was. His gear, such as it was, was gone. Frank had also checked in all his old familiar haunts, but there was no sign of him. Dylan Hodge, for the moment, was in the wind.

Hillary turned on the anglepoise lamp over her desk and scowled down at her watch. Only ten past three and already the light was failing. Outside, a darkening, grey, rain-spattered day scowled back, as if to tell her to get used to it.

As if in defiance of the gloom, somebody had hung gaudy red, blue, gold, silver and green tinsel around the 'Most Wanted' posters, whilst another joker had hung tinsel 'chandeliers' from several of the ceiling lights. As if in cahoots, a radio was playing softly somewhere, a brass band rendition of 'God Rest Ye, Merry Gentlemen'.

Hillary hadn't even thought about Christmas yet, although she noticed that some of the shops had started touting it at the end of October. Every year the celebrations seemed to start earlier and earlier. Before long they'd be advertising it along with bloody Easter eggs.

'You look like you could kick a dog,' a cheerful voice said, making her look up, and Hillary's scowl instantly turned into a smile.

'Doc,' she acknowledged cheerfully, pushing a chair with her foot towards him. 'Have a seat. Not often we see you here.' Like most police surgeons, he tended to hang out at the morgue, the path labs, or a pub.

'Just finished with your old lady. Flo Jenkins,' Steven Partridge said, by way of explanation.

Hillary blinked. 'I didn't realize you'd got around to her. Shit, I didn't assign an officer.' Normally, at least one member of the investigative team was obliged to attend the autopsy of a murder victim. You needed to get the information quick, first hand, and accurately. Vital clues were often forthcoming from the post-mortem, and she felt momentarily wrong-footed. 'Didn't you let us know? I'd have sent the new boy over. He has to be "bloodied" sometime.'

Steven looked at her curiously. 'Of course I let you know,' he said, with just a hint of reproach. 'In fact I spoke to the head honcho himself, the walking Adonis.'

Hillary blinked, momentarily puzzled, then grinned. 'Ah, Danvers.'

'That's right, your DCI. In fact, it was DCI Danvers himself who came to observe.'

Again Hillary had to blink. Nobody liked post-mortems, and by the time you got to the rank of DCI it was almost unheard of that you'd attend one yourself.

'I know,' Steven said, clearly reading her mind. 'You could have knocked me down with the proverbial feather. Must have been years since he last stood behind the ME trying not to be sick. But he was very stalwart. No passing out, not even any retching. He even asked a few good questions. Not everybody can take it when the old buzz-saw comes out.'

Hillary nodded, telling herself not to think about it.

Pointless, of course, because the moment she told herself that, she instantly pictured the old lady spread out on Steven's stainless-steel table. Naked and without dignity, being cut, probed and inspected.

'He must be one of those who likes to keep in touch with the grass roots,' Steven Partridge mused, and the scent of Old Spice wafted across the table towards her. Today, he was wearing a pair of spotless cream slacks and what looked like a boating blazer. Gold cufflinks shone at his wrists, and his too-dark hair gleamed in the overhead lighting with some kind of expensive hair oil.

Pushing aside speculation as to why Danvers had attended the autopsy, she focused her attention on the medico. 'Anything interesting?' she asked, but by now it was rhetorical. Partridge wouldn't have called by in person if everything had been strictly routine. She nodded to Keith Barrington, who was blatantly listening, and pointed at his notebook. Instantly, he grabbed it and wheeled his chair quickly over. 'By the way, this is Detective Constable Keith Barrington, my new DC. Keith, this is Steven Partridge, one of our police surgeons, and the best of the bunch.'

Steven reached across and shook hands casually. To those who didn't know him, the medical man was often mistaken for being gay. But Steven had a very wealthy, very lovely wife, whom he delighted in taking out and about to the opera, and dining with in 'the city'.

Barrington nodded politely.

'So, doc, what can you tell us about our victim?'

'Well, no surprises about cause of death,' he began, speaking slowly and clearly so Barrington could take notes. 'The knife wound was the direct cause of death. It nicked her aorta, causing the left heart chamber to fill with blood, and thus stop beating.'

'Would it have taken long?' Hillary asked curiously.

'No. Less than a minute, probably.'

Hillary felt herself sigh with relief. At least the poor old soul hadn't suffered too much. 'Any signs of a struggle?'

'Not one. No bruising, except for around the knife wound itself, caused by the handle of the knife pressing into her flesh. No defence wounds, nothing under nails. I suspect the lady was simply sitting in her chair and somebody just stabbed her before she could react. The angle is confirmed by the way. She was already seated.'

Hillary nodded. No help there then. 'And time of death?'

Steven looked pained. 'About what we thought, I'd say.'

Hillary nodded and raised an eyebrow. 'And now, on to the interesting bit?'

Steven grinned. 'You know me so well,' he drawled, and out of the corner of her eye she saw Keith Barrington look up quickly, sensing that the banter might just have a bit of a flirtatious edge to it. It probably did, but Hillary knew it was harmless. Steven was a one-woman man.

'She was already dying,' Partridge said flatly.

Hillary started up in her chair. 'What? You mean she'd been attacked earlier? Or poisoned?'

Steven shook his head. 'No, no, I don't mean literally dying, right at that moment. I mean she had advanced cancer in her pancreas, which was spreading towards her stomach and lower intestine. Inoperable, invasive, deadly. She was riddled with it, poor old girl. No wonder she had such a cornucopia of pills. Pain management alone must have been a nightmare.'

Hillary nodded, and before she could stop herself, heard herself saying, 'I knew she didn't look well.'

Partridge nodded. 'She wasn't. And she didn't have long left, either.'

Hillary glanced at him sharply. 'Just how long did she have? It would have been her birthday in just a day or two. And she was looking forward to Christmas, so all her friends said.'

'Oh, she'd have made her birthday,' Partridge said at once. 'Christmas? I don't know. A bit iffy.'

'So she'd have been dead within a matter of weeks?' Hillary said, talking almost to herself by now. 'Who the hell would want to kill a dying woman?'

'Someone who might not have known she was dying, guv?' Keith queried, then wondered if he was going to get his head bitten off for stating the obvious. If he'd been back at Blacklock he would have. His old sergeant never missed a trick to do him down.

Hillary Greene said nothing for a moment, but simply frowned. 'A stranger?' she mused softly. Was it possible? But a stranger wouldn't know about the lethally sharp murder weapon. Or that Flo lived alone. Besides, why would someone just randomly go to an old woman's house and knife her to death?

'Doesn't fit, does it?' she said at last, then glanced across at Partridge once more as an idea hit her. 'She must have known how bad it was?' she said, expecting a firm yes, and was surprised when Partridge hesitated. Catching it, he shrugged.

'It would depend on her GP,' he said slowly. 'If he knew her well, and what his personal views are. Some GPs elect not to tell terminally ill patients until the very last possible moment, for fear of suicide, or mental relapse. If a person's already dying, why make the poor so-and-sos depressed as well. You can understand their argument.'

Hillary nodded. 'But surely most people know? I mean, a GP has to explain test results and such, don't they?'

'Oh yes,' Partridge agreed. 'But they can couch their words in very careful terms. Talking about treatment crisis management, pain relief, diagnosis prognosis. Baffle 'em with science, and all that. And don't forget, people of Flo's generation and class tend to have had a very poor education. If her GP wanted to talk gobbledegook to her, he could have got away with it. On the other hand, he might simply have told her straight out. You'll have to talk to him and see.'

Hillary blinked. And instantly wondered what her own GP kept back from her. 'But Flo would have been in a lot of pain? I mean, she'd have known there was something definitely wrong?'

'Oh yes,' Steven said. 'But the old are more resilient than you think. They get used to bad indigestion, putting up with arthritis, gout, gammy legs, bad backs, you name it. They almost *expect* to hurt. So it's possible that she might not have realized how bad it was.'

Hillary nodded. Interesting, but it didn't necessarily help her much. 'Keith, find out who her GP is and make me an appointment, will you?'

'Guv.'

As he was making a note to himself, Janine walked into the office and made her way over, surprised to see the medico chatting to her boss. Hillary briefly filled her in on the path findings, omitting the fact that Danvers had attended in person. Hillary thought she might know why Danvers had done that, and Janine was sharp enough to guess as well.

'By the way, congratulations, sergeant,' Steven Partridge said to Janine when Hillary had finished. 'It's the big day soon, isn't it?'

Janine smiled. 'Friday lunchtime. Just the registrar.'

'They're not even going on honeymoon until next month,' Hillary said. She wasn't sure, herself, that she'd want to go to work, pop off to tie the knot, then go back to work afterwards. Even her marriage to Ronnie Greene hadn't totally dampened her sense of romance, and Mel and Janine's low-key ceremony seemed so low key as to be almost non-existent. Like slotting in just another piece of business in the working day. Still, that's how they wanted to play it, so it hardly mattered what she felt about it.

'Well, I hope you'll be very happy, sergeant,' Steven said, beaming and then rising to his feet. 'Well, must get back. Nice to meet you, DC Barrington.'

Hillary watched him go and shook her head. 'We'll have to re-interview all Flo's closest friends and neighbours,' Hillary said, making Janine groan. 'Find out if they knew how serious her illness was.'

'Does it really matter, boss?' Janine asked, dreading the thought of doing house-to-house yet again.

'Why would you kill a woman who'd be dead in three weeks' time anyway?' Hillary asked her bluntly.

Janine opened her mouth at once, then engaged her brain, thought about it, and slowly closed her mouth again.

'Exactly,' Hillary said succinctly. 'When we know that, I've got a feeling we'll know everything.'

She was just about to get up the nerve to go and thank her DCI for his unexpected dedication to duty, when the phone went. 'DI Greene. Sir,' she said smartly, making Janine's head swivel around at once. She knew Hillary never used quite that tone when talking to her old friend Mel. It had to be the chief super again. For the second time in as many days too, Janine mused, watching Hillary's face like a hawk. Just what the hell was going on? Even though she'd be out of here next week, curiosity still bit deep.

'Yes, sir, I'll be right up,' Hillary said, hung up, and rubbed a hand across her forehead. Suddenly, she had a raging headache. She stood up, tugged her jacket down to straighten out the hem and grabbed her bag.

Janine watched her go, then glanced across at Barrington. She was rather intrigued by his rep as a sergeant-slugger. He didn't seem the type, somehow. But you could never tell with redheads. 'Looks like she's going to see Donleavy again,' she said meaningfully. 'There's definitely something up, if you ask me.' She wished, suddenly, that Tommy Lynch was still here. She missed chatting to someone who had more heart and so many more brain cells than Frank Ross. Barrington seemed all right, but he wasn't one for talking. Now, he frowned.

'Wonderful.' The last thing he wanted was discord

between his immediate boss and the powers that be. A nice, quiet posting, where he could keep his head down and give the dust a chance to settle. That's all he'd asked of this place.

Janine grinned. 'Relax. Donleavy's our Hillary's biggest fan. He reckons she's one of the best working detectives we've got.' It irritated her to know that Mel felt the same. 'It's just that, ever since last summer, something's been a bit off. You ask me, it's got something to do with Superintendent Raleigh.'

'Raleigh?'

'Yeah, the man from the Met. The super who was brought in when Donleavy got kicked upstairs. Mel's got his old job now.'

'How come?' Barrington asked, intrigued. It was almost unheard of for a superintendent to stay in a posting just a few months.

Janine shrugged. 'Raleigh just upped and left. He headed the Fletcher raid which sort of went well and yet cockeyed at the same time. Hillary got shot, Fletcher died, Raleigh left, and Mel got promoted. And somewhere amongst that lot lurks something that, unless I'm mistaken, might just be about to bite our boss in the arse.'

Downstairs, a young man in uniform walked to his locker and shrugged off his heavy coat. He reached inside one of the pockets for his mobile phone before putting the coat away, glanced over his shoulder to confirm that he was alone, then called up the photo memory on the menu.

He began to scroll through the snapshots one by one, smiling at the images. All of them were of Detective Sergeant Janine Tyler, all of them taken around here, at the nick. Janine walking across the car park. Janine, back view, walking down a corridor. Janine, in profile, sitting at her desk. It was incredibly easy nowadays when you had a phone in your hand, to pretend to take a call but snap off a shot instead. Finally, he found the one he wanted. Janine Tyler, almost looking full on at the camera, walking through the door of the canteen.

He had a mate who was really clever with computers and digital photography and all that kind of stuff.

The young man began to whistle as he imagined what fun there was still to be had. He didn't see another young man, still in his outdoor coat, watch him walk away. He didn't know his name was Jem Titchmarsh. He didn't know what his dad had asked him to do.

If he had, he might not have whistled quite so jauntily.

Donleavy watched Hillary walk into his office and nodded to the chair in front of his desk. He didn't mince words. 'Falconer, the cop on vacation in Malta,' he began curtly. 'He's been given permission by his guv'nor to approach Raleigh. If it *is* Raleigh.'

Hillary nodded. 'It was bound to happen.'

'Yes,' Donleavy concurred. Given the state in which the Fletcher investigation had been left, he had to agree. 'But the ACC isn't keen to reopen the whole can of worms.' Unspoken went the obvious rider: so *maybe we'll get away with it.*

Hillary nodded wordlessly. But maybe, she thought gloomily, they wouldn't.

chapter eight

Hillary returned to her desk, her mind very much on the past, on her crooked husband, who'd amassed a fortune by running an illegal animal parts smuggling operation and died before she could divorce him. On the millions of pounds she'd found in his hidden bank account, and the man who'd stolen it and ran. On Luke Fletcher, a murderer, drug dealer, and thug, now dead himself, murdered during the raid last summer. But most of all she reflected on just what Chief Superintendent Marcus Donleavy knew, due to the anonymous report she'd written for him, and, more importantly, what he didn't know.

Of them all, the only person she really worried about was Jerome Raleigh, and what he might say if suddenly confronted by his past in the form of a nosy copper from his old nick.

Walking across the vast, open-plan office towards her desk, she tried to thrust it all to the back of her mind. After all, Raleigh was hardly likely to confess to cold-blooded murder, and what would he gain from telling anyone about the hidden money? Not when all he had to do was keep quiet. Besides, she had a murder investigation to cope with, here and now. Picking over the wounds of the past, or worrying about what might happen in the future, would have to wait.

Nevertheless, the wound in her hip twinged as she took her seat, as if it just couldn't help but give a sniggering nudge to all her hastily erected building blocks of self-confidence, and she bit back a curse.

Both Keith Barrington and Janine Tyler were studiously working at their desks, heads bent, fingers working the keyboards of their computers, but she had no doubts at all that they'd been discussing her, and her second summons to Donleavy's office. Hillary wondered how long it would be before the rest of the office twigged that something was amiss. If she knew station-house gossip, not long.

Too tense to drive back to Bicester yet again, she did something she seldom did, and reached for the telephone in order to question a witness. Normally she liked to see the face of the person she was talking to, thus giving herself the opportunity to read any betraying signs of their body language as well. She wasn't surprised, therefore, when Janine shot her a surprised look when she greeted Caroline Weekes.

'Hello, Mrs Weekes. This is Inspector Greene. Yes, how are you feeling now? Has your mother arrived? Good. Yes, I just want to ask you one quick question, I won't keep you long. Tell me, did you know that Mrs Jenkins was unwell?'

'Oh yes.' The voice in her ear sounded sleepy, and Hillary wondered if she'd taken anything.

'Did Mrs Jenkins tell you so or was it something you observed for yourself?' Hillary asked, leaning slowly back in her chair, aware that rigid tension in her shoulder blades was making her back ache.

Over the wire, she heard Caroline Weekes clear her throat. 'Well, a bit of both really. I knew she'd been to see the doctor a while back, because he referred her to the John Radcliffe for a specialist's appointment, and I drove her.'

'Did you ask her what the problem was?'

'Oh no,' Caroline Weekes breathed, sounding slightly shocked. 'But I could tell it was something serious. Later, I would remark on how ill she looked, and she'd say something like, "Well, love, it's not surprising is it?" And from other things she said, you know, it was clear that she wasn't expecting to see many more birthdays or Christmases. But things like that aren't something you dwell on, or talk about, is it?'

'No, I see,' Hillary said. 'Well, thank you, Mrs Weekes. Sorry to trouble you again so soon.'

She hung up thoughtfully, consulted the files, then dialled a second number. 'Mr Keane. This is Detective Inspector Greene. Yes, that's right. Hello again. Look, I'm sorry to bother you, but there was something I neglected to ask you the last time we talked.' She glanced across at Janine, who'd turned back to her computer screen, and wondered if the fact that she was going to be a married woman in just two days' time worried her at all. Janine, at nearly thirty, had always struck her as the type who liked being single. She only hoped her old friend Mel Mallow knew what he was doing.

'That's all right, ask away.' Walter Keane's voice in her ear brought her thoughts back to the task in hand.

'How was Mrs Jenkins' health the last few months, do you know?'

Walter Keane gave a bark of laughter. 'She was on her last legs, wasn't she? You know, on her way out. So it was bloody awful.'

Hillary's eyes narrowed thoughtfully. 'You think she was dying?' she asked softly.

'I bloody well know she was dying,' Walter corrected gruffly. 'She told me. Cancer,' he added succinctly.

'And how did she take it?' Hillary asked, then added quickly, 'I mean, I know it must have been a shock. I'm sure she was angry, and upset, but generally speaking – did it make her very depressed, or was she more inclined to be scared or introspective? I'm sorry to be asking such a question like this, especially over the telephone, but it might be important.'

Over the wire, Walter Keane sighed heavily. 'Well, it

rocked her a bit, of course,' he agreed. 'And she had a bit of a weep, like, when she told me. But Flo was never really one to let things get on top of her. She read up on this remission thing, where terminally ill people suddenly get better for a little while. Amazing thing that, not even the doctors know why. She often said she might go in for a bit of that, like. As if, by the power of positive thinking, she could make it happen.' Walter paused, as if to comment on what he thought of that, then seemed to think better of it. 'Then she read cases where doctors had given a poor sod just a week to live, and there they were, two years later, still walking around. She always said you might as well hope for the best, as go around fearing the worst.'

Hillary smiled. 'That sounds like a good attitude to take. She must have been a feisty lady.'

'Ah, she was. And determined to enjoy herself too. Often she said to me, seeing as how she might drop off her perch any minute, she was going to live the life of Riley while she could. Course, to Flo, that was going to bingo whenever she could, and buying the slightly dearer brand of gin from Tesco. But she wasn't suicidal or nothing like that,' he added firmly.

So, Hillary mused, she'd told Walter Keane all about her illness, but only hinted at it to Caroline Weekes. Interesting that. And maybe suggestive. 'Do you know if anyone else knew about her condition? I mean her close friends or near neighbours?' Hillary pressed.

Walter Keane grunted. 'Well, it weren't no secret,' he said. 'Flo didn't keep on about it, but I reckon everyone she was close to either knew, or could read the writing on the wall, like.'

Hillary thanked him and hung up. For a moment or two she doodled on her pad, then reached for the phone again. 'Doctor Partridge please. Yes, I'll wait. Oh good.' His lab assistant had just caught him before he'd started on his next autopsy.

'Yes?' His voice was hurried, and Hillary didn't hang about.

'Sorry, Steven, just a quick word. Florence Jenkins – can you just tell me what she might have expected from her last few weeks on earth?'

'Pain and more pain. Bowels going, liver function going, being sick all day, her whole body packing up. A quick visit to a hospice, if she couldn't get nursing at home and then, if she was lucky, not waking up from her last morphine shot.'

Hillary felt a cold hand clutch her stomach and swallowed hard. It sounded unbearable, just hearing about it. 'Right. That would be a lot of pain then?'

'Yes.'

'Thanks, that's all I needed to know.'

Steven Partridge said a quick goodbye and hung up.

Hillary replaced her receiver and glanced up. 'OK, you two,' she said, and waited until Janine and Keith had wheeled their chairs over. 'I'm a 76-year-old woman, who knows she's got a serious illness that's going to kill her in a very short while. The pain is bad, and I know it'll only get worse. Soon I'm going to be sick all the time, my body functions are going to go, and I'll have to either go into a hospice or struggle on in my own home. What do I do? Janine?'

'If it was me, I'd top myself, boss,' Janine said at once.

'Keith?'

'Dunno, guv. Depends. I mean, is there something I really wanted to do before I died? Maybe, if I was really terrified of death, I'd hang on because I had no other choice. Besides, where there's life there's hope.'

Hillary nodded. 'OK, that just about covers her options. Now, everyone keeps telling us Flo Jenkins was looking forward to her birthday party, looking forward to Christmas, was bearing up and being a good soldier about it all. In short, she was an optimist. Now, supposing that's just what she wanted people to think? Suppose she was really down, afraid, and simply wanting to get out of it all?'

'You mean suicide, boss?' Janine asked, amazed. 'Surely the old girl would just swallow all her pills at once? Or down a bottle of gin and tie a plastic bag over her head? Shit, even take a bath and toss in an electric fire. She wouldn't stab herself in the chest.'

'Right, guv,' Keith said. 'It's not something you'd think of, is it?'

'Agreed,' Hillary said. 'I never asked Doc Partridge if it could have been suicide because it was obviously a non-starter. Besides, her prints weren't on the handle of the dagger and she could hardly have stabbed herself, then wiped off her prints – even if death hadn't been practically instantaneous. But let's just think about it for a moment. She was sitting in her chair, and there were no defensive wounds of any kind on her body. Which means that she knew who was standing over her, and the fact that he or she had a lethally sharp blade in their hands either didn't worry her, or she didn't care. Now, what picture does that conjure up?'

Janine blinked, trying to see what she was getting at, but it was the new boy who got to it first. 'A mercy killing, guv? By a second party.'

'Right. Suppose Flo Jenkins didn't have the nerve to kill herself. Or maybe some kind of religious conviction stopped her. Maybe it just went against the grain to do it herself – but having somebody else do it for her, well, that was OK. It wasn't so bad then. The matter was more or less out of her hands. I can see how a pain-riddled, confused, tired old lady might think that way.'

Janine nodded slowly. 'OK guv, but again, why the knife? Why not ask them to crush up some pills in the gin and just quaff it down?'

'Because then *she'd* have to be the one to do the swallowing,' Keith said, following Hillary's reasoning. 'She'd have to take an active part in it. But being stabbed – well, she wouldn't actually have to *do* anything then, would she?'

'Except sit there and take it,' Hillary said flatly, and the image of that quickly dampened any enthusiasm they might have felt for the theory. As she knew it would.

'Can't see it boss,' Janine said at once. 'Suppose whoever it was bungled it? Bottled out, even. Only wounded her or scratched her? No, I don't think it would work. Besides, the thought of a cold blade piercing your flesh ...' She shuddered. 'No. I can't see anyone opting for that.'

'Nor me, guv,' Keith confirmed. And he didn't appear too worried that his new boss might not like having her thoughts shot down in flames by a mere DC.

Good, Hillary thought. He was beginning to trust her. 'No, neither can I. But what if she didn't know it was coming? Not specifically *then*, I mean?'

'I'm not with you, boss,' Janine said, intrigued by where Hillary was going with this, but in no way convinced.

Hillary sighed. 'When I was talking to Walter Keane, I noticed an old army photo of his. I'm not an expert on war uniforms or insignia, but I've got an idea he might have been in some sort of special ops corps. Commandos maybe. He's a man, anyway, who'd know how to go behind enemy lines in the dead of night and silently dispatch the enemy. With something like a very sharp knife. A man who would know just where to thrust a blade, quickly, cleanly, and painlessly.'

Janine blinked. 'I got the feeling from the other neighbours I questioned that Flo and Walter were close. Oh, not doing the terrible deed ...' Janine's face wrinkled with disgust at the thought, 'but proper friends. Tight knit, like. If she was going to ask anybody to help her out, I suppose it would be him.'

'But that still doesn't get us past her birthday, guv,' Keith said. 'I mean, everyone commented on how much she was looking forward to having this party. So, say she did ask her good friend Walter Keane to put her out of her misery, she'd wait until she'd had her birthday at least, wouldn't she? If not Christmas.'

'Not if she told him she didn't want to know when it was coming,' Janine said, then stopped, as if suddenly struck by the absurdity of what she was saying, and shook her head. 'Come off it, boss,' she scoffed. 'We're in cloud cuckoo land here. Can you honestly see some batty old lady asking her eighty-year-old ex-commando neighbour to sneak up on her at some point and bump her off before she knew what was happening?'

Hillary grinned widely. 'No. But I expect you to think about it, and then give it a little tweak.'

Janine stared at her, then slowly nodded. 'I get it,' she said softly. 'It was all Walter Keane's idea. Flo didn't know anything about it. Being genuinely fond of the old girl, he can't bear to see her suffering getting worse and worse, so one night he nips around to her place, takes the dagger and ends it all, quick and painless.'

'Now that could work, guv,' Keith Barrington said judiciously.

Hillary sighed. 'Not so fast. It answers a fair few questions, that's all,' she agreed. 'Questions like: why kill a woman who was already dying? And it would explain the lack of defence wounds, the neatness of the stabbing. As an old soldier, he'd be efficient at least. But it doesn't explain the inconsistencies, such as Flo's missing pension money or our favourite junkie spending so much cash the night Flo died.'

Janine frowned. 'Unless Hodge came to see his gran later that night and found her already stabbed.'

'Go on.'

'Well, what's he going to do? Pick up a phone and ring the police?' Janine snorted. 'Not bloody likely. Besides, he's got the shakes bad, seeing his old gran dead like that, and he needs a fix more than ever. He knows it's pension day, that's why he's there, so he goes through her bag.' She was talking faster now, warming up to her hypothesis.

'Right, she won't be needing the money now, will she?' Keith put in, putting himself in the mind of a junkie.

Janine shot him a quick impatient look and charged on. 'So he grabs the money and legs it to one of Benny Higgs' runners. Gets off his head. Probably doesn't even remember much about that night now.'

'But when we pull him in, something in his fried brain makes the connection.' Keith picked up the baton. 'And he has a flashback. Maybe even thinks he might have done the killing. Who knows?'

'And does a runner,' Janine finished triumphantly.

Hillary smiled and slowly clapped her hands. 'Well done. A lovely house of cards. Now let's see how it stands up to scrutiny. First, Keith, I want you to do some background research on Walter Keane. Find out what his regiment was, where he served, and see if you can prise out of the army any of his old records, especially any psychological evaluations he might have gone through. If he was special ops, I think they had the shrinks check them over for suitability.'

Janine laughed. 'For all the good that'll do. Psychology was in the dark ages in them days, boss.'

Hillary sighed. 'That's it, make me feel better.'

She watched her team set to work with renewed vigour, and wished she could feel so energized. The fact was, she had very little faith in their latest 'lead'. If it could even be called a lead at all, when the truth was, Hillary had just created it out of thin air. A chilling example of just how desperate she was. Forensics was no help. The few witnesses they had weren't really of much use. Unless they could find a motive, at the very least, the case was almost certainly going to stall.

'Janine, I want you to put on your best radio voice. Ask for anybody who might have visited Florence Jenkins that night to get in touch. Speak to the PR officer about it – see if they can get a piece in the *Bicester Advertiser*, the *Banbury Cake*, you know the drill.'

'Right boss,' Janine agreed.

'If it wasn't Hodge who was seen that night, I want to know who it was, and what he was doing there. What about …'

'Guv, I've got him.' Frank Ross' triumphant shout cut across the busy office, temporarily silencing the ever present murmur of voices, as Hillary, Janine and the new boy, all rose to their feet.

Frank Ross, charging across the room, a wide cheesy grin lighting up his features, puffed up to them. 'One of my snouts told me about this safe house near the railway station. Nothing more than an abandoned old electric shed – you know, six foot by six foot concrete block where there used to be an electricity sub-station. Used to service the railways when they were still using steam, by the looks of it. Anyway, Hodge was there, right enough, snoring away in a pool of his own piss.'

'Oh great,' Janine said, sitting back down. 'Barrington, you can take the interview if you like.'

Hillary laughed drily. 'Get the custody sergeant to clean him up a bit. Is he conscious? Talking sense?'

'More or less, guv,' Frank said cheerfully.

'Right then. Let's have another go at him.' She wanted to take Barrington with her, but it was Frank's collar. She sighed. 'Frank, you're with me.'

Hodge smelled of carbolic soap by the time he was led into interview room two. He was also wearing a loose white cotton overall, over a faded black T-shirt. Hillary glanced at them curiously, recognizing them as 'emergency togs'. These were old clothes donated, usually by serving officers, to be used as and whenever circumstances dictated. As Frank set up the tape and introduced all those present, she looked over at the constable standing by the door.

'I sincerely hope you didn't burn his clothes, constable.'

'No ma'am.'

'Good. I want them taken to forensics along with the rest of his gear. Frank, you retrieved his gear, right?' she asked sharply, and beside her Frank Ross sneered.

'Course I did. Logged it in to the evidence officer the moment I came in.'

Hillary nodded, but it wouldn't have been the first time Ross had ignored the protocols. Then she glanced sharply at Hodge. 'I hope you're listening to all this, Mr Hodge,' she said. 'We now have all your worldly possessions, which will be gone over by our forensics department. All we need is one speck of your grandmother's blood to place you at the murder scene.'

This was not, of course, strictly true. Any good defence barrister could argue that Hodge could have got his grandmother's blood on his clothes at any time. He was, after all, a regular visitor to her home. Perhaps she'd had a nose bleed, your Honour, or had even, given her condition, coughed up some blood into a handkerchief, which her dutiful grandson had then dealt with.

Hillary, ever mindful of the tricks lawyers liked to play, and even more mindful just how tenuous her evidence against this man was, knew she had to be careful now. And balanced against this need, as ever, was the even greater need to get the man talking. It was a tightrope every SIO had to walk, and sometimes it led to you falling flat on your face.

'We know you stole your grandmother's pension money, Dylan,' she said sharply. 'We've been having a word with Benny Higgs.'

At this, Dylan Hodge suddenly straightened up in his seat. He'd been lounging forward sleepily, like a lizard that hadn't quite had enough morning sun to heat his blood, but at the mention of his supplier, his torpor vanished.

Hillary smiled. 'Yes, thought that might interest you. He told me something very interesting. Know what that was?'

'Oh man,' Dylan Hodge whined. 'You ain't really been talking to Benny have you? Everyone knows Benny don't like talking to cops. That last stretch he did inside really bent him out of shape. Made him paranoid as hell. He won't want to know me now,' he wailed. 'I'll have to find another connection. You cow, you really screwed me.'

Hillary sighed heavily. 'Dylan, try and pay attention will you? Listen to what I say.' She leaned forward, forcing eye contact, and then said slowly and clearly, 'We know you visited your grandmother on the night of her murder. You were seen,' she said, being just a little bit over-indulgent with the truth there. 'We have a witness who can prove you were flush with money that night. We know your grandmother withdrew her old age pension that day. Your clothes and gear are with forensics now. All it takes is one scrap, one molecule, one little hair, and you'll be tied in to her murder. Why are you worried about finding another connection, when the chances are that you'll be serving life for first degree murder? Wise up, will you, and do yourself a favour.'

Dylan Hodge's jaw had slowly swung open during this speech, and now a trail of saliva trickled over his chin. Hillary sighed and leaned back in her chair.

'Look, Frank, why don't you explain to Mr Hodge the score, hmm? I'm running out of patience.' She knew she could trust Frank to handle this stage of the interview. In fact, he was very good at putting the wind up people.

For once, Frank was glad to oblige her. 'See, Hodge, when you're looking at a dead old lady, it's all in the details,' he began, rubbing his chin thoughtfully. 'Was it premeditated? Can you wangle manslaughter out of it? What about diminished responsibility? Then there's temporary insanity and mitigating circumstances. If you acted whilst under the influence of the old skank, well then, a clever lawyer might be able to get you off in ten years. But you've got to do yourself some good here and now. Get it?'

Frank Ross tapped his temple, but Hodge, as far as Hillary could tell, was only staring at him for something to do with his eyes. She doubted if any of it was getting through. He was still worrying about where he'd find a new connection.

'See, this is when the deals are done. Here and now.' Frank wasn't giving up. 'You scratch our back, make our job easier, and we scratch yours, know what I mean?'

Hodge obviously didn't.

Hillary stirred in her chair, one eye on the tape machine. Frank was sailing very close to the wind now. She coughed a warning, and when Frank flicked a glance at her, pointed at the machine. Frank scowled.

'Look, if you didn't really mean to do the old lady in, if she wouldn't let you have her pension money and you just lost it and grabbed the knife, well, see, that's not premeditation is it?' Frank ploughed on. 'That's not twenty-five to life.'

'I didn't kill her,' Dylan Hodge said flatly. Then glanced across at Hillary. 'I didn't. I didn't even touch her. Didn't go nowhere near her.' And then, quite suddenly and shockingly, he began to grin, a big, wide grin, as the wonderful truth seemed to dawn in his brain. 'So it don't matter if you've got my gear, or nothing else. I didn't do it, so you can't prove I did, see? Now, I want a lawyer.'

Frank sighed heavily and glanced guiltily over at Hillary Greene. Once they'd asked for the lawyer, and it was on tape, they had to stop questioning and bring one in.

Hillary nodded and without a word stood up. Outside, Frank Ross swore, long and hard. 'Sorry guv, don't know how I lost him.'

But Hillary was already shaking her head. She had the sinking feeling that forensics wouldn't find any of Florence Jenkins' blood on Dylan Hodge's clothes. She was, in fact, almost certain that he'd been speaking the truth – or at least, a junkie's version of it.

No, she suspected they had it right before. Hodge had called round to do his usual scrounging, and found his grandmother dead in her chair. He hadn't gone near her, just as he'd said, but simply stolen her money and ran.

'When his brief gets here, keep at him,' Hillary said. It had to be done, and it kept Ross out of her hair for a while. 'You never know, he might still give us something useful.'

'Right guv,' Frank said listlessly. Like herself, he could already sense it was a lost cause.

Hillary walked upstairs and towards her desk, but instead of sitting down, carried on to the nearest window and stared out over the dark car park. The orange street lights stared back at her and the wind threw raindrops against the window pane. No help there, then.

Hillary had headed up five murder investigations in her career to date, and she had solved and closed all of them. Now, fear of failure bit deep. This case seemed to be drifting away from her. It was as if she was floundering, forever looking in the wrong places, or chasing her own tail.

Then there was the dark cloud that was Jerome Raleigh, and the Luke Fletcher fiasco, threatening to break over her head, drowning her in hot water. No way around it, things were beginning to look distinctly bleak. And to cap it all, she was still feeling uneasy about her relationship with Mike Regis, and where it was going, or might end up.

Well, she mused grimly at her reflection, at least things couldn't get any worse.

And then Paul Danvers came out of his cubby hole, walked over, and rubbing his hands said brightly, 'Right everyone, what say we go for that drink I promised you?'

chapter nine

Mitch 'the Titch' Titchmarsh had not been idle since his unexpected call for help from Hillary Greene.

In truth, he was finding retirement something of a mixed blessing. At nearly seventy, he was glad to lie in of a morning, contemplating nothing more onerous than coaxing a spurt of growth in his Brussels sprouts so that the wife might have some home-grown fresh veg ready for Christmas dinner. The allotment had been her idea, of course, designed to get him out from under her feet, but Mitch hadn't objected too strenuously. He enjoyed sitting in the allotment shed during the long summer evenings, drinking cider with his fellow toilers of the soil, talking about the poor state of British football and, just for a laugh, the state of the Labour Party.

Even so, he missed the excitement of the old days back in uniform, and Hillary's call to arms was giving him a taste of it once more.

It hadn't taken him long to alert the three of his sons who were serving at Kidlington HQ to the problem, although Jonathan, the oldest, hadn't seemed that impressed. As far as he was concerned, a blonde bombshell sergeant from CID should be capable of looking after herself. Mitch soon put a flea in his ear however, and now all three were keeping their eyes and ears firmly open.

Geoff, the youngest, had alerted him to one PC Brian Conleve, who'd been at the nick for a year just before Mitch left. Conleve, it seemed, had a bit of a rep for being a misogynist, one of those men who never married but lived with his mother. Sainted mother excepted, he seemed to see the female gender as one step below him on the food chain.

Mitch remembered him only vaguely, but thought that anyone that openly anti-female was unlikely to be their man. In his experience, it was the ones who kept things bottled up who were most likely to explode into nasty action. No, a far better bet seemed to be one that Jonathan had noticed, a young PC in Traffic called Martin Pollock. Pollock, according to Jonathan, had been trying to get into plain clothes for some time now, without success. Thwarted ambition, as Mitch had seen only too often, could twist itself into dangerous paths. Added to that, he'd learned from an old mate only this morning that Pollock had been used to make up numbers on a house-to-house inquiry on an estate in the Leys – a particularly nasty mugging that had nearly killed a 42-year-old father of six. Janine Tyler, interestingly enough, had worked that case too, so their paths had definitely crossed.

But the thing that twitched Mitch's radar the most about Pollock was the news that he'd recently been given the elbow by his girlfriend – a pretty blonde, by all accounts. Apparently, according to one of Traffic's biggest gossips – a divisional section head who liked to tie one on on a Saturday night – the girl, who worked in a travel agency, had dumped young Pollock for the manager.

Mitch didn't need a degree in psychology to read a whole volume into that. Janine Tyler, pretty, blonde, a fully fledged member of CID, and about to marry her boss. Pollock might as well be walking around with arrows pointed at him.

Mitch, who was at that moment sitting in front of the telly pretending not to watch EastEnders, glanced at his watch, and once more reached for his mobile phone. He'd tried to call Hillary at work, only to learn she'd just left, but she wasn't answering her mobile. He called her number again and got the ring tone. He waited for several moments, and was about to switch it off and try again, when it was suddenly answered. A blast of jukebox music and some loud voices nearby told him she was in a pub.

He grinned into the phone. 'That's nice that is,' he bellowed loudly, so that she could hear him, and ignored the sigh his long-suffering wife gave, who really *was* trying to watch EastEnders. 'Here's us retired, poor old clapped-out buggers doing your work for you, when you so-called elite are swaggering about swilling it down at the boozer.'

Hillary, who was sitting at a table with her boss, Keith Barrington, Janine and Mel and, unfortunately, Frank Ross, kept her face perfectly straight. 'Yes, speaking,' she said flatly.

Mitch whistled. 'Can't talk, huh?'

'It's not really convenient right at this moment.'

'OK, just a quick update then. I think I've found your man. I'll let you know when it's more than an old copper's gut feeling and nasty suspicion.'

'Thanks,' Hillary said, and waited for Mitch to hang up before flipping her phone shut. She smiled across at Mel, who'd raised an eyebrow. 'An old snout, probably blowing bubbles,' she said dismissively. 'It's my round, isn't it? What's everyone having?'

When she got back to the bar, Barrington helping her to transport the drinks, Danvers was filling Mel in on her latest case, evidently bewailing the fact that there were no solid leads.

'Those sorts of cases can be a sod,' Mel said, catching Hillary's eye as she sat down. 'I know just how frustrating they can be. No apparent motive, or none that really stands up to scrutiny. Plenty of forensics, but nothing that tells you something useful. No witnesses to speak of, going nowhere fast. It's even worse when it's one of the elderly that's been victimized.'

Hillary shrugged. 'Early days yet. We've still got leads to follow up.'

Janine shot her a quick 'have we?' look that everyone at the table caught. Frank Ross smirked, and drank his beer. 'It'll be the scumbag grandson,' he said. 'We just won't be able to prove it.'

'Thanks for that, Frank.' Hillary smiled cheerfully at him. 'Always good to have the right attitude. Remember that, Keith.'

Ross scowled at Keith, who pretended not to hear.

'So, the big day Friday,' Paul Danvers said, glancing at his immediate superior. 'Still can't tempt you into a bit of a do afterwards?'

'No,' Mel grinned. 'Janine and I have plans for the weekend though.'

Janine beamed and reached across to take Mel's hand. Hillary watched them and sighed. If the Flo Jenkins case suddenly cracked open and they needed all hands on board, she knew who she wouldn't be calling. She saw Keith Barrington's lips twitch, and realized she'd telegraphed her thoughts. Barrington was bright and perceptive, no two ways about it. She'd have to remember that in the future.

Thinking about Barrington, it was time she hauled him out into the open, kicking and screaming if she had to. It might be cruel, but it had to be done. Everyone at the station was gossiping about him, and the sooner he was a known quantity the better. There was nothing else for it to be quick and brutal. It was far kinder that way.

'So, Keith,' she said, her voice, though quiet, instantly attracting everyone's attention. 'Just why did you put your old sergeant back at Blacklock Green in hospital?'

Keith went pale. It wasn't hard for him to do, given his colouring, but the unexpected attack, and the direction from which it came, clearly took the ground out from under him. Although it had only been a few days, he'd begun to feel comfortable in his new work environment and had begun to trust Hillary Greene. Now he shot her a look like a dog that had been unfairly kicked by its master.

'Yeah, let's ...' Frank began, but Hillary shot out, hard and fast.

'Shut up, Ross. I don't want to hear it from you.'

Ross went red. Danvers reached slowly for his beer, wondering what Hillary was doing, and if it was wise. Mel, who knew her better, said nothing, but simply waited. He knew only sketchy details himself, since the firm from the Smoke hadn't been very forthcoming. Not that that was surprising. No station liked to wash their dirty linen in public for all and sundry to laugh at.

Hillary waited until Keith looked at her again, before saying quietly, 'We need to know. Surely you can see that? I need to know what makes you lose control to that extent. And unless I can trust you, it's pointless you being a member of this team. And you're not deaf and blind – you must be aware of the idle speculation that's going around about you. It's far better to have the truth out in the open. And besides, I want to hear your version of it.'

Something about the steady way she spoke, and perhaps the unspoken promise that she was not about to judge him without a hearing, made Keith Barrington square up to her in his chair. 'OK guv,' he said flatly. If she wanted it, she could have it. 'Mick Barnes was a bastard. He was always a bastard, long before I joined the nick, and no doubt he still is. He was a natural born bully, often picking on those in uniform and making their life hell. When I was assigned to his team, he decided it would be more fun to have someone he could torment on a day to day basis. And I took it. I took the constant put-downs, the way he'd pull rank when he shouldn't, the way he'd take credit for my work, the bad-mouthing to the brass and everything else that went with it.'

He paused, took a breath, aware that everyone was hanging on his every word, took up his glass with a hand that wasn't quite steady, and took a pull of draught bitter.

'But it wasn't as bad as it sounds,' he carried on thoughtfully, determined to be scrupulously honest. 'Everyone knew he was a bastard, and it didn't take long for it to get around that he had it in for me. So Barnes couldn't really do me that much harm. Our DI knew what he was about, all right, and the rest of the team made it their business that he got to know when I did well, because Barnes sure as hell wasn't going to. My mates were supportive and let me blow off steam when I needed to. And maybe Barnes began to realize that he wasn't doing himself any favours either, because after the first six months or so, he slackened off a bit.' Barrington sighed. 'I got used to dodging the worst of it, and like I said, the lads rallied around, never letting him get me down too much. And it would have gone on like that, I expect, until I could transfer away from the bastard. I was determined I wasn't going to let him win, see. But then we got a tip-off about a body shop on our manor. This was right up our alley, because car theft figures had been rising steadily, and it had put the crime rate way up. And you know how the brass sing about that.'

Mel, being 'brass' merely smiled. The rest simply waited for him to go on.

'Well, a chop shop made sense. Young kids, working as a ring, lifting middle-range vehicles for the parts, all added up. We just didn't know the chop shop was on our patch. Once a snitch let on, Barnes was all over it. Well, he would be, it had glory written all over it, and he wanted the kudos.' Barrington took another sip of bitter and sighed again.

'Anyway, this young kid, Jimmy Grigson, Grigsy we called him, volunteered to go undercover, posing as a young twocker. He looked like one too – he was nineteen, but could have passed for fourteen on a good day. Stick thin, gawky, spots and all. I didn't think he was ready for it, to be honest. He'd only been in the force ten months, eager and all, and a good head on his shoulders, don't think I'm doing him down. But not ...' Keith, as if aware of his own youth, looked suddenly embarrassed. 'Well, he just didn't have the experience to be thrown in at the deep end. Of course, he shouldn't have volunteered in the first place, and I tried to talk him out of it, but once Barnes heard about it, he sold it to the super. Get a man on the inside, get a raid organized, find 'em bang to rights, and hey presto, the crime rates for the next month would fall by magical numbers.'

Hillary had a very bad feeling about where this was going. Glancing across at Paul Danvers, she saw a similar tension in his own body language, so she obviously wasn't the only one.

'Well, at first, it all seemed to go OK,' Barrington carried on. 'Grigsy teamed up with this known car thief, who after a bit took him along on a job. He didn't take him to the chop shop of course, just used him as a lookout. But then he used him again, then began to teach him the tricks of the trade. We knew it would only be a matter of time before Grigsy was trusted to do his own thieving, and take the car to the body shop, then we'd have 'em.'

By now even Frank Ross was looking more interested in the story than his own sulking, and Hillary nodded encouragement. 'And they did?' she prompted softly.

'Oh yeah, they did. We set up the car, of course, one from the motor pool. We watched Grigsy steal it, but Barnes was all for putting a tracer on it, the dozy bastard. As if people who butchered cars for a living wouldn't spot it. Naturally, the DI vetoed it, but we didn't follow Grigsy in case they spotted us. The plan was for Grigsy just to ascertain the location of the garage, and then we'd raid it another night.

'Nothing wrong with that plan. It was simple, relatively safe for Grigsy, and it would probably have worked. But Barnes wanted more. He wanted to make sure the big fish was caught as well as the minnows. He wanted to know who was behind the garage and if he had more chop shops.

So he persuaded the DI to hold off a bit.' Barrington shook his head. 'Of course, Grigsy was all for it. He was a bit of an adrenaline junkie, and still green enough behind the ears to think he was indestructible.'

Hillary leaned slowly back in her chair. The writing was so clearly on the wall, she hardly needed to have it spelled out. But she'd asked for it, after all, so now she was going to take it.

'Next day, we ran a trace on the garage, and sure enough it was a front for a man only too well known to us – a Kray wannabe called Wilkie Dalton. He'd done time for GBH, and was running one of the biggest protection rackets on our patch. Of course, the DI and Barnes went wild. If we could get Dalton dead to rights, the whole division would be celebrating for a week. So they let Grigsy run with it. We set up another car for him, this time got him to wear a wire. See if he could get them talking. And sure enough, we got one or two nibbles about Dalton being behind it all, but nothing we could take to court. Then Grigsy started to push it, suggesting they do something bigger and better – maybe start nicking top-of-the-range gear, shipping and selling it abroad. Pushing to have a word with the boss so that he could sell him on the idea.'

Hillary shook her head and groaned. That was a mistake that no seasoned undercover officer would make.

'I'll bet the minnows loved that,' Frank grunted. 'As if they'd let a newcomer come in and start getting ideas above his station. What was your DI using for a brain?'

'It wasn't the DI,' Barrington said flatly. 'He'd gone into hospital with appendicitis by this point. This was all Barnes' idea. The super let him run the investigation, thinking the DI would be back in a week. But Barnes saw the chance for glory, didn't he, and egged Grigsy on. Well, one night, after he'd taken a Range Rover, me, another PC, Barnes and one of his cronies, were listening in on the wire, and a good job we were. The guy who'd brought Grigsy in on the scheme and two of his mates decided to teach him a lesson about hierarchy.' Barrington's voice became bitter now. 'We got in there fast, but they'd already broken his jaw, collapsed his right lung, knocked out all but eight of his teeth, and punched him in the right eye so bad it detached his retina.'

Janine Tyler drew in a sharp breath.

'We cuffed the bastards and called the paramedics. Me and this other PC were lying on the ground with Grigsy, holding him, trying to keep him upright so that he could breathe better. Then Barnes started cursing about losing his chance to nab Dalton.' Barrington drew in a ragged breath. 'He didn't even look at Grigsy. Just went on and on about Dalton wriggling off the hook. So I got up and belted him one,' he finished abruptly.

Hillary let the silence linger for a moment, and then said softly, 'You only hit him once?'

Keith Barrington met her eye and smiled grimly. 'Just the once, guv. But I made it count.'

Frank Ross snorted, but it was one of admiration. Hillary could almost hear the wheels turning in his head. Barrington, it seemed, in spite of all the signs to the contrary, was turning out to be a man after his own heart after all.

Hillary, however, rather doubted it. Frank Ross wouldn't be able to take the months of bullying Barrington had obviously put up with. And that one single blow told Hillary that Barrington, more importantly, hadn't totally lost control, if he'd lost it at all.

'Of course, Barnes cut up rough. Tried to get me for assault, but no one was willing to back him up – not even his own mate. I couldn't deny I'd belted him one, though, so …' Keith shrugged and looked around, as if to say, here I am.

Hillary nodded. She knew that by lunchtime tomorrow the story would be common knowledge and, as a result, Barrington's life would start getting easier. 'Well, as far as

I'm concerned, it's all over and done with,' Hillary said, catching Paul Danvers' eye. She hadn't forgotten his offer to get Barrington off her team if she wanted his help, and wanted to make it clear that, as far as she was concerned, Barrington was all right. Unless he proved otherwise.

Paul smiled. 'My round I think?'

Everyone began to talk of something else.

EastEnders had just finished, and the familiar theme tune had just woken Mitch from a light doze, when his mobile began trilling the opening lines of the *Z cars* theme. His youngest daughter, Amanda, had got it for Christmas – a bit of a joker that Mandy, Mitch thought fondly. She'd spent nearly all Christmas Day and Boxing Day teaching him how to use the camera and camcorder on it, as well as how to text his messages. Thing was, none of his old cronies would know how to answer them. Well, it kept the kid amused.

Now Mitch answered the humble telephone facility on the mini computer in his hand, and opened his sleepy eyes a little bit wider. The caller was young Freddy McCollins, Martin Pollock's panda car co-driver. McCollins, who was dating a girl who used to date Jem, his third son at HQ, was only too glad to do the legendary Mitch the Titch a favour. Although why he should be interested in 'Pillock Pollock' was a mystery to him.

'Yeah, Mitch, it's me, Fred. You said you wanted to know if the Pillock did anything out of the ordinary. Well, he just called and said he couldn't pick me up tomorrow morning. Doesn't sound much, I know, but he always picks me up in the morning. He lives a couple of miles out, and has to pass my place on the way in to work. But he said he had to do something tomorrow before going in. Don't know if that's the kind of thing you had in mind, like? Perhaps I shouldn't have bothered you with it?'

'No, that's fine, lad,' Mitch said fulsomely. 'Keep up the

good work. That's just the sort of thing I want to know.' But as he hung up he wondered if it was.

So, the Pillock had things to do, did he? Learning Martin Pollock's nickname was interesting in itself. Usually uniforms who drove a panda together were tight. The fact that young Fred didn't seem to mind dropping his co-driver in it, spoke volumes about Martin Pollock. However, with all the ill will in the world, Pollock could have any number of reasons for not picking up his work mate tomorrow. Perhaps he was having a quickie with his girlfriend. Hell, maybe he was visiting his old mother. Then again, Mitch mused with a smile, it would make a nice change to go to bed, knowing that in the morning he had to get up and do some point duty. Follow a suspect. Report back to his 'boss'.

Oh yes, when Mitch the Titch went to bed that night, he was whistling 'Yellow Rose of Texas'. And even gave Mrs Titchmarsh a suggestive squeeze.

That night, Dylan Hodge was flying. He was back at the old squat because he'd heard that his girlfriend had scored some good stuff, and he'd managed to find her stash. She'd tried to hide it down her knickers, silly cow, but he'd simply waited until she'd passed out, before fishing out a little baggie for himself.

Hodge heated the spoon over his empty can of Heinz Baked Beans, and watched the coarse grains liquefy. Soon he'd be where the cold wet air didn't make his bones ache, and the cops didn't hassle him about his old granny's death. He pulled the liquid up into a used needle, uncaring about cross-infection, wanting only the hit.

To be free, and happy and out of it all. That was all he wanted.

Who cared who killed the old girl? She was on her last legs anyway. Something cruel, her pain was at times. He remembered going round there once, and she was almost bent double with it, being sick into a bowl between her feet. Who'd want months more of that? No, as far as Hodge could see, whoever had done her in had done her a favour.

He quickly pulled a rubber tube around his leg, injecting into the back of his knee. The rush was almost instant, and seemed to take the top of his head off. In fact, it was so instant, he didn't even have time to remove the needle before he launched into orbit.

He didn't know it, but it was a great pity that he'd raided his girlfriend's knickers so skilfully that he hadn't woken her up. If he had, she might have warned him that the horse she'd scored was really high grade. A one off, really, a bit of luck she'd stumbled across that was never to be repeated.

If she'd told him that, he wouldn't have used quite so much. And if he hadn't used quite so much, he would have woken up the next morning.

It was bitterly cold the next morning. The wild wet weather had given way to a hard frost that had coated everything with ice.

Janine Tyler was the first to notice it, stepping outside in her long quilted, Japanese-style housecoat to pick up the paper and the morning milk. The bitter air numbed her fingers and had her scooting back inside, almost before she'd registered the piece of mail left inside the newspaper, which had already been thrust through the letter box.

The all-invading cold also meant that she didn't linger outside, and so didn't notice a young man, sitting in a second-hand Mazda parked a few doors down, who was watching her with avid anticipation.

But then, she wasn't the only one that morning to be less than observant. For PC Martin Pollock, of Traffic Division, didn't notice an even older, second-hand Granada, parked three cars down, or the old man who sat in it, peering down at his mobile phone.

Well, well, well, Mitch thought, somewhat bemused, as

he watched the results of his own, rather inexpert fumbling with the camcorder facility of his daughter's Christmas present. Despite being a bit overexposed and distinctly wobbly when he'd lifted the phone to get a better view through his windshield, Mitch was watching a perfectly recognizable image of a young copper in uniform. Captured on the tiny screen, he headed up the garden path of a private residence and thrust a plain brown envelope into the letter box, which already contained a copy of the *Daily Telegraph*.

Mitch kept his head down as a chuckling PC Pollock drove past him. Then he stored the piece of film to the phone's computer memory – or at least, he *hoped* that's what he'd done – and turned it off.

He didn't know for sure whose house Martin Pollock had just visited, but given the fact that a very pretty blonde had just appeared and brought in the milk and mail, he wouldn't be at all surprised to learn that it belonged to one Superintendent Philip Mallow.

Just as Dylan Hodge's girlfriend turned over in her sleeping bag and shivered, wondering why Dylan felt so cold, Janine Tyler poured herself a glass of orange juice and reached for the paper.

Hodge's girlfriend, Phoebe Cole, had once been pretty, with a ripe figure and long auburn hair. The figure was now stick thin and in urgent need of warmth, the long hair having long since turned thin and straggly. She frowned, shivering, and cuddled up to Hodge, who felt like a block of ice. She frowned and forced her eyes open. The crack which had made her loose her hair, also gummed up her eyes, and she had to knuckle the crud away from her lids before forcing them open. When she did, she raised herself up to one elbow and looked down at her sleeping partner.

And swore softly. Quickly, she reached down to pat herself on the bum, and wailed when she encountered only bony flesh. 'You stupid idiot,' she wailed, pummelling the lifeless body of the man she'd shared the last six months of her life with. 'That stash would have lasted me a week!'

As Phoebe Cole mourned her loss – of the horse, not of Hodge – Janine Tyler frowned as a brown envelope slipped from the morning newspaper and fell onto the breakfast table. In the kitchen she could hear Mel puttering about getting the coffee, listening to Radio Four as he always did.

She was about to toss the envelope in the recycling basket, thinking it was just one more of those 'free offers' that seemed to come with every paper nowadays, when she noticed her name – handwritten in green ink – on the front.

She went cold.

A moment later, she realized there was no stamp or address on the envelope. Whoever had delivered it, had done so by hand. He knew where she lived. That morning, as she'd lain in bed beside Mel, someone had walked through the icy cold air, up her garden path, and thrust this through her letter box.

Quickly, before Mel could come to the table with the coffee, she got up and went upstairs. Once sitting on her bed, she opened the envelope and stared down at a picture of herself. At first, she couldn't quite make out what she was seeing. A woman, a fully naked woman, was standing in the doorway to what was recognizably the canteen at HQ. The naked woman had her face.

Once she'd stopped gaping and got her mind in gear, it was obvious what had happened. The cretin had taken her picture coming through the door, then, using a computer, had morphed a naked woman's body onto her head.

Angrily, she screwed it up and then began to tear it into pieces. But as she did so, she wondered, how many more copies did this man have? Had he sent any more through the post, to Mel, or her mother maybe, or friends, or just colleagues at work? What if she went in this morning and found one of them pinned up to the notice board?

No! She took a long, slow breath. No, she mustn't panic like this. It was exactly what the bastard wanted. Anybody could see the photo was a fake. A hideously embarrassing, humiliating fake.

Almost against her will, she got up and walked, crab-like, to the window, careful not to be seen. She pulled the curtain aside and looked out.

The next-door neighbour was busy wiping his car windshield free of ice. A car, exhaust pipe puffing heavy white smoke, drove away down the road. She recognized it as belonging to a neighbour, Margaret Peterson, a chartered accountant.

There was nobody out there. She told herself to pull herself together and go to work. She reminded herself that tomorrow was her wedding day. But she felt only like crying.

chapter ten

Phoebe Cole stuffed her arms into a ragged duffel coat that had padding oozing out of tears on the right elbow and left shoulder pad, and a large dirty stain that spread across the left breast. Her hands were shaking, more from anger now than cold.

She'd never get another stash like it.

The old duffer who'd wandered in last night slowly uncurled himself from a ball, like a hedgehog sensing hibernation was over. Also like a hedgehog he was covered in fleas. Phoebe had seen him around, and reckoned he'd come to the squat only to get shelter from the cold. Usually he liked to beg around Bonn Square in Oxford, and slept on the park benches nearby.

'He dead then?' he asked, his voice raspy from the damage done by the meths he drank.

Phoebe shrugged, grabbing her bag. She had everything packed. She wasn't hanging around to talk to the cops.

The old man pushed stringy grey hair out of his eyes and watched the girl leave. Then, vaguely curious, he crawled over to the still body in the filthy sleeping bag. He couldn't be bothered to straighten up just yet. His arthritis played him up something cruel when he fell asleep hugging his knees for warmth.

The boy was definitely dead, and beginning to stiffen. At this, the old man perked up. He'd call the cops and report it. Not that he was civic minded, of course, but they'd be bound to take him down to HQ for questioning – he'd refuse to talk to them here – and that meant a warm radiator where he could defrost, and at least two cups of tea. If he strung it out to lunchtime, someone usually gave him some grub too. He doubted he could swing a night in the cells though.

Oh well. Beggars couldn't be choosers. With a sigh, the old man began the long, painful process of getting to his feet.

Martin Pollock drove away from the Moors area of Kidlington, feeling particularly pleased with himself. The posh suburb where Superintendent Mellow Mallow lived, as a result of a profitable divorce from his second, wealthy wife, was just beginning to stir. By now, he thought, the blonde bombshell should be opening the envelope. Shit, how he'd love to see her face. Not so smug then, he'd bet.

The cold snap had caught many people by surprise and there was little traffic in this old part of the town. He was just approaching a T-junction, when something ginger on the side of the road made him look. A dead fox, maybe. No, not quite big enough.

Suddenly a thought hit him and he indicated to pull over and let a red Vauxhall pass him before getting out and jogging back towards the casualty. As he'd thought it was someone's pet cat, a handsome ginger tom. It hadn't been dead long, for when he reached down to touch it, it was still vaguely warm. Like a lot of moggies killed by cars, this one didn't seem to have a scratch on it. No blood, nothing.

PC Martin Pollock grinned as he picked up the pathetic bundle and walked back to his car. There he emptied a Tesco bag of a loaf of bread he'd bought yesterday and forgot to take in, and carefully wrapped up the corpse. He knew just what use he could make of it. But he'd have to be quick. Before it started to pong.

Whistling happily, Martin Pollock drove to Thames

Valley Police Headquarters. Behind him, Mitch Titchmarsh, who'd watched the whole manoeuvre from a hundred yards away, nodded his head grimly.

Now they'd have the sick little bastard.

Hillary was first at her desk, closely followed by Keith Barrington, who looked just a little ill at ease. Hillary, in no mood to babysit, said briskly, 'Any luck on tracing that old photograph I gave you?'

'I've had a few ideas, guv,' he said quickly. 'I ran a few copies off on the computer and posted them to all the local parish magazines, asking them to print them with the caption DO YOU KNOW THIS MAN? I've noticed they nearly always include old photographs in their issues. Probably because their readership is so old, and nostalgia is always appreciated.'

Hillary nodded, impressed. 'Good thinking.'

'I've also given copies to the ladies at the local libraries – here, Bicester of course, Oxford and Banbury. I've asked them to display it with the same question. I've done the same with drop-in centres for the elderly. If we don't get any hits soon, guv, I don't think he'll have been local.'

Hillary nodded. 'You've done well. But I think we might get lucky. Flo didn't travel much in her lifetime – she spent most of her life in Bicester. I can't see her boyfriend, if that's what he was, being anything other than local as well.'

Barrington nodded, then reached for his phone as it shrilled. 'DC Barrington. Yes. What? When? He's downstairs. OK.'

Frank Ross, just arrived, caught the excitement in the new boy's voice and paused in the act of shrugging off his heavy overcoat.

'Guv, Dylan Hodge is dead,' Barrington said, trying to keep the eagerness out of his voice. 'Some old codger living at the squat reported finding his body this morning. He's downstairs.'

'Bloody hell,' Frank said, whistling softly. 'Do you think it's the same killer?'

'Whoa, hold on,' Hillary said, putting a brakes on the rampant testosterone. 'Do we know yet how he died?' she asked Barrington.

'No guv,' Keith said. 'Uniform want the go-ahead to call out SOCO. They also want to know if you want to take it. The duty sergeant recognized Hodge's name from our case. He'll assign it to us if we want it.'

Hillary sighed and nodded. 'OK, Frank, get over to the crime scene and supervise. Barrington, you can talk to the witness.'

'Guv,' Barrington said, hardly believing his luck. Lead interview already. Last nights show and tell at the pub was already forgotten.

'And Keith,' Hillary said, stopping him in his tracks. 'If he's old and spent last night in the squat, he'll be cold and hungry. Feed him and make sure he has plenty of hot cups of tea. If he looks in a really bad way, crawl to the custody sergeant and see if you can find him a bed for tonight. I heard on the weather forecast we're going to have a perishing frost again tonight.'

Keith blinked. 'Right guv,' he said slowly, feeling ashamed because he knew that thought would never have occurred to him.

'And Frank, don't get ahead of yourself,' Hillary warned. 'We don't know yet if this death is even connected to Flo's. Personally, I think it's far more likely Hodge just overdosed, or got hold of some bad gear.'

'Guv,' Frank said sourly. Trust her to rain on his parade.

Hillary sighed and let them go. They'd probably been watching too many crime dramas on the telly. But in her experience, one murder rarely led to a whole series of them. And she'd never worked a serial killer case, and never expected to. Still, the death of Hodge might complicate things, so it was best to check it out thoroughly.

Spotting Janine's empty chair, she frowned and glanced at her watch. It wasn't like her sergeant to be this late. Granted, she was getting married tomorrow, but if she'd wanted time off, all she'd had to do was ask.

Grimly, she wondered if her stalker had been busy.

With a sigh, she began to tackle her In tray, which, as usual, had somehow magically filled up overnight.

Janine parked her car carefully in plain view of the CCTV camera nearest the main entrance, and locked it up. She was dressed in smart olive-green trousers, with a matching jacket and a bright orange blouse. She'd put her hair up with tortoiseshell combs, and been extra careful with her make-up.

Two cheeky PCs wolf-whistled as they pulled out in their panda car, and she grinned and automatically lifted a finger. Then, as she turned for the door, she suddenly thought – *was he one of them?* She turned, but the panda car was already out of sight. Then she shook her head and told herself to stop it. She couldn't look at every cop in HQ and keep on wondering the same thing. It would drive her mad – which was just what he wanted. She'd be out of here next week. She could hold on till then. But she couldn't help but wonder what he had planned for tomorrow – her wedding day. Somehow she didn't think he would resist the challenge of doing something extra special.

It made her feel sick.

When she got to the main open-plan office, she could see that Hillary Greene was already in and ploughing through her paperwork. Barrington had been in – she recognized his jacket slung around the back of his chair – but had obviously gone out again. Of Frank Ross, naturally, there was no sign. She straightened her shoulders and marched purposefully across the large office.

Hillary, sensing her approach, glanced up from the folder she was reading. The neatly typed, perfectly spelled memo was from the new boy, reporting that Walter Keane had indeed been a commando during the war. He'd photocopied the relevant documents, which showed that Keane had been decorated twice for bravery.

Hillary watched Janine slip off her long Burberry coat, and her eyes narrowed at the uplifting outfit, the new hairdo and makeover. Oh yes, Hillary thought grimly, the stalker has been up to some trick or other. She recognized defensive dressing when she saw it. It made a woman feel good and confident to look her best.

'Walter Keane,' Hillary said, deciding to take her mind off things fast. She shoved the report over and watched as Janine read it.

'So he'd definitely know how to knife someone in the chest then,' Janine said flatly, when she'd finished.

'Yes. I think we'd better have another word.'

Which was fine with Janine. She couldn't wait to get out of this place. Somewhere, down in one of the offices below, he was somewhere about. She could just feel it.

Hillary didn't miss the alacrity with which her sergeant grabbed her bag, and she bit back the anger that threatened to engulf her. Normally Janine was tough and hot-headed, and ultra-confident. But this bastard was obviously beginning to get on her nerves. She only hoped Mitch was right, and that he knew who it was. The sooner he was given a taste of his own medicine, the better.

Downstairs, in the men's locker rooms, Martin Pollock hefted his duffel bag to the bench nearest his locker and began to change into his uniform. He purposely dawdled until only one other man was present – Jem Titchmarsh, who primarily worked Burglary. Jem nodded, stuffed his coat into his own locker, and walked away. He walked heavily and noisily on his big sturdy boots, got to the door, opened it and then closed it again noisily. Then he walked without a sound to the bank of lockers overlooking Pollock's, and carefully peered around.

Pollock was carefully putting something wrapped in a Tesco bag into his locker. It looked oddly shaped, soft and yielding. When he started to look over his shoulder, Jem quickly drew back. Whatever he was up to, he obviously didn't want witnesses. He moved silently around the back of the lockers and watched Pollock leave, then reached for his phone.

When it was answered, he said quietly, 'Dad? It's me, Jem.' He told his old man what he'd seen, then listened, his young face getting grimmer and grimmer as he listened to Mitch's reply.

Janine and Hillary took the stairs, rather than wait for the lift. As they walked, Hillary filled her in on the news about Hodge.

'You really don't think they're connected, boss?' Janine was saying, as they stepped from the bottom step into the lobby. 'Bit of a coincidence, though, isn't it?'

'Not really,' Hillary replied. 'You know the statistics as well as I do. Nobody in Hodge's position tends to live a long and happy life.'

'Even so,' Janine began, but then stopped, as the desk sergeant called them over.

'Hey, you two lovely ladies. Heard the latest?'

Hillary, suspecting he wanted to talk about Keith Barrington and the reason he'd taken a pop at his old sergeant, sighed heavily. 'Not really, sarge,' she called. 'We're on our way to question an important witness.'

Seeing her turn towards the main entrance, and a valuable source of gossip slipping from his grasp, the desk sergeant all but bellowed, 'They've only gone and arrested Jerome Raleigh, haven't they?'

Hillary felt herself stumble. It was as if she'd taken a step forward and found an expected drop beneath her. She saw Janine shoot her a quick look, and knew she must have gone pale. Her mind whirled. Arrested Raleigh? Was it possible?

She managed a wan smile and a graphic sigh for Janine's

benefit, then turned and headed over. 'No kidding?' she said, seeing the desk sergeant beam with satisfaction. Like the rest of the nick, he knew that Hillary Greene, as a participant of the Fletcher raid, and heroine of the hour, knew something that none of the rest of them did. It hadn't gone unnoticed that when Raleigh had up and resigned so suddenly, Hillary Greene hadn't been at all surprised. Besides, everyone from Donleavy down to the tea lady knew that Hillary Greene had brains. If anyone could have figured out what had been going on, it was DI Greene.

'Yeah, somewhere abroad he was. Costa Brava, Costa del Sol. Somewhere hot and balmy anyway,' the desk sergeant said, leaning on his elbows over the counter top and lowering his voice conspiratorially.

Close, Hillary thought. It was Malta, actually, but she wasn't about to enlighten him. 'But what have they arrested him for exactly?' Hillary asked. 'Don't tell me the local cops caught him drinking and driving? Soliciting? What?' She was deliberately underplaying it, and feared that the other two must realize as much.

The desk sergeant frowned. 'No. Nothing like that,' he denied impatiently. 'Scuttlebutt has it, it has something to do with the Fletcher inquiry. You know, he left before they'd reported their findings.'

As he spoke, he glanced at Hillary keenly, but she was frowning and shaking her head. 'Can't be that,' she said flatly. 'The Fletcher inquiry is done and dusted and closed.'

'If you say so,' the desk sergeant said cannily, and added, 'You'd know.'

Hillary smiled and shrugged. 'Well, when you find out, let us know,' she said casually. 'Now we've got to be going.'

She was glad of the cold air as she stepped out into the car park. Damn, it couldn't really be true, could it?

Walter Keane answered the door quickly. Obviously the old man had no trouble moving fast when he wanted to.

Janine smiled and held out her ID card. 'Detective Sergeant Tyler, sir. I believe you've already met DI Greene?'

'Course I have. Come in. You found him yet?'

Janine blinked, her heart lurching. For one moment of madness, she thought he was asking her if she'd found her stalker. Then she realized, of course, that he meant Flo's killer. 'Inquiries are still ongoing, sir,' she said blandly. 'It's early days yet.' In truth, Janine knew that most murders were solved in their first week or not at all. But she was hardly going to tell Walter Keane that.

Hillary nodded pleasantly at the old man as he stepped aside, then followed as he led the way to the kitchen. 'Cuppa?'

'Lovely,' Hillary said, though she'd have preferred coffee.

'Have a seat. I tend to spend more of my time in here than in the living room,' the octogenarian apologized.

The kitchen, though not big, had enough room for a tiny table and two comfortable-looking chairs. A small portable television rested on a Formica worktop. On the table was a copy of the *Daily Mirror*, opened to the crossword page.

Hillary noticed that he was filling in the Quizword section, and doing very well too. So, his mental faculties were still sharp. 'Fourteen down,' Hillary said, as she accepted a steaming mug from him. 'John Donne.'

Walter Keane glanced at the question. 'Poet known as the father of the Metaphysical School ...' and grunted a thank you before penning it in. 'But you didn't come here to help me do the crossword,' he commented cannily, putting the pen down and looking steadily across at her. He'd taken the second chair at the table, since Janine had opted to stand leaning against the wall, jotting into her notebook.

Hillary smiled. 'No. I understand you were a commando during the war. Decorated for it too.'

Walter glanced at her quickly, his old face as calm as a rock pool, the eyes wide and guileless. Then he smiled. 'You saw the war photo of me and my mates. Recognized the insignia? Don't miss much, do you?' he added admiringly.

Hillary smiled. 'Not much, no,' she admitted.

Walter Keane nodded, knowing at once that she wasn't boasting, or trying to scare him, but merely stating a fact. Although it had been over forty years since he'd been in the army – he'd stuck it until 1963 – he could feel himself slipping back into the old way of thinking. In his day, women were there to make the tea and man the phones, but Hillary Greene was, without doubt, a superior officer. He could almost feel his spine stiffening to attention. He smiled at the thought and reached for his tea.

Some of his so-called 'superior' officers during the war he wouldn't have pissed on if they were on fire. Then there were the other sort – the sort who knew what they were doing. Hard as iron, those, like terriers with a rat. And brains. They always had brains. And whilst Walter wouldn't have said this woman was exactly made of iron, she had something of a steel spine about her. And brains. Definitely brains. He was suddenly glad that she was heading Flo's case.

Janine Tyler glanced sharply from her boss to the old man, and bit back a familiar feeling of respect and jealousy. Once again, Hillary Greene was weaving her magic on a suspect. Just how she did it, Janine had never been able to tell. But time and time again, she'd watched her boss tease and winkle and trick and cajole or simply magic the answers from any number of unwilling, bemused, frightened or downright shifty witnesses.

Now she saw it happening again. It was as if the old man and she were somehow telepathically linked. She saw Hillary nod, as if in acceptance of some silent question, then the old man smiled. 'So, DI Greene, what can I tell you?' Walter said affably. But his eyes were watchful.

Hillary decided that there was really only one way to go here. The Police Manual was insistent that an officer, when interviewing a suspect, gave away no information, only sought it. And ninety-nine times out of a hundred, Hillary agreed with that whole-heartedly. But there were always exceptions. And looking into the old soldier's unwavering eyes, she could tell that this was one such time.

She took a sip of unwanted tea and sighed softly. 'See, the thing is, Walter, we're having a hard time finding a motive for anyone to kill Flo. Her grandson needed her alive, so he could continue leeching off her. Her friends were urging her on, planning to make her birthday party a big success. Caroline Weekes was planning to make a big chocolate cake for example. And you yourself were planning on helping out with the sandwiches and stuff. Flo had no fortune to leave, and hadn't made any enemies as far as we can tell. What's more, she was going to die soon anyway,' Hillary continued softly, and spread her hands helplessly. 'So why would anyone want to kill her? Her house wasn't burgled, so it's not as if she was some random victim of a mugger or thief. So what's left?'

Walter nodded. 'I see the problem. I've been wracking my brains too, trying to think. But there isn't an answer is there?' He sounded genuinely baffled.

Hillary smiled. 'Well, there might be. See, the thing is, our medical man tells us that Flo must have been suffering these last few months or so.'

Walter nodded grimly. 'Yeah, she was.'

'Even with the pills and therapy, it must have been hard,' Hillary agreed. 'So hard, in fact, that who could blame her if she'd had enough?'

Walter's slightly watery blue eyes suddenly sharpened. 'Take the easy way out you mean? No, not Flo. Besides, she was stabbed in the chest, weren't she?'

Hillary nodded. 'We're not saying she did it herself. But perhaps she asked someone to help her? An old, dear and trusted friend, maybe? Someone she knew could make a clean, painless, neat job of it?'

Walter Keane stared at her, then slowly smiled. 'Oh,' he said. 'I get it.' He leaned back in his chair, slowly nodding. 'Now I follow you. Mercy killing. You think I might have bumped her off.'

Hillary watched the old man carefully. 'Nobody would blame you if you did, Mr Keane,' she said softly. 'We've had cases like this before. The judges are nearly always lenient. It might not even come to trial. The public prosecutions office, given your age, and the fact that you're no danger to society, might even decline to prosecute.'

Walter grinned, not sure how much he believed her, but instantly taking her point. 'Meaning, if I did it, I've nothing to lose by saying so? Well, that maybe true, it may not. But I'm not scared of going to prison anyway. My wife's gone, nobody would miss me or care if I did go down. So if I'd killed Flo, I'd just say straight out that I did it. There's only one problem.'

Hillary smiled softly. 'You didn't do it.'

'Nope.'

'Would you have done, if Flo had asked?'

'Yep.'

Janine blinked, and wrote the reply down, verbatim in her book, then glanced across curiously at her boss. Was she buying this? Yes, it looked as if she was, for Hillary was slowly rising to her feet.

'You've got it all wrong, you know,' Walter said, rising along with her. 'Flo would never have taken that way out. She loved life too much. Yes, she had bad days, but that only made her more determined to live it up on the good days. She took the simple pleasures in life and magnified them. Like having a takeout on pension day. Like conning her friends out of a campari and soda when she managed to get down to the local. On a sunny day, Caroline used to drive her down to the park to feed the ducks. There was no way Flo would have killed herself. She wanted that birthday party and was determined to see one last Christmas.'

Hillary nodded. 'I believe you, Mr Keane,' she said truthfully. 'Thank you for your time.'

Once outside, Hillary waited until she heard the door close behind her, then glanced around. Beside her, Janine shivered. 'Well that was a waste of time,' the blonde woman complained.

'Not quite. Weren't you listening?' Hillary prompted.

Janine, who hated it when her boss suddenly put her on the spot like this, realized that she hadn't been. Not really. 'Sorry boss,' she muttered, expecting a lecture. Instead, Hillary glanced at her sharply, and Janine felt herself go cold. It was almost as if her DI knew what she was going through. But that was impossible. She'd been careful to keep it well hidden. The last thing she wanted to do was leave her old nick on a tide of sympathy or sniggering.

'He said that Flo liked to have a takeout on pension night,' Hillary prompted. 'Well, she was killed on pension night, wasn't she? And Barrington's witnesses said they saw a man, maybe carrying something, go to Flo's house that night.'

Janine groaned and felt like kicking herself. 'I'll get right on it, boss,' she promised. In a small town like Bicester, there couldn't be that many places that delivered to the door.

As Hillary drove back to HQ, leaving Janine behind to follow up their new lead, her phone rang. 'DI Greene.'

'We've got him,' Mitch's voice said grimly. 'His name is Martin Pollock. He works Traffic. What's more, he's got something nasty planned for your little DS, and I've got a fair idea of what it is and when he's going to play it. What you doing tonight?'

Hillary, thinking of her distracted sergeant, smiled wolfishly. 'What did you have in mind?'

She hadn't stepped two paces into the lobby when the desk sergeant nobbled her again. 'Hey, DI Greene!'

Hillary bit back a groan. 'Sarge?'

'The Silver Marauder wants a word.'

Hillary grimaced, guessing only too well what Marcus Donleavy wanted to talk about. 'OK, I'll go right up.'

She glanced at her watch. It wasn't yet 10.30, and already her day was in the crapper. But for once, her pessimism was unwarranted. The moment she stepped into Donleavy's office, she could tell the news was good.

Today, Donleavy was living up to his nickname, wearing a silver-grey spotless suit, with a pale pink shirt and an electric blue tie. His silver eyes watched her take a seat, and when she was comfortable, said simply, 'They've questioned Raleigh. He says he left the force for personal reasons that had nothing to do with the Fletcher debacle. He claims an old friend rang to tell him that the internal inquiry had cleared him, so he felt he was morally clear to leave. He apologized very prettily, so I'm told, for not working out his notice, and basically told our man in Malta to sod off. Incidentally, he has no plans on returning to the UK in the future.'

Hillary cleared her throat, but said nothing.

'What's more, the brass aren't willing to take it any further, and prefer to take his explanation at face value. I think we can safely say we've heard the last of it.'

Hillary didn't try to hide her sigh of relief. So it was over. Finally. 'That all, sir?'

Donleavy nodded, his silver hair catching the daylight streaming through the window, giving him a very deceptive-looking halo. He waited until she'd turned and was halfway to the door, before saying softly, 'Oh Hillary, one last thing. The officer questioning him reported that Raleigh seemed to be living well. Very well indeed. Renting a top-end villa, driving an Aston Martin classic no less. Dressed by Armani. That kind of thing. Any idea where he got the money?'

Hillary, who knew damned well where he'd got the money, turned and looked at him blankly. And in the instant that she met those unnerving, reflective silver eyes, she knew that Marcus Donleavy knew as well.

Somewhere in the back of her mind, she'd always known that it was only a matter of time before he worked it all out. Donleavy was too smart not to realize that, if anyone could track down where her dead husband's dirty money had been stashed, it was herself.

She blurted out, before she could stop herself, 'I never touched a penny of it.' Then she clamped her lips shut hard. She knew that Marcus Donleavy rated her highly – though she'd never taken advantage of that fact. What she didn't know was what Donleavy would do now.

A detective inspector working under him had just admitted to knowing the whereabouts of illegal money, and hadn't reported it. He could suspend her on the spot and if he reopened the internal inquiry into Ronnie Greene's activities, who knew where it would end? Now that he knew where the money was – namely, in Jerome Raleigh's possession – he had a good place to start. If the banks cooperated, it could probably be traced back to Ronnie Greene.

But not to her. She'd been careful to leave no traces that she'd ever discovered its whereabouts. Yet the suspicion would be enough to actively finish her career. Even if they couldn't dismiss her, and she'd fight any such move to the bitter end, they could easily sideline her. Move her over to Missing Persons. Or Records even. Her life as an investigative CID officer would be over.

It all rested on what this man decided to do.

Donleavy pretended not to hear her. Or understand her. He said mildly, 'Well, I expect ex-Superintendent Raleigh had private means. He always struck me as a man who was well heeled.'

Hillary swallowed hard. 'Yes sir,' she whispered, barely able to believe it. He was letting her off the hook. Giving her another chance.

He almost certainly believed that she'd never touched the

money, because she knew him well enough to know that he'd have had her guts for garters if she had. So he was willing to turn a blind eye. Maybe he simply didn't want to lose a good officer, especially not one who had been recently decorated for valour. Perhaps he simply didn't want another scandal. She might never know.

Without another word, she turned and walked out of his office.

She felt about two inches tall.

chapter eleven

Keith Barrington scratched the top of his arm as he pulled out his chair and glanced across at his boss, who was talking on the phone. A quick glance at his watch told him it was just gone eleven, and the old boy he'd left downstairs should, by now, be digging in to bacon sandwiches.

He scratched his arm again as he drew out his notebook and began to type up the interview. It had seemed to go well. He didn't think he'd missed anything, or failed to ask anything obvious, but he was nervous as he typed, nonetheless. He just couldn't afford to screw up something so routine, but potentially as important as this.

So far, Hillary Greene had been scrupulously fair in the way she handed out assignments to her team. The search of the victim's house had been necessary, and he hadn't minded the hours spent on hands and knees, or the dust he'd inhaled in searching Flo Jenkins' house for evidence. Handing him off on the old photo, when Ross didn't want it, might have smacked of downgrading, except that he genuinely believed Hillary Greene was the type of officer who left no stone unturned. So, one no-hoper assignment in a case like this wasn't that surprising. Certainly Frank Ross had been given his share of footwork and even Janine Tyler had been left with more than her fair share of paperwork.

Now he'd been given a primary interview on the Hodge death. A feather in his cap, albeit a modest one. After nearly a year of being given nothing but shit work from his old boss at Blacklock Green, it felt good. Bloody good.

OK, last night he'd felt a bit mauled by his DI's ambush, but he'd sensed that his explanation of the situation back on his home turf hadn't done him too much harm. Maybe even some good. He'd still been smarting over it this morning, but since nobody had mentioned it, he'd been more than willing to play along. Now he was beginning to feel as if the first major hurdles were all behind him, and things looked set fair.

Apart from Ross, of course. But nobody liked him, and Keith had already decided that the best way to keep out from under him, was to ignore him, like everyone else.

He heard his DI hang up the phone and spun his chair away from the VDU. 'Want a verbal update on the interview, guv? I'll have my notes typed up in ten minutes.'

Hillary shrugged. 'Might as well. How's it looking?'

Keith, using his feet to push off on the floor, wheeled his chair closer to her desk. 'Witness is Brian Chestin, or Braz, as he's known on the street. Wino who usually hangs around Oxford, apparently. Last night, knowing it was going to be brass monkey weather, he went to the squat in Ardley – apparently he's got some sort of running feud with another wino, and didn't want to kip in the city. When he got there, Hodge, his girlfriend and several others were already in residence. One of them tried to roll him, found only a bottle of meths that he wouldn't touch with a barge-pole, and after that, left him alone. He says he was awake most of the night, and thinks he heard rustlings from Hodge's sleeping bag. Some time later, he saw a small flame – can't say for sure what, but it was probably Hodge stewing up some horse. Next morning, he wakes up when Phoebe Cole starts wailing and moaning.'

Barrington frowned and scratched his arm again. What the hell was wrong with it? It was itching like a son of a bitch. 'Anyway, he rolls over, which is a bit hard, since he says he seizes up of a morning, and sees Phoebe thumping Hodge's arm and railing at him for stealing her stash. According to Braz, she seemed particularly upset because it was an unusually good "hit". A friend of a friend stole it from a pusher before it got its third or fourth cut.'

Hillary grunted in instant understanding. Drugs, as a rule, were purchased by the first in a chain of runners, who cut it – or mixed it with other materials to bulk it up and maximize profits – then sold it down the chain to someone else, who then cut it again, and so on. By the time it reached the street, and your average junkie, it could be as much as eighty per cent baby milk – or something far less benign. If Phoebe Cole had managed to get a stash from higher up the chain, the drug would be much stronger than she'd be used to.

'Anyway,' Barrington said, still scratching feverishly, 'Braz asks if the boyfriend is dead, but by now Phoebe is dressing and packing, getting ready to split. When she's gone, the old man goes over and finds him dead, then wanders outside and dials 999.'

Hillary grinned at Barrington's frowning face, and said calmly, 'Fleas.'

Keith looked up. 'Huh?'

'The itching. You've probably got a tiny hitchhiker from our Wit. If I were you, I'd head downstairs to the locker room, shower, and give your clothes a good shaking out.'

'Shit!' Barrington yelped, getting up and looking down at himself comically, as if expecting to see little black things jumping.

Hillary grinned. 'Before you go – did our wino say if he heard anyone else coming into the room during the night?'

'No guv,' Keith said miserably. Ignoring the urge to start scratching everywhere, he carried on gamely. 'Neither did he hear any sounds of a struggle or an argument, either between Hodge and his girlfriend or Hodge and anyone else.'

Hillary nodded. 'He gets the impression that Hodge stole the stash from the girlfriend without her knowledge?'

'Yes guv. And Phoebe didn't let on how strong it was.'

'The ME will probably find he died of a massive overdose,' Hillary said flatly. 'But liaise with Frank, make sure you cross all the t's and dot all the i's.'

'Right guv,' Keith said, and flushed when Hillary laughed, and waved him off. He all but jogged across the office, scratching viciously as he did so. Sam Waterstone, from his desk midway in the office, glanced across with a raised eyebrow, and Hillary grinned and shook her head, silently passing on that all was well. By the amused look several others gave the young DC, some had probably guessed what the problem was. After all, they'd all been there themselves. Hillary herself had had a close encounter with head lice during her young uniform days giving lectures to schoolgirls on the perils of drug use.

When her phone rang again, she reached for it automatically, wondering if it was Janine. So it took a moment to register the deep, sexy voice of DI Mike Regis. 'Hey, it's me. Think you can get free to meet me for lunch? The Old Oak?'

Hillary glanced at her watch. Barely twelve. It was a bit early, but what the heck. 'Sure, but it'll have to be quick. You already there?'

'And waiting,' Mike's voice sounded warm and suggestive. It was so long since she'd had a sexy phone call from a man – literally years, in fact – that she felt her face getting warm. Damn it! But why the change in their policy of not making personal phone calls to the workplace?

'I'll see you soon,' she said, a shade abruptly, and hung up. Once again, she felt that vague sense of unease that plagued her whenever her relationship with Mike protruded into her working life. What was it? Had she been celibate so long that she couldn't bring herself to believe there was life after Ronnie Greene?

Sighing, and telling herself not to be such a twit, she grabbed her bag and headed out the door.

The Old Oak was one of those large, modern, characterless pubs that had sprung up everywhere over the last couple of years. Built just out of town, often within sight of a super-store like Tesco or Sainsbury's, it had huge parking lots, and was no-smoking throughout. The decor was bland and pleasant, the menu reasonably priced and extensive, if correspondingly bland. The drink was reasonably cheap. For all that such pubs were popular, she preferred her more scruffy, lived-in, local.

She saw Mike the moment she stepped away from the bar with a pineapple juice in her hand, and headed towards the left-hand side of the huge seating area. He spotted her at the same moment and half rose. He was seated not far from a window, next to a tub of one of the many huge, fake ferns and bamboo that dotted the interior.

He smiled at her as she approached, remembering the first time he'd met her. She'd been SIO on her first murder case, and he'd been instantly attracted by the curvy figure, the intelligent eyes, the no-nonsense, experienced air she wore like most women wore expensive perfume.

He'd known her rep, of course – the disastrous marriage to a bent cop, the solid work, the fine conviction rate. She was popular with both the brass and the rank-and-file, and it hadn't taken him ten minutes in her company to realize that she was his kind of copper. Despite the fact that she was OEC (Regis was strictly comprehensive school reject) they thought the same about crime, and fighting it.

Things had got off to a dodgy start when she'd realized he was still technically married, and for a few months there, he'd worried that he might have lost his chance with her. But he'd persevered, and now, here they were.

He noticed several of the men, dining early to make way for long and tedious business meetings that afternoon, turn in their chairs slightly, the better to watch her go by, and felt a warm glow that came with pride of ownership. Not that he'd ever put it quite that way, of course, and certainly not in Hillary's presence.

But it was not surprising he felt that way. Even in her mid-forties, Hillary had the curvaceous figure of a Hollywood siren of the 1930s. Her skin was still flawless, her nut-brown hair well cut and always shining. Even dressed in a no-frills business suit of dark nutmeg, with a cream blouse, she managed to look both feminine and capable. Mike wondered how many of the horny gits were imagining her in stockings and suspenders, brandishing a whip.

The thought made him smile and catch his breath at the same time. Hillary, now nearly at his table, saw the flash of his teeth and wondered what had amused him. She put her glass down and pulled back her chair. 'Thanks for getting me out of the office,' she said, and meant it. It was beginning to feel as if she'd lived there for the last week.

'No problems. Case still stalled?'

Hillary shrugged. 'There are developments, but nothing major.' As she filled him in, she checked the menu. The smoked salmon salad looked good.

'Everything all right otherwise? At the office I mean?' Regis asked, and Hillary stared at him blankly for a moment, before she caught on.

'Oh, Danvers. No, that's fine. Well, he did attend the Jenkins autopsy for me.'

Regis smiled, but it didn't reach his eyes. 'Earning himself some brownie points?'

'I fear so,' Hillary sighed. 'Let's not talk about him.'

'Let's not,' Regis agreed. Danvers was younger than himself, a rank above, was better looking, and no doubt had a better body too. And he had an eye on his girl. He was going to have to do something about Danvers. And soon.

'You think you're gonna be free Saturday night?' he asked, after she'd beckoned over a waiter and given her order. Regis plumped for the steak and kidney pie.

'Might be. Why?'

'Gilbert and Sullivan at the Oxford Playhouse.'

Hillary wrinkled her nose. 'Think I'll pass.' Music wasn't her thing, but when she did listen to it, she liked the 60s stuff. Stuff that had a tune, and people who could – more or less – sing.

'OK.'

As if sensing she'd disappointed him, she found herself saying, 'When are you due some time off? I thought we could take the boat up to Stratford, catch up with an old neighbour of mine, watch a show. Not a tragedy but something light. *Much Ado*, maybe?' Now why had she said that? Spending five or six days on a small narrowboat with no escape from another person would normally have been her idea of hell. She instantly found herself regretting it.

'I've got the weekend after next off,' Regis said quickly, as if sensing it, and Hillary felt herself wilting with relief.

'Not enough time,' she said, shaking her head. 'Maybe sometime in the spring. The weather will be better anyway.' She took a rueful glance outside.

'Not enough time?' Mike frowned, not getting it. 'The whole weekend?'

'It'll take a couple of days to get the *Mollern* to Stratford,' Hillary grinned. 'She's only allowed to go at four mph remember?'

'We don't have to take the boat,' Regis said quickly. Just a shade *too* quickly. 'We can book into a hotel. I know a place.'

Hillary bit back a sharp retort. Yes, she bet he knew a place all right. What was it with men, and all the 'nice little hotels' they knew? Then, realising that she was hardly being consistent – let alone fair – shook her head. 'Well, I can't really think about it until my case is over anyway.'

The waiter came with their orders just then, and for a moment they busied themselves with buttering bread and adding sauces. When Hillary lifted her fork to half-heartedly spear a tomato, she glanced up and thought she saw a worried look in his dark green eyes. Then he smiled, and began to talk about a film they both wanted to see, and the moment passed.

Janine Tyler was feeling pleased with herself when she pulled in at HQ, a nervous young lad sitting beside her. Tariq Kahn worked at the Golden Empress, just off Dean's Court in central Bicester. It was an Indian restaurant that had a fairly large clientele of takeout customers, to whom it delivered on a more or less regular basis.

She parked her car, again near a CCTV camera, and smiled encouragingly across at him. 'This shouldn't take long, Mr Kahn.' She wasn't sure whether that was the truth or not, but he wasn't to know that.

She'd tracked the Golden Empress down via the phone, the proprietor, a Mr Ram, confessing at once to knowing the name of Florence Jenkins. Janine had quickly driven over for a word, and Mr Ram confirmed that Flo Jenkins sometimes used their home delivery service. Not often enough to be called a regular, but often enough for the delivery boy, Tariq to remember where she lived without needing to consult his residential map.

Mr Ram, a fifty-something with shiny cheeks and equally shining, bald dome, had obligingly checked his records, and confirmed that the old woman had ordered a meal that night – the mildest chicken tikka masala they had, with a slice of blueberry cheesecake to follow. His wife, Mr Ram had said modestly, was famous for her cheesecakes. The owner also agreed that Tariq had delivered said meal, and had, with some reluctance, handed over the young man's address.

Tariq lived in a small bedsit in Glory Farm, a large,

modern estate on the town's outskirts. She'd roused him from bed. Since it must be after midnight before the kitchen worker and general dog's body usually got home, no doubt he liked to sleep late.

He'd been bemused to find a pretty blonde outside his door asking for him, then alarmed at the police identification, and just a bit scared at the mention of Florence Jenkins' name.

Knowing that her boss liked to be in on important interviews, she'd done her best to curb her curiosity, and had asked him to come down to Kidlington HQ to make a statement. Just how long that would take, however, depended on what he had to say.

Now, she walked with him to the entrance, then escorted him through to the front desk. The desk sergeant looked up, eyes narrowing speculatively on the DS and the nervous-looking, stick-thin young man with her.

'We need an interview room, sarge,' Janine said cheerfully. 'What's available?'

'You can have …' the desk sergeant checked the roster by leaning slightly backwards and consulting a wall chart. 'Six, two or nine.'

'Two will be fine,' Janine said, as if it made any difference. They were all uniformly sized and uncomfortable. She signed herself and Tariq Kahn in, then said, 'Can you call DI Greene down to interview, sarge?'

'Think she's out,' the desk sergeant said. Then added sorrowfully, 'Ross is back though.'

Janine cursed. 'New boy?'

'In the showers. Don't ask.'

Janine sighed wearily. Great. That was just what she needed. 'OK, send Ross down,' she muttered.

When Hillary Greene returned to HQ barely forty-five minutes after leaving it, she was once again beckoned over by the desk sergeant, and was tempted to pretend she hadn't seen him. But things like that tended to give him the hump, and since desk sergeants were the hub of what went on in the nick, it didn't do to offend one. So she put on a smile and went over, dreading yet another grilling about Jerome bloody Raleigh. Instead, the old man pointed a thumb downstairs.

'Your DS Tyler wants you down in number two.'

Hillary nodded. Good. Sounds like she found herself a delivery boy. 'Thanks, sarge.'

She went downstairs to where the interview rooms were lodged, and discovered, in the observation room for interview two, that Janine and Frank Ross were both present. Sitting facing them was a young Indian lad who looked petrified. Not surprising, she realized a moment later, when Frank Ross opened his mouth.

'Don't go denying it, laddie,' Ross all but snarled. 'We know you delivered to the murdered woman the night she was killed. You were seen.'

'But I don't deny it, sir,' the lad replied self-righteously, looking to Janine for help.

Janine moved restlessly on her seat, wishing Frank would cool it. She wasn't sure that any strong-arm tactics were really needed here, and she was damned sure this wasn't how DI Greene would have played it.

'Your boss, Mr Ram, is it?' Frank ploughed on, 'Gave you up. He says you went out with Florence Jenkins' order at roughly 6.40 that night.'

'That's right. I had two more deliveries in the same area,' the lad squeaked nervously. 'No, not two. Three. I think. I'm not sure.'

Sensing the rising panic, and knowing he'd only get more incoherent the more Ross pushed him, Hillary swore softly and walked quickly to the door.

Janine looked up with a definite feeling of relief when Hillary Greene walked into the interview room. Beside her, she heard Frank mutter something, and felt like giving him a sharp kick under the table. But then, Janine often felt like kicking Frank.

'Detective Inspector Hillary Greene has just entered the room,' Janine said, for the benefit of the tape.

Hillary took a chair and said flatly, 'Thank you DS Ross, that'll be all for now.'

Frank flushed, pushed back his chair violently, and stalked out of the room. The bewildered Tariq watched him go, and whispered across to Janine, 'Why is he so angry?'

Janine's lips twisted. A good question. But then, the likes of Frank Ross probably didn't need a specific reason to be pissed off.

'Now, Mr Kahn,' Hillary said, smiling gently. 'You were about to tell us about the night you delivered some take-away to Mrs Jenkins? What time was it, do you think, when you got to her door?'

'I'm not sure exactly,' the young man said, anxious to be helpful. He was glad the other man had gone, but something about this new officer reminded him of his mother. So he'd better get things right. 'I think it must have been about 6.50, something like that.'

Hillary nodded. 'Did you notice anything unusual at all? A car parked outside Mrs Jenkins' house? Somebody maybe watching the house?'

'No ma'am, nothing like that.'

'You parked your van outside?'

'Yes. Right outside.' Tariq's young face lit up. 'Ah, yes, so there was no car parked there. There never is. Mrs Jenkins can't drive. Often we joke about it – that I can always park right outside her door, so the food is nice and hot.'

Hillary smiled and nodded. 'It sounds as if you liked Mrs Jenkins.'

Tariq nodded his head vigorously. 'Oh yes, very nice lady. Always gave me a pound coin tip. I don't think she could really afford it, but she would insist.'

'You heard that she's been murdered?'

Tariq's face darkened, and for the first time he dropped his eyes. He stared at the table miserably and nodded.

'But you didn't come forward, when we asked for anyone who'd been in the vicinity that night to get in touch. You did hear the appeals on the radio, didn't you Tariq?' Hillary added firmly.

He shot her a cow-eyed look, a quick look full of guilt, and nodded again.

'So why didn't you get in touch?'

Silence.

Hillary regarded him thoughtfully. A young, well-brought up Indian boy, he was probably dying to tell the truth. Only one thing could be holding him back.

'Did your parents tell you not to? It's all right if they did,' she went on as he shot her a hopeful look. 'I can understand why they would. Lots of people don't like to get involved with the police. And murder is particularly nasty. They probably thought that they were giving you good advice. But now that we've found you, off our own bat as it were, you have to cooperate. You do understand that don't you? It's your duty to help the police – not only is it a legal requirement, but as a good citizen too, you need to answer our questions.'

Tariq heaved a sigh, but looked better for being let off the hook. 'Of course.' He straightened his shoulders and beamed at her. 'I will tell you all that I know.'

'OK then,' Hillary nodded sombrely. 'You walked up the path and rang the bell. Did she answer right away?'

'Oh no. It takes Mrs Jenkins some time to get to the door. She used to be quicker, but I noticed lately she's getting slower. And she loses weight – too much, I think. I don't think she was well,' he added, lowering his voice confidentially.

Hillary smiled. His earnestness was so genuine it was almost painful. 'When she answered, did she seem her usual self?'

'Oh yes.'

'She didn't seem nervous or upset?'

'Oh no.'

'Did you get the impression that she had someone in the house with her?'

Tariq frowned. 'No. What do you mean?'

Hillary spread her hands helplessly. 'Did she look over her shoulder a couple of times, or lower her voice? Anything that made you think there was someone there with her?'

'Oh no. She was much the same as ever. She says, "Hello Tariq, got my hot chicken have you?" And I laugh and say, as I always do, "Not that hot, Mrs J." She couldn't stand too much spices, so she always said, on account of having had her gall bladder out. So then she reached for the box, and I hand it over. She always had the right money and the pound coin.' Tariq paused for a much-needed breath. 'Anyway, I take the money, and says, "You enjoy it now. Mrs Ram put extra blueberries in the cheesecake just for you." She didn't of course,' Tariq added with a blush, 'but I liked to josh her along. You know?'

Hillary nodded patiently. 'And then?'

'Well, then she closes the door and I go back to my van and drive off,' Tariq said, slightly puzzled.

'When you got in your van, did you drive straight back to the restaurant, or did you have another delivery to make?' Hillary persisted.

'Oh, another delivery. Near the big church, not far away. St Eckberts or something like that it's called. Those old people's flats near the library. You know?'

Hillary nodded, although she didn't, and said, 'So you would have driven to the end of the road. Did you see anyone walking down the pavement?'

'A woman. And a man the other side, with a dog.'

'Did you see either of them turn into Mrs Jenkins' garden?'

'No, I was turning off by then.'

Hillary sighed. 'All right, Mr Kahn. My sergeant here will get a statement form. We'll ask you to write out a statement, just covering what you've said in our interview here – Janine will help you with it – then once you've read it through and are happy with it, you need to sign it and then you can go. Janine, you can drop Mr Kahn back at Bicester.' On a piece of paper, she scribbled, '*Check his other deliveries that night, and times he called,*' and handed it over.

Janine read it, bland faced, and nodded. 'Boss.' She didn't need to be told to run a background check on Kahn to check for priors. But Janine didn't think the boy was a very serious suspect.

Upstairs, the newly washed and hopefully flea-free Keith Barrington was just laying a copy of his freshly printed interview notes with Braz on Hillary's desk. He reached for his phone when it rang, and glanced across to see Hillary Greene returning to her desk. 'Hello. DC Barrington.' The voice in his ear was female, sounded middle-aged and friendly, but with an edge of efficiency in it that rang a bell.

'This is Jessica Mainwaring here. The assistant librarian, Bicester branch?'

'Oh yes, Ms Mainwaring. What can I do for you?'

'It's about that photograph you left, of a young man, taken, we thought, just after the war? Well, one of my regulars has just been in and thinks he knows who it was. I asked him, and he said he'd be glad to speak to you. Shall I give you his name and address?'

Keith grinned widely. 'Yes please.' After his recent confidence-sapping episode with the parasite, he felt in need of a boost. And dropping a little morsel into his new boss's lap was just the sort of boost he had in mind. Eagerly, he reached for a pen and began to write.

chapter twelve

Keith Barrington drove nervously along the narrow country lane, not sure where the turn-off might be. Although he'd followed Hillary's advice to spend his spare time driving around the countryside, getting to know his patch, he hadn't yet come this far out.

The address the librarian had given him was for a small village called Fritwell, not far from Bicester. He glanced over the bridge they were crossing and saw, to his surprise, a busy motorway. Unnervingly, this major thoroughfare wasn't even noted on the old atlas he was using, which he'd been given by a sergeant in Traffic. At the time, Keith had wondered why he'd grinned so widely. Now he knew.

He glanced across at Hillary, who was sitting in the passenger seat staring out at the wet, cold countryside, seemingly unaware of his predicament. Everywhere he looked it was either damp green or water-clogged brown, with none of the bright neon lights, enclosing buildings, or the hustle and bustle of human presence that he was used to.

Suddenly he came upon a crooked crossroads, and on one of those old-fashioned, white-painted wooden signposts, pointing off to the left, was a sign for Fritwell. Hiding a sigh of relief, Keith indicated.

Peter Woodsman lived in a small cul-de-sac of one-time council houses, about halfway down, and Keith was able to park directly in front of the cream-painted semi. The garden looked neat and tidy, if unoriginal, with a paved path right down the middle, leading from garden gate to front door. On either side were lawns, each with a round flower bed cut into the middle, in which were planted two identical, dwarf weeping cherry trees. Bordering the hedges on all four sides were scraggly, dead-looking woody shrubs that would probably look wonderful in the spring.

The door was opened quickly, as if the occupant of the house had been looking out for them – as he probably had been. In this quiet backwater, Keith supposed uncharitably, even a visit from the cops was something to look forward to, in order to break the monotony.

Peter Woodsman was a fit late sixty-something, and looked like one of those men who was determined to enjoy retirement. The sort who took up golf, or a whole slew of hobbies. He had fine, white hair that had almost certainly once been blond, and thin, delicate hands. Not a manual worker then, Hillary thought at once. More likely he'd enjoyed a mid-level management career, which had been cut short by enforced redundancy. It would explain the now privately owned house, which was well maintained, but not the 'real' thing, as in a genuine country cottage.

'Hello.' The voice was surprisingly hearty for such a slim man. 'You the fuzz?' he asked, a wide smile taking any sting out of the sobriquet.

'DI Greene, this is DC Barrington,' Hillary confirmed, holding out her card. Peter Woodsman barely glanced at it before standing to one side.

'Well, come in, come in. I must say, I was rather intrigued by Miss Mainwaring. I went down to change my Erle Stanley Gardner for an Ian Rankin, and stepped into a real-life mystery.'

Hillary smiled, recognizing both the names as belonging to authors of crime fiction. 'Well, I'm hardly an Inspector Rebus, and even more certainly not a Perry Mason, but I hope we can measure up,' she said cheerfully.

Peter Woodsman looked delighted at the riposte, and opened a door that led into a long room that had obviously at some point been two rooms, knocked into one. Two large windows framed either end – one looking out over the road, the other over a back garden.

Woodsman led them to the furthest end near the garden, and ushered them onto a sofa. Through the window, Hillary could see the outlines of a small pond and a sundial. A recent patio held creosote-covered tubs that were, at this time of the year, empty. In the summer no doubt they'd be choc-a-block with scarlet geraniums. On an easel set up to one side, catching most of the cold white winter sunlight, was a small watercolour. Peter Woodsman saw her looking, and smiled. 'Trying my hand at a bit of art,' he said. 'Not sure I'm any good at it, though.'

Hillary didn't think so either, but was hardly about to say so. 'Did Miss Mainwaring tell you anything about our inquiry, sir?' she asked instead.

'Oh no. Very discreet is our Miss Mainwaring,' Peter Woodsman said, sitting down in a matching leather armchair and crossing his legs neatly at the ankle. 'She just asked me if, by any chance, I recognized the man in the photograph, and when I said I thought I did, asked me if I'd be willing to talk to the police. Well, naturally, I was intrigued.' He spread his hands and shrugged, trying to look shame-faced, but was obviously too busy enjoying himself to make any real effort.

Hillary smiled, unoffended. In fact, it made rather a nice change. Usually, members of the public were either too busy, too uneasy, or too downright antagonistic to want to talk to coppers in their living room. It was refreshing to be looked upon as a delightful diversion.

Beside her she felt Keith Barrington shift restlessly, and sensed his impatience. Janine had been like him once too. Young and raring to go. But Hillary had taught her DS the rewards that could come with taking things slowly and carefully. And this chap would learn too, given time.

'So, Mr Woodsman. You think you recognize the man in the photo?' she asked conversationally.

'Yes. Well, I was only a lad at the time, but my dad played in the St Mary's Eleven, and I always turned out to cheer him on. Course, the war stopped all that. I think nearly all of the team were wiped out overseas.'

Hillary smiled. 'St Mary's Eleven?'

'Yes. Our local football team. Oh, here, I forgot,' he replied, and reaching forward, picked up a faded red-velvet photo album that had been lying in wait for them on the coffee table beside his chair. 'When I got back from the library, I brought this out, just to make sure. See ...' He turned the pages quickly, and nodded in satisfaction when he reached the spot he wanted. He then turned the album around and handed it to her, leaning forward to tap one particular snapshot with his finger. 'This one here. Fourth man from the right, front row.'

Hillary pulled the album onto her lap and felt Keith Barrington lean a little closer for a look. The photograph was in black and white, and large, one of those posed, professional shots taken by a travelling photographer. Inscribed in a neat hand on a white strip of paper at the bottom, were the words: 'St Mary's Eleven, 1940.'

'Constable, a copy of the original please,' Hillary said, and Keith quickly reached into his inside pocket for a copy of the photograph. She peered at the picture of the young man that Florence Jenkins had kept in her own photograph album, and checked the features against that of the man, fourth from right, front row. Although the face was small, and taken from a distance, it did indeed look to be the same man. He had distinctive, beetling brows and rather sticky-out ears.

'Do you happen to know his name?' Hillary asked without much hope, and wasn't surprised when Peter Woodsman shook his head.

'No, sorry.'

Hillary looked somewhat sadly at the picture of eleven young men, most of whom were to die in the next few years, victims of the vast bloodshed caused by the Second World War. 'Which one's your father?' she asked, and Woodsman pointed to a young man on the back row, far right.

'That's him. Goalie.'

'I don't suppose he's still alive?'

'No. Killed in 1944,' Peter said. 'Mother remarried in 1948.'

'I don't suppose you know if any of these other men are still alive?'

Again, Woodsman shook his head. 'No. But I know who might be able to help you. Old Albie. Mr Albert Finch to you and me. He used to coach the football team back in the fifties. Took over the job from his dad, who used to do the same. He lives opposite the pub, in the cottage that looks as if it's going to fall down any minute. He's unofficial archive keeper for anything to do with the local football team, so I'm sure he could help. Even though he's ninety-odd, he's still sharp as a button. Marvellous, isn't it, when you can reach that age and still be right as rain?'

Hillary agreed that it was, thanked him and left.

Back at HQ, Martin Pollock sauntered over to the duty roster and checked the lists. The major changeover shift was scheduled for 7.15 that night. He himself was officially off duty at 6.40, but he could hang around and wait. Nobody questioned you doing unpaid overtime.

If he timed it just right, he reckoned he could get into the women's locker room without being seen, no problem. By eight o'clock it would be deserted, with the last of the day-shift stragglers gone, and the new shift all beavering away upstairs.

He was almost sure that the locker room wouldn't be locked, but just in case, he had a plan. Whistling as he went, he strode into Records, where WPC Felicity Burke was busy tapping away, inputting that morning's business into the database. She looked up, then away again without interest on spotting Pillock Pollock. The man, in her opinion, was well named.

'Hello darlin', just wanna check something from the vault.' The vault was where the very old, pre-computer case files were kept.

'Help yourself,' Felicity said, her flying fingers never pausing in their work.

'Mind if I help myself to some paper clips?'

'No. Second drawer down, over there.' She waved vaguely to a large, all-purpose desk, at the moment unmanned.

Martin Pollock nodded and walked over, bent down and glanced quickly over his shoulder. He opened the last drawer, and saw, as he knew he would, her handbag. He'd been in here before, and seen the way the staff used this desk as a general storage unit. Whistling softly, he reached inside her bag and extracted the large set of keys. The car keys were obvious, as was the Yale key to her front door. Silly cow, anyone could make a copy of them, then come and pay her a visit one dark night. One key, however, was smaller and simpler than the rest, with a square-shaped head and a single hole in it, and was obviously a locker key. Attached to it was a slightly larger Yale key. Yes! It had to be the key to the locker-room door.

'Need to open a new box darlin',' he called over his shoulder, careful to keep his back to her, blocking her vision of what he was doing.

'Yeah, yeah, whatever,' Felicity muttered, sighing heavily.

Sarky cow, Martin thought sourly, and neatly slipped off the pair of keys. Rising, he used his upward motion to slip them into his back pocket. 'Thanks. Won't be long.'

Felicity continued to tap assiduously at the keyboard.

The cottage did indeed look as if it was about to tumble down. It leaned drunkenly against its neighbour on one side, a more substantial younger cottage, whilst an old garden wall propped it up at the other. The window frames were rotten, and Hillary wondered how long it would be before a strong winter gale blew the glass inwards. The front door was so old and overpainted, it was obvious it hadn't been used in years. Decades probably.

Without a word, the two police officers went around the back, where a flimsy looking French window, looking incongruously out of place, led straight into a kitchen that could have featured in a 1950s *House and Garden* magazine.

Hillary tapped on a pane of glass and peered inside. If old Albie was in his nineties, he might have difficulty hearing them, but there was no door bell or knocker. However she needn't have worried, for a moment later she saw a door open from the other side of the kitchen and an old man slowly shuffling across the floor. He stood for a moment on the other side of the glass, eyeing them carefully. Then he looked from one to the other and shouted, 'Don't want no Jehovah's Witnesses asking me if I'm saved. I bloody well am, so sod off.'

Hillary grinned and held up her card. 'Police, sir. Nothing to be alarmed about, we'd just like a word.'

The old man didn't look any more pleased to receive coppers than he did Jehovah's Witnesses, but he reluctantly opened the door. 'I ain't paying my council tax, and that's that. If you've come to cart me off to prison, that's fine by me. It'll be warmer and dryer than this place, no doubt. I told that council woman, or social worker or whatever the hell she was last time. I ain't paying it.'

Hillary smiled widely. 'We're not here about that, Mr Finch. We have a few questions for you about the St Mary's Eleven, circa 1940. Think you can help?'

Albie Finch, when standing straight, was probably nearing the six foot mark. Bent and stooped as he was, he more or less met Hillary's dark and friendly eyes straight on. 'Football? You wanna talk football?' His wrinkled, cantankerous face fairly lit up with joy. 'In that case, you can come on through.'

Hillary thanked him and stepped inside, and instantly felt the damp and cold invade her flesh. She glanced at the old-fashioned stove, which was unlit and giving off no heat. If the rest of the house was like this, she hoped that someone from the council *did* come and take him off to a nice warm cell.

'Through to the living room then,' Albie Finch said, shuffling ahead and leading them through to a corridor so dark she almost bumped into the back of him when he stopped without warning to lift the latch on an old-fashioned oak door.

The living room had a fireplace where there was at least a cheerful fire spluttering and spitting in the grate. The wood was obviously as damp as the rest of the house, she mused, as she avoided a particularly ferocious bit of spitting, and watched as a piece of burning wood landed on a rather threadbare sheepskin rug and began to smoulder. Keith stood on it abruptly, grinding it out underfoot.

'Now then, sit yerselves down. I ain't offering you tea, so don't ask me.'

Hillary bit back yet another wide grin. 'I should think not, price of tea nowadays sir. It's tantamount to accepting a bribe, accepting a cup of tea.'

Albie Finch fell down onto a chair, as opposed to sitting down, and eyed her suspiciously. Then a reluctant smile tugged one end of his lips, revealing a toothless section of gum. 'Saucy bint, aren't you?' he said admiringly.

'So I've been told, sir. Now, we're trying to trace the identity of one of your football players who was in the 1940 squad. Constable?' She nodded at Keith, who quickly handed over the reproduction of Flo's snapshot.

'Oh ah,' the old man said at once. He had wide white caterpillar eyebrows and a hooked nose that rather reminded Hillary of a bald eagle. Not that she'd ever seen a bald eagle, even in a zoo.

'Know that face all right. You, whippersnapper.' Albie clicked his fingers in Keith's direction, who snapped to attention. 'That bookshelf behind you. Yes, yes, turn around, you ain't got eyes in the back of your head, have you?' he demanded, and Hillary bit back a guffaw as her bewildered constable turned obediently around. 'Bottom shelf, see the numbers?'

Keith, obligingly crouching down, saw a row of amateurish, but perfectly legible bound books, all bearing the name St Mary's Eleven, and a date.

'You want 1940, you say? Bring it out and let's have a butchers,' old Albie chivvied him along.

Keith duly selected the one they wanted and handed it over to the old man, who reached into his baggy cardigan pocket and produced a pair of small glasses that he perched onto the end of his nose and peered down through. He then shot a sudden look up at them, to see if either Hillary or the young man were laughing at him, and gave a small grunt of satisfaction to see that they weren't. 'Damn doctor insisted I get my peelers checked,' Albie Finch muttered. 'Told him I can see perfectly well, but bloody optician made me have 'em. Never cost me a penny though,' he added fiercely.

Hillary nodded. She wasn't sure whether the elderly were still entitled to free glasses on the NHS, but they probably thought, in Albie's case, it was easier just to give them to him, rather than try and pry money out of him.

'Huh, here we are. Full team. Now then, let's have a look-see. Not him. Nope. Nuh-uh. Ah, here he is. Roger Glennister.'

Keith walked over to peer over the old man's shoulder, and got a fierce glare for his trouble.

'I'm perfectly capable of matching one photograph to another, sonny. I ain't senile yet.'

'No sir, I can see you're not,' Keith said soothingly, and

nodded briefly at Hillary, confirming the identification. Not that Hillary was in much doubt. If her memory served her right, Flo had written on the back of the original the man's initials: RG.

'Do you remember this man, Mr Finch?' Hillary asked hopefully, but the old man shook his head.

'Not really. Dad was running the show then.'

'Any idea what happened to him?'

'Dunno. Killed in the war, I 'spect, like most of 'em.' Albie sighed heavily. 'I was with Montgomery meself. Bloody desert. Bloody hot. Bloody flies. I was glad to get home, I can tell you.'

Hillary nodded, thanked him and left.

Back in the car, she smiled across at Barrington. 'Well, constable, now you have a name to play with, I want to know all about Mr Glennister. Did he die in the war? Has he got any family still living around here? And what connection did he have to our victim?'

'Guv,' Barrington said happily.

Martin Pollock pushed his way through the door from the vault, still whistling, and glanced across at the WPC still typing furiously on her keyboard. It looked as if she hadn't moved during the five minutes he'd been gone. But she had.

'Much thanks, darling.' He walked to the desk drawer and bent down. 'Just returning your paper clips.'

He quickly reattached the keys to her key ring and left, still whistling happily. In his pocket, wrapped carefully in a piece of tissue, was a wad of Blu-tack with the impression of a key pressed into it.

Felicity Burke carried on typing for a moment, then stopped, walked to the door, opened it cautiously, and looked around. Once she was sure he was gone, she went back to her desk, dialled a single number that put her onto the internal phone system, and dialled an extension number she knew off by heart. 'Hello Jem? Yeah, it's me, Flick. You were right. He just lifted my keys. Yeah, the keys to my locker and the women's locker room. How did you know that?' She listened grimly for a moment, then smiled savagely. 'OK, have fun. And give my love to your Dad. Tell him I've still got a list of all the advice he ever gave me, tacked up on my bedroom wall.' She listened to Jem Titchmarsh's laconic reply, grinned widely, and hung up. Before she turned back to her keyboard, she gave a two-fingered salute to the closed door. 'And screw you too, *darlin'*,' she murmured.

Keith Barrington hit the Internet running, and logged first onto Friends Reunited. Using St Mary's Eleven, Fritwell, Football, 1940 and other key words, the search engine was soon spewing out names and contact numbers.

Next he tried the Registrar of Births, Deaths and Marriages, then the office of the Census, and finally, the myriad number of websites that dealt with planning permission, building permits, and the like. It would take him hours to sort out, but he was sure, come tomorrow lunchtime, he'd have something to show Hillary Greene.

Hillary was at her desk when Frank Ross checked back in. She looked up, expecting a quick update on the Hodge inquiry, and was surprised to see the fat-faced sergeant walking at a fast clip across the office. He was deathly pale and looked sick to his stomach.

Janine, who was wondering if she should ask the boss if she could leave early to get her hair done in preparation for tomorrow's ceremony, did a quick double take too. It wasn't often you saw Frank Ross hurry anywhere.

'Guv, you heard?' Ross hissed loudly, which was his version of a discreet whisper. Probably only herself, Tyler, Barrington, and anyone sitting within two desk-lengths of them heard it.

'What Frank?' Hillary sighed.

'They've arrested Raleigh.'

Hillary's eyes sharpened on him in warning. 'Relax Frank, that's old news.' She wasn't surprised Ross had only just got to hear about it, though. Even though it must have been all over the station for hours, nobody ever volunteered information to Frank. 'And wrong, as usual,' she said calmly. 'Raleigh was spotted in Malta, and the brass were interested enough to ask a local lad on holiday out there to have a word.'

Frank, his knees feeling distinctly weak, sat down heavily in his chair. 'And?' He noticed Janine give him a hard-eyed stare, but ignored her.

'And nothing,' she said flatly, her eyes warning him to calm down. 'Superintendent Raleigh left the force for personal reasons, and won't be coming back. And that's that,' Hillary added, an unmistakably hard edge in her voice now. 'Not that it's any of our business, right Frank?'

Ross flushed angrily. 'Right guv,' he muttered. But they both knew that wasn't quite true. After all, Raleigh had been ready to frame Frank for the Fletcher killing, if the internal inquiry hadn't gone the way he wanted. And they both knew it was Hillary who'd saved Frank's worthless neck, yet again.

Now Janine glanced across at Barrington and rolled her eyes. She'd already told him that there'd been something iffy about Jerome Raleigh and the whole Luke Fletcher raid last summer, and here was yet more proof that Hillary Greene knew far more about it than anyone else. And Frank Ross too, by the looks of it.

It made Janine's blood boil to think that Ross knew more than she did, and couldn't wait for the day that she'd be out of there. Next week couldn't come soon enough as far as she was concerned. 'Boss, I need to leave early today, that OK?' she said, her tone of voice making it clear that it would be just too bloody bad if she didn't.

Hillary, who was in no mood to make anything of it,

merely nodded. Just then her phone rang, and she reached to answer it.

'Hello, is that Inspector Greene?'

Hillary recognized the halting, female voice at once. 'Yes, Mrs Weekes, isn't it?'

'Yes. I was wondering if you were going to be in Bicester today?'

Hillary glanced at her watch. 'I can be there in thirty minutes,' she said at once.

'Oh, it's not important. That is, I haven't remembered anything or anything like that. But I wouldn't mind having a quick word, if you were in the area,' Caroline said.

'It's no problem, Mrs Weekes,' Hillary assured her, and hung up. When she reached for her car keys, Barrington looked at her hopefully, but she shook her head. She didn't need a sidekick for this. 'I'll be back within the hour,' she said, to nobody in particular.

As she drove out of the car park, she passed, without knowing it, PC Martin the Pillock Pollock, who was just coming back from a quick visit to Oxford, and a small key-cutting shop that he knew on St Michael's Street.

Caroline Weekes looked terrible. When she opened the door to Hillary's ring, the policewoman almost didn't recognize her.

'Oh, you didn't need to come right over,' Caroline said, obviously flustered. 'Please, come on through.'

She seemed to have lost weight drastically over the last few days, and huge black bags had been deposited under her eyes. She led Hillary through to the same elegant room as before, but the policewoman could hear sounds coming from the kitchen.

'My mother,' Caroline said, spotting her quick glance towards the sounds of crockery clanking. 'She's been staying with me for a few days, but she's going back to Cowley tomorrow.' She smiled miserably. 'My husband gets on really well with his mother-in-law, but, well, it's not a good idea for her to stay too long is it?' Caroline said, as if unaware that her words, and their intended meaning, totally gainsaid each other.

Hillary nodded, not sure what to say. The other woman looked and sounded so fragile, she was almost expecting her to break any minute.

Just then, a buxom woman with wildly improbable bright-red hair pushed through into the living room carrying a tray. A delicate rose-patterned tea service resided on it, complete with a plate bearing a triumphant Victoria sponge. 'Hello there, I'm Martha Hoey. Caroline's mum.'

Hillary rose to shake hands, and watched as Martha Hoey put the tray down. She cut a large slice of cake, transferred it to a matching plate, and handed it to her daughter, who stared down at it blankly. 'You eat up, lovey. You need to take the pills, and the doctor said it's best to take them with food. My daughter's trying to conceive,' she said conversationally to Hillary, as if discussing the best way to grow daffodil bulbs. 'I never had any difficulty in that department, I have to say, having three boys and two girls ... Cake?'

Hillary eyed the delicious looking sponge, sighed regretfully and shook her head. 'No, thank you.'

'That husband of hers is dead keen to get a bun in her oven, but I've told him, she's not well. He shouldn't be thinking of things like that at a time like this. I mean, you can see she's not well, can't you?' Martha Hoey ploughed on, and Hillary wasn't surprised that Caroline's husband wanted her gone. Although she agreed that Caroline Weekes probably shouldn't be worrying about IVF treatment and such like, when she was obviously feeling so distressed.

'Mum, please,' Caroline said weakly. 'We're here to talk about Flo, remember? DI Greene, are you any closer to catching who did it?'

Meeting the other woman's eyes without flinching, Hillary nodded. 'Oh yes, progress is ongoing.'

'There, see, what did I tell you?' Martha Hoey said at once, obviously anxious to change the subject. 'Now, eat your cake.'

Caroline Weekes obediently picked up her piece of cake, but made no attempt to eat. 'I saw Walter this morning, Walter Keane,' Caroline said. 'He told me you thought Flo might have wanted to die? I mean euthanasia. Do you really think that's true?'

Hillary smiled briefly. 'It's hard to say at this point, Mrs Weekes. We have to consider every eventuality.'

Caroline Weekes nodded, then slowly broke off a tiny piece of cake and put it into her mouth. She had to force herself to chew and swallow, the effort being so obvious that Hillary had to quickly avert her gaze.

She took her gently through things again, but as she'd expected, Caroline Weekes had nothing new to offer the investigation. Hillary, sensing her need to talk, let her ramble on anyway, watched over by her fretful mother.

It was dark by the time she drove back to HQ and she still had lots to do.

chapter thirteen

Hillary glanced at her watch and saw it was nearly a quarter to eight. Outside, she could see a few residential houses, already lit up with multicoloured Christmas lights and gave herself a mental shake. She hadn't even started her food shopping yet, and as for presents – her mind was the usual blank.

She sighed, then hid a smile as she glanced across at Keith Barrington. No doubt the new boy was planning on hanging on to the grim death, only leaving after she herself had gone. She wasn't surprised that Barrington felt that he still had to prove himself, and normally she'd let him, but tonight she had other plans. 'OK Keith, that's it for the night. See you tomorrow,' she said firmly.

'Guv,' Barrington said, gathering his things. He wondered how much longer she'd stay at the office, and as he walked outside to his old banger, he felt a decided spring in his step. His new boss couldn't be more different from his lazy, good-for-nothing old one, and for the first time in months, he felt a distinct sense of optimism. Perhaps this posting to the middle of the sticks wasn't going to be so bad after all.

Back upstairs, Hillary noticed that most of the night shift were now ensconced, and she gave a loud yawn, getting up from her chair and stretching. Stuffing her bits and pieces into her handbag, she snapped off the anglepoise lamp on her desk, and headed for the main door, scattering 'good-nights' in her wake.

Once on the stairwell, however, she carried straight on down to the basement level and cautiously pushed open the fire door. As expected, down there, the corridors were deserted. Dim lighting gave the building a horror-film ambience that made her smile. In here, the horrors were real. For crooks, that is.

She glanced left, then right, then turned towards the woman's locker room. Why Mitch wanted them to meet here she wasn't sure. Unless the old reprobate had simply wanted to see what they were like.

The thought that a grizzled old veteran like Mitch might harbour such schoolboy curiosity made her grin. At the door to the locker room, she paused and listened. Hearing nothing, she pushed the door open and walked inside. It had been many years since she'd maintained a locker herself, preferring to keep a large bag for all her knick-knacks. But she knew a lot of officers were glad of the extra storage space.

She looked around sharply as a shadow fell across one wall, the ancient cream paint looking dirty and dingy under the low-watt light bulbs. The shadow disappeared, then quickly emerged in the very substantial form of Mitch the Titch Titchmarsh.

'So this is where you girls hang out,' he said, glancing around the ancient wire-racked dividers, the battered tin lockers and cold, rather dirty, red tiled floor. 'Very chic.'

Hillary grinned. 'Only the best will do. Why are we here?'

Mitch turned his head to indicate a row between the lockers, where a backless wooden bench stretched nearly the entire length of the room. He took a seat about halfway down and Hillary joined him. 'I think our boy is about to place a dead cat in Tyler's locker,' Mitch said, and recounted Martin Pollock's adventures that morning. Hillary listened, grim-faced, then nodded when Mitch finished.

'I agree,' she murmured quietly. 'A dead cat's a real find, and not one he'd be likely to pass up.'

'And he'll want to stash it before it gets too ripe, and if your DS comes in here tomorrow morning, on the very day of her wedding, and finds a little wedding present waiting, it would be right up the sick puppy's alley.'

Hillary nodded. 'He hasn't been in yet?'

'Nope, he's lingering though. I've got a WPC from MisPer keeping an eye on him.'

Hillary looked at him carefully. 'No regrets, Mitch?' she asked softly. Pollock, to all intents and purposes, was still one of 'his lads' – which was how Mitch had always looked upon the uniform rank and file. It must rankle, just a bit, to be setting him up like this.

Mitch grunted. 'Force is better off without him,' he said. 'If he's like this now, when he's only twenty-three, what would the cocky sod be like by the time he hits forty, when he's had a chance to accumulate some real anger? Nah, you can't afford to let his sort get away with shit like this. He's the kind who likes to spread the rot and all. Before long, he'd have his own little band of merry men, making life for the lasses nigh on unbearable.'

Satisfied, Hillary slowly leaned her head back against the locker behind her and closed her eyes. Now it was just a question of sitting and waiting.

Back at their house in the Moors, Janine Tyler soaked in a hot bubble bath. Tomorrow she'd become Mrs Janine Mallow. Her mother was coming down from Liverpool on the morning train, and seemed determined to pretend that she wasn't disappointed that her only daughter wasn't have a big white wedding. Her father, remarried and living in France, wasn't able to make it, which wasn't much of a loss as far as Janine was concerned. It wasn't as if he was needed to walk her down the aisle, after all.

She sighed and reached for a foam loofah, squeezing a dollop of honeysuckle-scented liquid soap onto it.

While she didn't really mind the registry office herself –

she was hardly a church and orange blossom sort of gal – she wouldn't have minded a bit more pomp and ceremony to go with it, at least to have the day off and go for a meal in a posh hotel afterwards. Just a touch of romance to make the day special would be nice. To go to work before and afterwards smacked of taking the business-as-usual thing a shade too far, but she understood Mel's reasoning. They wanted to give the brass nothing to beat them over the head with. And he *had* promised to take her on a spectacular belated honeymoon to the Maldives later that spring.

She heard the door bell ring, and her heart leaped. Clambering quickly out of the bath, she grabbed a terry cloth robe and struggled into it. Next, she padded out onto the landing and peered over the railings and was just in time to see Mel cross the hall and open the front door.

But it wasn't the postman (who sometimes managed to squeeze in an evening delivery) as she'd feared, but only the paper boy, calling for his monthly payment.

She trooped back to the bath and climbed in again, but it was no use. The water felt too cool to relax her suddenly tense shoulders. There was no reason to suppose that Mel would get a delivery of the fake pictures anyway, but as she closed her eyes and began to soap her arms, Janine could only hope and pray that her stalker wouldn't put in an appearance at the wedding tomorrow.

It might not be a big do, but it *was* her wedding, and she wanted to enjoy it in peace. Such as it was.

Keith Barrington parked his car on the side street, as close to a street light as it was possible to get, and climbed out. He didn't think the car would get stolen – it was too much of a rust bucket to tempt any self-respecting car thief, but it might attract the attention of joy riders or vandals. Not that Summertown had much of that element – not like his old stomping grounds. It was tame by comparison around here.

But with money so tight, losing his transport at this juncture would be a catastrophe.

His room was on top of a laundromat, overlooking a set of traffic lights, and as he climbed the creaking wooden stairs, he suddenly felt dog tired. Reaching for his key, he unlocked the black-painted door and pushed it open, then froze, his hand halfway up to the light switch.

He could smell cologne. And, in the corner of the room, his solitary arm chair creaked, as if someone was sitting on it and had moved their weight.

Swallowing hard, Keith slowly moved his hand up a few inches and flicked the light switch.

'What a dump,' a voice drawled from the far corner of the room. 'Don't tell me you left me for this rat hole?'

Hillary felt Mitch tense beside her, and quickly opened her eyes. She too had heard the quiet 'snick' of the outer door as it opened. Mitch instinctively froze, and Hillary did the same. Whoever had just come in had paused inside the door and was listening hard. Why would anyone who had legitimate business in here be doing that?

In her mind's eye, Hillary could see a young man, waiting and poised for flight, one hand still on the door handle as he stood straining his ears for the slightest sound. One tiny indication that he wasn't alone, and he'd be gone.

For several moments, all three occupants of the locker room acted like statues. Then, eventually, Hillary heard the second quiet 'snick' as the door was carefully shut.

She knew Mitch would have chosen their location carefully, being fully out of sight, yet within easy reach of Janine's locker. She herself had no idea where that might be.

A moment later they could hear the soft suck-suck-suck noises of rubber-soled shoes on hard ceramic flooring, and then Mitch rose carefully to his feet. It was an old trick her own sergeant back at Headington had taught her. Once a target was moving, his ears were full of the sound of his own movements – the rustle of his trouser legs as they rubbed against each other with every step, his footfalls, his own breathing even. It made it far more difficult for him to hear someone else softly moving some distance away.

When the sounds of footsteps stopped, so did Hillary and Mitch. It wasn't until they heard the metallic rasp of a jemmy against metal that they moved again, rounding the end of the row of lockers and peering round.

With no need for finesse, Martin Pollock was using a tyre iron to jemmy open Janine's locker. At his feet was a shopping bag. Without a word, Mitch unhinged his phone, turning away slightly as he pressed a series of buttons, so that the sound would be muffled and couldn't possibly reach their quarry.

Hillary was impressed. Her own mobile phone did nothing more exotic than put through and receive phone calls. But then, it *was* ancient. Perhaps it was time for that upgrade she'd been promising herself for the past two years.

She watched, smiling grimly, as Mitch turned the viewfinder back towards Martin Pollock and taped him reaching down into the bag and taking out the carcass of a dead cat.

Martin Pollock carefully moved aside Janine's gym bag on the second shelf and positioned the cat inside. Apparently, he wasn't satisfied with the dramatic effect it presented, because he took it out again and placed it on the shelf above, letting the stiffened head poke out. In the morning, when rigor had passed, Hillary guessed that its head would hang pathetically down, dangling over the top shelf and onto the shelf below. Far more artistic.

Martin Pollock grinned at his handiwork, pushed the door on the locker so that it looked, at first glance, to be shut, then turned around to walk away and yelled.

Mitch was walking towards him, looking into the lens of his mobile. 'Very photogenic you are, Pillock old son,' Mitch rumbled. He was wearing a pair of new-looking dungarees and a well-worn, well-washed white shirt underneath. With his leonine head and large feet, encased in a disreputable pair of white sneakers, he looked like most people's idea of an off-season Father Christmas.

'Shit, Mitch, you scared the daylights out of me,' Martin Pollock said, with a high, painfully false laugh. His face was pasty white, and when his gaze slid over Mitch's meaty shoulder to Hillary Greene, his colour turned to a sickly grey. 'What you doing down here, Mitch?' Martin asked, only now noticing the phone in his hand, and registering his opening words. His colour, if anything, became worse.

Hillary saw a rather nondescript young man, neither ugly nor handsome, and supposed, sadly, that that was probably part of his problem. She would have, and must have, passed him any number of times around the place, and never given him a single thought. Was that why he'd taken to stalking the beautiful, bright, successful Janine Tyler? In order to be noticed? In order to make a difference, no matter how unwanted and ugly a difference?

The human condition. We all wanted to be noticed. Acknowledged. Hillary began to feel depressed.

'We've got it all on here, old son,' Mitch said, walking up to Martin and draping an arm over his shoulders. Martin's knees almost buckled under the weight, and she could tell by the way he winced that Mitch was putting a lot of pressure on that friendly looking arm.

'What? Sorry, I'm not with you,' Martin Pollock mumbled.

Mitch, still with one arm draped around the stricken man's shoulders, leaned forward and opened up Janine's locker. Then, raising his phone, keeping Martin Pollock's profile firmly in shot, he filmed the inside of the locker. 'We've got you bang to rights on this,' Mitch said. 'I've also got you on film this morning making unsolicited deliveries to Mel Mallow's place.' He turned to look at Hillary, his big meaty arm turning the hapless Martin in the same direction.

'What do you think, Hill? Was he delivering a Happy Wedding Day card?'

Hillary regarded Martin Pollock and shrugged. 'I somehow doubt it, Mitch.'

'I do too. So what was it Martin?'

'I don't ... shit, you're breaking my neck,' Martin Pollock hissed as Mitch bent his elbow, the better to cradle Pollock's neck in the crook of his arm.

'What was it Pollock?' Mitch said again, not altering his tone by so much as a note. Even Hillary felt a sense of menace.

Martin Pollock swallowed – with some difficulty – and gave another false laugh. 'It was only a joke, Mitch. You know, a laugh.'

Mitch grinned mirthlessly. 'Well, we all like a good laugh as much as the next man, right, Hill?'

'Too right. Never have too many laughs, that's what I say.'

'So let us in on it,' Mitch carried on conversationally. 'What did you put through Miss Tyler's letter box this morning, Martin? And don't lie to me.'

'It's nothing, I told you. Just a joke photograph. I was playing around on the computer, thought the sarge would appreciate the joke. DS Mallow too, maybe. You know a bit of stag-night humour for his wedding day.'

'I'm sure Sergeant Tyler would have thought so too,' Hillary said drily. 'She's no prude. Shall I phone her and ask her what it was?' she continued, reaching into the bag for her phone. 'I'm sure she'd let me in on it. After all, she's off to Witney next week, and I won't be her guv'nor any more. She won't mind sharing with me.'

'It was just a photo. An obvious fake,' Martin said desperately, staring at Hillary like a mouse would stare at a snake. 'A naked lady, with her face on it, nothing more. Nothing major. It was taken in the canteen, for Pete's sake. Just a lark, see?'

'And who else did you send these joke pictures to?' Hillary asked quietly, thinking how mortified Janine must have felt. Fake or not, having your family, friends or colleagues see images of a naked body with your face on it would be hard to live down. For a serving police officer, saving face and maintaining the respect of others was essential. As this little bastard knew only too well.

As did Mitch. 'If any of those pictures show up, Pollock ...' he said softly, and Martin Pollock abruptly bent forward and threw up all over his shoes.

Mitch stepped smartly back, as did Hillary. When he was finished, Pollock wiped his mouth with the back of his hand and straightened up. He was now visibly trembling. 'I'll delete them off the computer,' Pollock said, his voice little more than a whisper.

'Then you'll write a letter of resignation,' Mitch said, and when Martin Pollock's head shot up and around, his eyes narrowing with half-hearted defiance, Mitch smiled grimly. 'Oh no, I can't make you,' he agreed, as if Pollock had actually said the words aloud. 'But if you don't, I'll have a few words in a few ears. And you know how many ears listen to me, don't you, Pollock? You won't be able to function in this nick or any other.'

Martin Pollock began to cry.

'And Pollock,' Hillary said, waiting until he'd turned and looked at her. 'I'll be keeping tabs on Janine. If I even get so much as a hint that you've gone anywhere near her ...'

Mitch shook his phone in front of Pollock's face. 'This makes its way to the desk of a woman DI I know in Sex Crimes who's always happy to put away one of her own. Her ex made her very bitter.'

Hillary nodded. 'And you don't want to do jail time, Pollock,' she advised softly. 'You really don't.'

'Now piss off out of our sight,' Mitch said, withdrawing his arm. When Martin moved to step around him, he added, 'Aren't you forgetting something?'

Pollock looked at him blankly, and Mitch opened the locker door a bit wider. 'Tiddles?'

Without a word, Martin Pollock collected his dead cat and crept away.

'My treat, what you having?' Hillary asked pushing open the door of the Boat and glancing around. Her local at Thrupp wasn't very busy on a week night, but the first person she saw was Mike Regis.

She saw his eyes widen as he realized she was coming in with a man, then smile as he recognized the legendary Mitch the Titch.

'A friend of mine from Vice is in,' Hillary said quietly, as Mitch let the door close behind him.

'OK,' Mitch said, understanding at once that she didn't want anyone else to know about Janine's woes. 'Do I know him?'

'Mike Regis,' Hillary said casually.

'Only by rep. Seems solid,' Mitch agreed.

Hillary led the way, and made the introductions. 'Mike, Mitch. An old friend from way back. We meet up for a brew every now and then and to have a good moan.'

Mike shook hands, smiled and said, 'What you having?'

'My shout,' Hillary repeated, wondering if she sounded as awkward as she felt. 'Mitch?'

'Pint of cider, thanks.'

Mike indicated his still full glass and Hillary went to the bar. She was just ordering herself a large gin and tonic when she spotted a flash of blond hair out of the corner of her eye. She turned around and felt her heart do a little jig. She almost groaned out loud. This was not good. Not good at all.

Chief Inspector Paul Danvers spotted her at the bar, and smiled. 'Hello. I was hoping to catch you. Just a quick word about the Jenkins case.'

'Sir,' Hillary said, wishing she'd made the drink a treble.

With no other option, she led Danvers and his pint of Guinness to the table where Mitch sat and who lifted an eyebrow in silent inquiry.

'DCI Danvers, ex-Sergeant Mitch Titchmarsh. Mitch, my boss.'

Danvers nodded, but if he was aware of Mitch's legendary status, he gave no sign of it. Being originally from York, he might genuinely not have known him. Instead his eyes went immediately to Regis, and the smile on his face stretched just a little bit wider.

'Chief Inspector,' Regis said unenthusiastically.

'Paul, please. It's DI Regis, right?'

As if he didn't remember, Hillary thought, wondering why men had to play such silly buggers. Mitch, who could never be accused of being slow on the uptake, looked from Danvers to Regis, then gave Hillary a sly wink.

Hillary kicked him sharply under the table.

She awoke the next morning feeling deeply unhappy. She stared at the ceiling, barely a foot above her head, and frowned. Talk about getting up on the wrong side of the bed.

Then it all came back. That ugly business with the pathetic Martin Pollock. Then the fiasco in the pub. With a groan she pushed the covers aside and took a step to the right, coming out into a tiny narrow corridor, and then taking two steps forward and one to the left, which put her in the tiny cubicle that was her shower. She'd got the two-minute shower down to a fine art, and five minutes later she was dressed and heading down the narrow corridor to her tiny galley.

At first living on the boat had seemed like a nightmare, but now she couldn't imagine herself living in a house. All those acres of carpets to hoover. All those dirty, inaccessible windows to wash. Now she spent about half an hour a week on housekeeping, if that. And, come the summer, all she needed was a few days off, and she could push off from her mooring and tootle off to Oxford for a spell, or head out towards the Cotswolds, taking her home with her. Instant stress relief.

She put on the coffee pot and popped two slices of bread into the toaster, trying not to remember last night. Not that that was possible. Regis and Danvers had been like two fighting dogs sniffing each other's backsides, each getting ready to launch into the fray and land the first bite. Only the presence of the highly entertained Mitch, and Hillary's warning, flashing eyes had stopped them.

Well, one thing was for sure. Her romance with Regis was now well and truly out of the bag. Danvers could hardly have failed to read the signs, even if Mike hadn't gone out of his way to drop hints the size of house bricks that he and she were now a couple. And Mitch would certainly foghorn the news all over the county. Like all men, he loved to gossip.

Hillary had felt so cheesed off, she'd refused to go back to Mike's place last night, even though he'd practically begged, and she wondered now with a flash of defiance if she'd ever go back again.

She didn't like to be claimed, as if she was a mining stake in the Yukon. She was nobody's property. Damn it, what was it with men?

She got to HQ early, and was in no mood to find Keith Barrington already there. Not that he said much by way of greeting. In fact, he seemed uncharacteristically preoccupied.

When Janine came in, dead on time, a small ragged cheer went up. Anyone who could make it was invited to the registry office that afternoon at two o'clock for the ceremony, and most of her colleagues were genuinely happy for her and Mel. Some, no doubt, would be glad to see her go to Witney, but on a girl's wedding day, most people were willing to give her a break.

She grinned widely and gave the room a general good-natured finger, but Hillary saw the tension around her eyes. The moment she sat down at her desk, Hillary handed her a large card. 'For you.'

Janine smiled a somewhat awkward thanks and opened it, reading the inscription without much thought. Then her face went pale, then red, then pale again.

Inside, written underneath the usual Hallmark pleasantries, Hillary had scrawled:

One wedding gift – no more hassle. No more fake photographs. No more little notes. No more stalking. The bastard's resigned and gone and won't dare bother you again. If he does, just let me know, and he'll do time. Happy honeymoon. Your old boss, Hillary Greene.

Janine swallowed hard, and felt tears flood her eyes. She swallowed them back, and when she finally looked up, her face was shining. 'You're the bloody best, boss,' Janine whispered hoarsely. 'Sometimes I think there's nothing you can't do.'

Hillary grunted and shook her head. 'I wish! This Jenkins case has got me baffled for a start.'

She didn't know, then, that she would solve the case before the day was out.

chapter fourteen

Keith Barrington gave his computer the command to print, and watched the piece of paper go through the machine. His thoughts, however, were firmly back at his bedsit, and his unexpected visitor. He blinked when the machine beeped at him, letting him know that the function had been completed, and he keyed back onto his screen-saver and collected the sheet of paper.

He glanced across at Frank Ross' desk, more than usually relieved to see it empty. He knew only too well what the likes of Frank Ross would have had to say about Keith's visitor. And although he was almost sure that Hillary Greene wouldn't agree with him, Keith had no desire to put it to the test.

He was already treading on thin ice as it was. So far, it seemed that the fiasco back at Blacklock Green wasn't going to be held against him here. But that didn't mean that he wanted another question mark, if not a black mark, held against him so soon.

'Guv, I've got the name of Roger Glennister's nearest living relative – a younger brother called Paul.' He handed her the piece of paper and recounted his researches.

'Glennister's parents both died in the sixties, and his brother moved to Fife. Now he's retired, and moved back to his old stomping ground. The Glennisters did live in Bicester, as you thought they might have, but now Paul's retired to a dot on the map called Northbrook. Know it?'

Hillary did. 'It's a tiny hamlet not far from here. Funnily enough, my first murder case involved a body found in the canal near there.' She took the sheet of paper and read it through quickly. The Glennisters were a typical working-class family, the father a roofer, the mother a home help. Paul had been the only one to go to university, and had subsequently gone into the oil industry. Hence his move to Scotland, she supposed. Married, but now widowed with one child, a boy, who was following in daddy's footsteps.

'OK, let's go and talk to him,' Hillary said. They might as well – they had nothing else to do. Ominous thought for a murder case that was nearing the end of its first week. 'Janine, when Frank gets in, if he ever does, tell him I want a full report on the Hodge case to date.'

Janine rolled her eyes. 'You know he'll be stringing it out from here to eternity, right boss?'

Hillary did. It wasn't often she left him in charge of anything, much less gave him so much carte blanche to spend time away from the office. Still, it kept him out of her hair. 'Just do it. If you need to take a long lunch break, you go ahead.' With the ceremony at two, she might appreciate it.

'Thanks boss.'

Keith was staring at his screensaver when Hillary turned back. 'Ready, constable?' she asked sharply, and Keith leaped to his feet.

Janine grinned and hid her face in a forensics file.

Driving back to Northbrook brought back only a few memories of her first case as SIO in what turned out to be a murder case. But then it had been high summer, with wheat gleaming under bright sunlight, and the sounds and sights and smells of the canal at the height of the boating season. Now, as they turned off onto the single lane that led down into the valley, the fields were ploughed brown, heavy-looking and waterlogged. Trees were bare, raising blackened, stick-like forms against a buffeting grey sky, and the only sound was that quintessential sound of winter in England – that of arguing crows. Or was it rooks? The hamlet of Northbrook looked utterly deserted, with not even a dog or cat trotting in the lane.

'Canal cottage, guv,' Barrington said, peering through his car window, trying to make out the name on the building opposite him. He couldn't imagine living in such a tiny settlement, nestled in such a remote valley. What on earth possessed a man to move from a city to a place like this?

'Up on the left,' Hillary said, suddenly spotting it.

Canal cottage had a low, grey-tiled roof, and was built of Cotswold stone. A large porch, also with a grey-tiled roof, guarded a pale lemon-coloured front door. Newly installed double-glazed windows gave the old house an incongruously modern look. A neat, well-tended garden added to the air of modest affluence.

Hillary, who knew the cost of house prices after recently selling her own marital home, whistled softly. 'Not bad for a working-class boy from Bicester,' she said to Barrington, who looked at the cottage and shuddered. He might only have a bedsit over a laundromat, but he still preferred his place. At least it had a touch of life. In the mornings, he could hear Lal, the owner of the shop, opening up and cheerily greeting his customers who were dropping things off for dry-cleaning before heading off to work. In the evenings came the loud and sometimes humorous catcalls of those just turfed out of the pub up the road. But what did anyone get to see around here? Unless it was those noisy black birds, kicking up a racket in a large, dead-looking tree?

'Engineer, guv,' Barrington said. 'Must be money in oil.'

Probably not for much longer though, Hillary thought gloomily, and sighed. She shut the car door behind her, mindful that Puff the Tragic Wagon couldn't always be relied upon to be totally waterproof in bad weather – and definitely not if the wind was in a certain direction.

Barrington led the way to the front door, and rang the bell. The Westminster chimes could be heard clearly inside, and the sound brought on a sudden and savage pang of homesickness, which made Barrington half shake his head. He knew why he was feeling so unsettled of course. His visitor had brought more than potential trouble and strife. Now nostalgia bit him like a hungry dog. But there was no going back to London. No matter what.

'Something wrong, constable?' Hillary asked mildly, and Keith jerked a half-panicked glance in her direction. Shit, she was quick on the uptake.

'No guv,' he lied brightly.

Just then the door opened, revealing a man who couldn't have stood at more than five feet five. He was dressed in slippers, which didn't help, and wore a chunky-knit, Arran sweater and beige slacks. 'Yes?'

'Mr Paul Glennister?'

'Yes?' he answered a shade more sharply.

Hillary displayed her ID card. 'DI Greene, Thames Valley Police. DC Barrington. Nothing to be alarmed about, sir, we're just making routine inquiries. Mind if we step inside? It's a bit damp out here.'

Paul Glennister nodded wordlessly and stepped aside to allow them access. Once they were in the tiny foyer, however, he firmly barred the way. 'If you don't mind, I'd just like to ring Kidlington myself and confirm your identity. There's been a spate of robberies locally, people talking their way into people's homes and then robbing them and so forth. I'm sure you won't object to that.'

Hillary smiled. 'Not at all, sir. I wish more people were like you.' She waited patiently, listening in as Paul Glennister called HQ, using the landline phone resting on the hall table. She showed him her card again so he could quote the serial number then hid a smile as the home owner demanded a physical description of both DI Hillary Greene and DC Keith Barrington.

Once he was satisfied that they had the necessary bona fides he hung up and, without apology, led them through into a small but pleasant lounge. He made no offer of coffee though.

Hillary took a seat near the grate, where a real fire crackled a welcome, and nodded to Barrington to sit in a harder, wooden-backed chair by the wall and take notes.

'Now, what can I do for you?' Paul Glennister asked, sitting on the sofa opposite the fireplace. He had thinning sandy-coloured hair and rather dark circles under pale blue eyes. His hands, she noticed, were very gnarled, and she wondered if arthritis was the problem.

'It's to do with your brother, sir,' Hillary said.

'Roger? Good grief, he's been dead for over fifty years!'

'Yes sir. Can you tell me when he died exactly?'

'March fifth, 1951.'

So he had survived the war then, after all, Hillary mused. 'And how did he die, sir?'

Paul Glennister glanced down at his hands. 'Can I ask what all this is about?' he demanded shortly.

'I'm sorry, sir, I can't say. I can only tell you that his name has come up in an ongoing inquiry. I'm sorry if this is dragging up bad memories, but I wouldn't ask if it wasn't important.'

Paul Glennister regarded her silently for a few moments, then sighed heavily. 'Very well, I must accept that, I suppose,' he replied grudgingly. 'My brother killed himself.' He answered her question flatly.

Hillary blinked. 'I see. That must have upset your parents very much.'

'Of course it did,' Paul said with some asperity. 'Mother never really got over it.'

'May I ask ... how?'

'Hung himself in the garden shed.'

'This would be at the family home in Bicester?'

'Yes.'

'You must have been very shocked as well?'

'Yes.' Then, as if aware that his monosyllabic answers weren't going down too well, sighed. 'He was my elder brother, I looked up to him. Things had been difficult for some time. Roger was a conscientious objector in the war. Oh, he wasn't interned, and he worked for the medical corps, with some distinction, on the battlefields. But he wasn't really cut out for that kind of thing. He'd always been a shy, sensitive boy. He felt things more than most. He was never what you might call all that stable. He was shy, a loner. Never one for joining in things.'

'Yet he played football for Fritwell?'

'How the blazes did you know that?' Paul asked, amazed, then nodded. 'Yes, that was Dad's idea. Thought it would toughen him up. Dad was born and bred in Fritwell you see, before his family moved to Bicester. I don't think it really worked. He wasn't a very good football player.'

'Does the name Florence Jenkins mean anything to you, Mr Glennister? Or Florence Miller.' Miller was their vic's maiden name.

The older man finally smiled, a genuine smile with real warmth. 'My word, you are bringing back old times. Florrie. Yes, she was my brother's girlfriend for a short time. I think Mum had despaired of Roger ever having a girl-friend, so she almost fell on Florrie's neck when Roger brought her home. I was only a boy at the time, of course, but I remember Florrie all right. She was a pretty thing. Laughing, full of life. Even made old sober-sides – that's what I used to call Roger – even made him see the funny side of things every now and then. When they got engaged, Mum was over the moon.'

Hillary nodded. 'What happened?'

'Oh, it never happened. Just sort of petered out. Well, I think it was only to be expected really. Roger never had any pep, any sort of get up and go. He used to have the night sweats, remembering the war. Couldn't hold down a job from one month to the next. I think Florrie eventually wised up and dumped him. Some time later, Roger killed himself.'

Hillary glanced at Barrington, who was scribbling furiously in his notebook. 'I see. Did you blame Florrie for what happened? Did your parents?' She hoped her voice didn't sound as tense as she suddenly felt. Because, right now, this was the only sniff of a motive they had.

'No, I don't think so,' Paul said, after some thought. 'Roger, like I said, had been having problems all his life. He just didn't fit in. He wasn't all that bright, to be honest. He was the sort of man other people looked at and just wanted to kick. Defeatist through and through. Nobody was really surprised when Florrie dumped him. It was almost inevitable. She was only eighteen herself, and probably only felt sorry for him. But a young girl's got to look out for herself, hasn't she?' Paul, who was now leaning back against the sofa, his face looking thoughtful, and softer somehow with reminiscence, sighed and shook his head. 'We heard she married someone else soon after. Obviously some man called Jenkins.' He looked questioningly at Hillary, who nodded.

'Did your brother leave a suicide note, Mr Glennister?' Hillary asked softly.

Paul shrugged. 'Probably. But nothing I was allowed to read or hear about. I was packed off to an aunt up North for a couple of weeks, right after it happened. In that day and age, it was instinctive for people of my parents' generation to protect the young. Nowadays, of course, they'd have sent me to a counsellor and urged me to "talk about it".'

'So you don't know if your brother laid the blame for his actions on anyone or anything in particular?'

'No. But I can assure you, Mum and Dad never blamed Florrie. I'd have known about it if they had. You can't live in a house with someone until you're eighteen and not know what they're thinking and feeling. Has something happened to Florrie?' he asked abruptly, then frowned. 'Wait a minute. Jenkins. Didn't I read in the paper earlier this week that some old woman had been murdered in her home in Bicester? Was that Florrie?'

Hillary didn't deny or confirm it. 'Could you please tell me your whereabouts last Tuesday night, Mr Glennister? Say, from six o'clock to midnight. Strictly routine,' she added, before he could object.

But Glennister, strangely enough, showed no signs of objecting. For someone who was obviously officious, he'd become almost suspiciously compliant. 'As it happens I can. Tuesday night is Finds Night.'

Hillary, having no idea what he was talking about, repeated gently, 'Finds Night?'

'I'm afraid I'm one of those people who go about the countryside with a metal detector, inspector. Caulcott, just up the road, has a Roman road, and I've found quite a few coins since I returned to Oxfordshire. Our club meets at our chairman's house in Kirtlington, every first Tuesday of the month. We compare notes and findings, make sure every find is meticulously logged, trade areas of expertise, give advice on treasure troves and all that sort of thing. Fascinating. We meet at seven, and break up about ten. Or thereabouts. I can give you the chairman's name and number. Before and after those times, I was here. Alone.'

Hillary accepted the piece of paper he wrote on and thanked him. Outside in the car she passed it over to Barrington, telling him to check it out. Not that she seriously suspected the alibi would prove to be false. The old photograph of a past lover had only led to yet another dead end. She was going to have to go back to HQ and start right from the beginning again. Like it or not, it was starting to look as if the dead grandson was now the only contender in the running.

Frank Ross would be pleased.

*

Hillary pulled the pile of paperwork generated by the Jenkins case so far into several stacks around her, and reached for the first file.

Her stomach was rumbling, having long since dealt with two meagre slices of toast, but lunch was still more than an hour away. She refilled her coffee mug, grabbed a fresh pad and, trying to push all petty worries and niggling doubts to one side, took a deep breath and started from the top.

She'd done this before on cases that seemed to have stalled. Sometimes it shook something free, sometimes she got nothing more out of it than wasted hours and a raging headache. The thing was, until you did it, you could never be sure which it was that you'd get.

Janine, recognizing the signs, kept her head down and cast a surreptitious glance at her watch. Barrington, on the phone to the Kirtlington chairman of Gold Diggers Anonymous diligently confirmed Paul Glennister's alibi.

Hillary opened the file and stared at the picture of the dead woman. Flo Jenkins still looked as if she was asleep in that chair – only the protruding handle of the narrow-bladed paperknife showing that she wasn't.

Right, Hill, she admonished herself grimly, start at the beginning.

On her pad she wrote: 'Florence Mavis Jenkins, née Miller. Date of birth 9/12/30.' Beside it she wrote the date of her death. Then the date of her marriage: '14/2/49', and the name of her husband. She probably didn't need to bother with the name of her school and …

Abruptly, Hillary stopped writing and stared down at her pad. A funny feeling gripped her stomach, making her swallow hard. She blinked.

The numbers. There was something about the numbers. What the hell? She'd seen them before somewhere. Somewhere recently. She shook her head, telling herself not to be a mope. Of course she'd seen them before. If she'd read Florence Jenkins' file once, she'd probably been through it a hundred times.

But there was something about the numbers, written like this ... What the hell was it? Her palms felt sweaty and she took a deep breath, knowing that she was on the verge of a breakthrough. She'd felt like this once before, when investigating the murder of a young French student. The sense of scales about to tip over. Of revelation hovering just on the edge of her vision.

She reached for the pen and wrote the sequence of numbers again: 9,12,30,14,2,49. Not quite right. She tried writing them backwards, then randomly, then without the commas. Still not quite right.

Think damn it, think. Six sets of numbers. Not a telephone number, not a National Insurance number. Damn it, she could feel her body almost buzzing. Where had she seen those numbers before? When?

And then, in a flash, she remembered. Tuesday morning, before she'd even got the call-out to Florence Jenkins' house.

And then she knew.

She knew who had killed Florence, and almost more importantly, why.

'I'll be a son of a bitch!' Hillary snarled.

Barrington's head shot up from his desk, and Janine swivelled her chair around.

'You stupid, barmy, brainless dunderhead!' Hillary chastised herself. 'It was right there all along, staring you in the face. An idiot with the IQ of a gnat would have seen it.'

'Boss?' Janine said sharply.

Hillary glanced at her, self-disgust written all over her face. 'Janine, I want you to get a warrant for a murder charge.' She stood up and then abruptly sat down again. Wait a minute, they'd need a second warrant. Not such an easy one to get, because this time they'd be up against a big and powerful corporation. And judges always thought twice when that happened.

'What name?' Janine asked. Beside her, she felt Barrington get slowly to his feet. 'Boss, who should I make the warrant for?' Janine repeated loudly, seeing that Hillary was thinking furiously and hadn't heard her.

Hillary glanced at her. 'What? Oh, for Caroline Weekes.' Then she got up and moved quickly towards Paul Danvers' office.

Janine let her breath out in a whoosh. 'Weekes?' She hadn't even seriously considered Weekes as a suspect. And she was damned sure Hillary hadn't really rated her either. So what had changed?

'The guv OK?' Barrington asked nervously.

Janine glanced at him, saw the worry and guessed the reason behind it, and laughed out loud. 'Don't worry, she hasn't gone doolally. She's just had a brainstorm, that's all. It happens that way sometimes with the boss. You'll get used to it.' She reached for the phone. 'And don't fret about Weekes either. I've never known the boss get it wrong yet.'

Paul Danvers glanced up as Hillary Greene knocked on his door and, without waiting for a reply or gesture to come in, entered.

Paul had had a bad night. He'd lain awake for many hours, wondering just how serious it was between Hillary and that git from Vice, Mike Regis. And just when had Regis moved in on her? Why had Hillary been so coy about it? Surely she couldn't really rate the man. And how was he going to split them up?

Now, seeing her coming through his door, he wondered how he should play it. Then all such personal considerations took second place, as Hillary said crisply, 'The Jenkins case. I've cracked it. But I'm going to need a warrant for disclosure, and I don't think they're going to be pleased about it. We might need to gear up the legal eagles.'

Danvers, who wasn't aware of anybody, even on the fringes of the Jenkins case who might have such serious juice, sat up straighter. 'Who are we taking on?' he asked sharply.

Hillary, taking a seat in front of his desk, smiled grimly. 'Camelot.'

Janine glanced at her watch, and swore. It was nearly 1.30. She had half an hour to get to the registry office. Damn, why did the case have to break now? Hillary had spent nearly twenty minutes in Danvers' office, and then a team of lawyers had arrived. Danvers had come out and given Janine the necessary facts to get the warrant to serve on Weekes, and she'd sent Barrington over to get it. Once it arrived, she knew Hillary would be going over to Bicester to serve it and bring Weekes in. Janine was dying to know what the hell was going on, the whys and wherefores, and sit in on the interview. The case had been going nowhere ever since it started and now, just when she couldn't possibly get in on the act, it broke. She felt like screaming.

Then she looked up and saw Detective Superintendent Philip Mallow standing outside the door of the main office, tapping his watch. He was dressed in a beautiful steel-grey suit, and had a pale pink carnation in his button hole. He looked handsome, successful, wealthy and happy.

Janine sighed, grabbed her bag, and left. Somehow, she didn't think Hillary was going to make it to her wedding.

An hour later, after being processed, Caroline Weekes was ushered into interview room three.

Hillary looked up from her position seated to one side of the table and glanced behind her. Where was her solicitor?

Just as Janine had predicted, she had gone to Bicester, with Keith Barrington, to make the formal arrest and charge. She'd expected either her mother or husband to be at home, and wasn't particularly happy to find the woman alone.

Caroline Weekes hadn't said anything whilst her rights were being read out to her by the word-perfect DC

Barrington, and had been similarly silent on the drive to Kidlington, a fact that Hillary was grateful for. The back of a police car was no place for chit-chat. By-the-book-barristers had been known to get cases thrown out of court because of idle conversationn, carried out without the presence of the accused's legal representative.

'DC Barrington,' Hillary said quietly. 'Has Mrs Weekes' solicitor arrived yet?'

'No guv,' Barrington said. And Caroline Weekes spoke for the first time.

'I don't want a solicitor. I waive my rights to one. That's the correct term, isn't it?' she asked listlessly.

Hillary glanced at the tape recorder, whirring obligingly on the table. She sighed, and introduced herself for the tape, with Keith following suit, and said firmly, 'Mrs Weekes, I must ask you yet again, for the record, if you want to call a legal representative. If you can't afford to hire one, we can appoint one for you.' She repeated her rights in this matter again.

But Caroline Weekes shook her head. She was sitting opposite Hillary, lightly resting her hands on the table, her fingers looped to make a double fist. 'I don't want a solicitor,' she said stubbornly. She looked exhausted and ill. She was wearing a long black and grey dress and her hair was pulled back in a ponytail. She wasn't wearing make-up. Her eyes stared blankly down at her hands.

'Your husband then?' Hillary pressed, and saw Keith Barrington look at her with a slightly puzzled frown. Hillary knew they now had Caroline Weekes safely on tape, eschewing the need for a lawyer. Legally they were covered. But she wasn't going to take any chances.

'Oh no. I don't want my husband here,' Caroline said quickly, her voice rising to a squeak.

'As you wish,' Hillary said calmly. She was determined to make sure that everything was as watertight as it was possible to get. There would be no retraction of any confession later, not on her watch. Nobody would be able to listen to the tapes, either, and even hint that there had been any coercion or even a breath of bullying going on in this interview room.

'Mrs Weekes, do you understand that you've been arrested for the murder of Florence Jenkins?' Hillary continued, softly softly.

Caroline nodded.

'Mrs Weekes has just nodded her head,' Keith Barrington said automatically for the tape.

'Can you confirm that please, Mrs Weekes,' Hillary prompted.

'Yes.' It came out slightly strangled, and Caroline Weekes cleared her throat. 'Yes, I understand I've been arrested for killing Flo,' she repeated clearly.

'And I have to tell you now, Mrs Weekes, that you will almost certainly be charged, the moment this interview is over. Do you understand that also?'

Caroline's eyes filled with tears and she nodded, then gave a little start, looked at the tape, and leaning forward said huskily, 'Yes. I understand.'

Hillary let out a slow breath. Right then. No wriggling room there. Taking her time, she eyed Caroline thoughtfully. There were two possibilities here. Either she knew the game was up, and had decided to act for all she was worth, and try to lay down a case for mitigating circumstances. Or she really was as defeated as she seemed to be.

Hillary was inclined to think it was the latter, but she was going to keep a sharp eye out for any signs of the former. 'We know you used to do errands for Florence Jenkins, Mrs Weekes,' Hillary began carefully. 'You did the odd grocery shopping for her. Ran her into town to collect her pension, that sort of thing. You said as much in your original statement. Do you remember that?'

Caroline Weekes nodded. Then, when Barrington said flatly, 'Mrs Weekes has just nodded her head,' winced.

'Yes, that's right,' Caroline said, making some effort to sit straighter in her chair and pay attention, as if determined to pull her socks up and get things right.

Hillary nodded. In the observation room, she knew that Paul Danvers was listening carefully. 'And did these errands sometimes mean that you got Florence's lottery ticket?' Hillary asked softly.

Caroline Weekes drew in a harsh shuddering breath. But speech seemed suddenly beyond her. She opened her mouth, then closed it again. Her eyes flooded once more and tears oozed out, but she never sobbed. She simply stared at Hillary, like a cow facing the man taking her to the abattoir.

Hillary opened the folder in front of her, and said quietly, 'Do you remember telling me how much Florence was looking forward to her birthday party? It would have been today, wouldn't it? She would have been seventy-seven?'

Caroline licked her lips and nodded. 'I was going to make her her favourite chocolate cake,' she whispered.

'Yes, that's right. She was born on 9 December, 1930.' Hillary wrote three numbers on a blank piece of paper. 'Do you know what day Mrs Jenkins celebrated her wedding anniversary, Mrs Weekes?'

Caroline Weekes shook her head, then, remembering the tape, said, before Keith Barrington could respond, 'No, I don't.' She spoke it rather loudly, and looked surprised at the strength of her own voice.

On the table, the machine carried on recording the interview, oblivious to the tension in the room.

'It was on Valentine's Day, in 1949,' Hillary said, writing three more numbers on the piece of paper. This she then turned around to show Caroline Weekes. 'Do these six sets of numbers mean anything to you, Mrs Weekes?' she asked, then added, 'For the benefit of the tape, I am showing Mrs Caroline Weekes a piece of paper with the numbers, 2,9,12,14,30 and 49 written on it. The mixed numbers of Mrs Florence Jenkins' date of birth and wedding date.'

Caroline Weekes stared at the paper. 'No,' she whispered again.

Hillary nodded and, reaching into the folder, withdrew a sheet of newspaper. 'For the tape, I'm now showing Mrs Caroline Weekes a copy of last Monday's *Oxford Mail* newspaper. In it is an article that concerns an uncollected lottery win.' Hillary went on to describe the story, about how the ticket had been bought in Oxfordshire, and how the time was running out for whoever held it to collect the jackpot. When she was finished, she carefully folded it up and put it back in the file.

Caroline Weekes watched her, as if fascinated by her neat, precise movements.

'Florence always used these same numbers, every week, for the Saturday lottery draw, didn't she, Mrs Weekes?' Hillary asked. 'Her neighbour, Mr Walter Keane, confirmed as much for us just this afternoon.'

Caroline Weekes nodded. 'Yes,' she agreed.

'And you sometimes got the ticket for her, didn't you? If she felt too unwell to get it herself?' Hillary carried on gently.

'Yes.'

'And you got the ticket for her that week, didn't you, Mrs Weekes? The day those numbers came up?'

Caroline Weekes said nothing.

'We've contacted Camelot, Mrs Weekes. They've confirmed the serial number of the winning ticket.'

'Yes.'

Hillary tensed. 'Yes, what, Mrs Weekes?'

Caroline licked her lips again. 'I got the ticket for Flo that week. The week the numbers came up. I got it Friday, just after work. I was going to take it to Flo the next day, but something came up. So I still had it the following Monday morning.'

Hillary nodded. 'And when you saw the numbers, you realized Florence had won.'

'Yes.'

Hillary nodded, and paused for a moment. It was deathly quiet in the room, with only the gentle whirr of the recorder breaking the hush. 'So you went to Flo's that morning, expecting her to be cock-a-hoop. You thought she'd be celebrating, waiting to kiss you and hug you when you came through the door,' Hillary said, letting her voice soften.

Caroline nodded, her eyes once more threatening to brim over. 'Yes. But when I went in … there was nothing,' she said, sounding amazed. 'She was just the same as usual. She talked about having had a bad night, and I realized that she hadn't checked the numbers, that she'd probably forgotten to do so because of feeling so ill.'

'So you just never mentioned it,' Hillary said, careful to keep her voice calm and soft, without any hint of judgement.

'Yes. I kept expecting her to cotton on. You know, all that summer, every time I went to her house, I kept thinking, Today's the day she'll remember. She'll ask me about the ticket. And I had it all planned if she did,' Caroline said, looking at Hillary earnestly. 'I would tell her the ticket must be in my old purse. I'd go and fetch it and show it to her, and that would be that. But she never did. And I began to think.… I began to think it might all work out for me.'

Hillary nodded. 'You knew Florence Jenkins was dying?' she said softly.

'Oh yes. She was so desperately ill. I thought … any moment now, she'll just go to bed and never get up again. But the months went on and on, and still she clung on. She was so determined not to die!' Caroline's voice rose to a squeak again, and she slapped a hand against her mouth, hearing her own hysteria and being somehow shocked by it.

In the observation room, Janine Mallow, having come straight from her wedding, was now sitting next to Paul Danvers, hanging on to every word. Occasionally, she'd shake her head in disbelief. Trust the boss to nail it on the head.

In the interview room, Hillary sensed they were coming to the crux of the matter, and hoped Caroline Weekes would hold out just a little longer. 'Yes, Flo enjoyed life, didn't she?' Hillary said softly. 'No matter how ill she sometimes felt. And time was running out for you. You knew you only had so long left to claim the ticket, before it became invalid. Which put you in a bit of a bind, didn't it, Caroline?' Hillary said softly, then shut up. She wanted Weekes herself to lay it all out for the tape. That way, once it got to court, no weasely lawyer would be able to say that she'd put words into his poor, distraught client's mouth.

'Yes,' Caroline sighed heavily. 'But I kept hoping she'd just ... you know. Die.' She sighed again, and stared down at her hands. 'And then disaster struck,' she said quietly. 'That day, Monday, I was at work. One of the secretaries had bought a paper in her lunch break, and I saw that they'd rehashed the story and run the numbers again. I knew if Flo saw it, she'd realize they were her numbers.'

'But you knew Florence had the papers delivered at night?' Hillary chipped in.

Caroline nodded.

'For the tape, Mrs Weekes has just nodded her head,' Keith Barrington said again.

'So what did you do, Caroline?' Hillary asked.

'I went over that night. I thought, if she already knew about the numbers, then that was it. It was all over. But she didn't. She invited me in just as usual. She went straight to her chair and began to watch the telly, without a care in the world. But I felt sick. I was shaking. I felt so much worse than she did!' Again Caroline Weekes' voice rose to a fever pitch of self-pity, and again she broke off abruptly to take a deep breath.

Hillary nodded. 'You felt so bad because you knew what it was you had to do?' she murmured.

Caroline's eyes overflowed again, and she nodded. Quickly, before Barrington could speak and break the flow,

Hillary went on, 'And just what was it that you had to do, Mrs Weekes?'

Caroline looked at her, as if asking permission to speak. Hillary nodded encouragement. 'I had to kill her,' Caroline finally whispered the dreadful truth out loud. Hillary was glad the tape was sensitive enough to pick up even the softest sound, but she knew she couldn't leave anything to chance.

'Please speak loudly and clearly for the tape, Mrs Weekes.'

'I had to kill Flo,' Caroline repeated obediently, and in the observation room, Paul Danvers let out a long, slow breath of relief.

'I knew about the paper knife, about how sharp it was.' Caroline Weekes spoke quickly now. 'And Flo wasn't watching me, she was watching the television. She was so used to me being there, doing a bit of dusting or tidying, you see, she never really took much notice of me. I just reached up for the paperknife, went up to her and ... pushed it down into her chest.' Caroline took a deep, shaken breath. 'It was so easy. I never expected it to be so easy. I stood there for a moment, not realizing it was all over. Flo never made a sound. She didn't even bleed much. I just stood there, looking down at her, and realized, well, that was it. It was done.' She shook her head, seeming to be genuinely amazed. 'I thought it would have been harder. Wouldn't you have thought so too?'

Hillary ignored the question. 'What did you do next?' she asked instead, keeping her voice matter of fact.

As if picking up on it, Caroline Weekes suddenly did the same. 'I knew my fingerprints must be on the handle of the paperknife, so I used the hem of my skirt to wipe them off. Then I went out, making sure the door latched behind me, and went home. Later that night, I realized I would have to go back in the morning, and be the first one to "find" her again. Just in case I'd done something silly. Made a mistake or whatever.'

Hillary nodded. 'So, the next morning, you went to "find" Mrs Jenkins, played the part for any neighbours who might be watching, and reported finding her.' She waited a moment, knowing this next bit was crucial. 'You did it because you needed the money of course?' she asked casually, almost as if it didn't matter.

And Caroline fell for it, merely nodding absently. 'Yes.'

'For the IVF treatment. You and your husband were trying to have a baby, that's right isn't it?'

'Yes. But I'm too old, and the National Health wouldn't pay for it. My husband has a good job, and so do I, but we live right up to our income. The treatments could last for months – maybe even years. I *needed* that baby. You have to understand – I knew I'd lose him if I couldn't give him a child. He'd find someone younger, someone who could conceive at the drop of a hat!'

The voice was rising yet again, and Hillary nodded soothingly. 'Don't distress yourself,' she murmured the words almost automatically.

But Caroline Weekes had just admitted to the premeditated, cold-blooded murder of an elderly woman strictly for monetary gain. No jury in the world, surely, would show her leniency now.

'I understand. You needed money badly. And Flo – well, she was an old woman, wasn't she?' Hillary said, raising an eyebrow.

'Exactly,' Caroline rushed in, glad that the policewoman seemed to understand at last. 'She was in her seventies. She'd already had *her* child. She was ill and dying. What did she need the money for? She only had that dreadful drug-addict grandson, and what would he use the money for? Drugs,' Caroline spat. 'I wanted it to create another life. I knew Flo would understand.'

If Flo would understand, Hillary suddenly thought savagely, why didn't you just tell her about the lottery ticket and ask her for a loan to see you through the IVF? Knowing

Florence Jenkins, she probably would have done so without a single thought. However her face registered none of her thoughts.

'So you killed Florence Jenkins for her winning lottery ticket, and then gave it to your mother to claim it. Did she know it was Florence's?' Hillary asked abruptly.

Camelot, when legally required to, had indeed coughed up the name of the person with the winning ticket. But it had not been Caroline Weekes, but one Martha Hoey who'd claimed it.

'Oh no!' Caroline said, appalled. 'Mother knows nothing about this. I told her I wanted her to claim it because I didn't want my husband to know. And Mother – well, Mother doesn't like John much, so she was happy to.'

'But in reality, you didn't want to claim it yourself, just in case it got back to us, and we began to wonder?' Hillary offered.

Caroline nodded, her eyes tearing up once more.

'For the tape, Mrs Weekes has just nodded her head,' Keith Barrington repeated one last time.

'So, that's it then,' Paul Danvers said later that night. It was dark outside, and below stairs, Caroline Weekes was spending the first of what would, Hillary hoped, be many years behind bars.

The newlyweds, herself, Barrington and Danvers were all squashed together in his office, drinking champagne supplied by Mel, partly as a wedding celebration, partly as a case-closed party.

'I feel kind of sorry for her,' Janine said thoughtfully, glancing across at Mel. She would have kids one day, she supposed vaguely. Not yet, but one day. 'It must be hard to really want a baby, and not be able to have one.'

'Yeah, and I think she was right about that husband of hers too,' Barrington said. 'I reinterviewed him during follow-ups, and he came across as the sort who'd cut his losses and go for a newer model, if the old one couldn't provide the goods.'

Hillary grunted. 'Save your pity for Flo Jenkins,' she advised them both sharply. 'That old lady wanted nothing more than to enjoy her birthday and one last Christmas. And if she'd had that lottery win back when she'd been entitled to it, her last few months could have been spent having a high old time. She'd have liked that. Instead, a woman she thought of as her friend, a woman she trusted, put a paperknife through her heart. If you want to feel sorry for someone, feel sorry for her.'

In the somewhat awkward silence that followed, Mel said softly, 'Hillary Greene, champion of the dead.'

Hillary smiled wryly. 'Damn right!'

Barrington excused himself first, and his departure triggered the newly-weds to go as well. Hillary also rose, but just as she reached the door, Paul Danvers raised his head. 'Hillary, just a minute. How about a bite to eat?'

Hillary, one hand on the door handle, turned and glanced at him. He had to be kidding right? She had Regis breathing down her neck to move in with him, and now her boss, her *boss*, for Pete's sake, was asking her out on a date. It wasn't as if she even fancied him. She'd have to be insane to accept. 'OK,' she heard her voice say.

And Paul Danvers, totally but happily surprised, grinned as if he'd just won the national lottery.